her guilty
secret

BOOKS BY EMILY CAVANAGH

The Bloom Girls
This Bright Beauty
Everybody Lies

her guilty secret

emily cavanagh

Bookouture

Published by Bookouture in 2021

An imprint of Storyfire Ltd.
Carmelite House
50 Victoria Embankment
London EC4Y 0DZ
www.bookouture.com

ISBN: 978-180019-165-5
eBook ISBN: 978-1-80019-164-8

To my mother, my first and best girlfriend

ELISE

Facebook status update: Heading out to see my ladies! Hope the kids don't burn the house down while I'm away.

Hunched over her iPad, Elise Kelly-Ryan deleted the last sentence. Surely it was bad luck to joke about something like that. *I'll miss my chickens when I'm away*, she wrote instead, then deleted that too. People would think she meant actual chickens, not her children. Everyone seemed to be raising chickens these days. Backyard poultry and planting their own gardens. Now that it was spring, at afternoon pickup all the other mothers would be talking about their peas, or how the wild turkeys had gotten into the lettuce. Was there something so wrong with buying your food in the grocery store? At least she tried to buy organic.

Elise posted the status update with just the first sentence, then tagged Ada, Ivy, and Libby. She closed the iPad and surveyed the kitchen. The counter was sticky with maple syrup. Everything was always sticky with maple syrup. Marianna insisted on waffles every day, and Elise had finally stopped resisting. For a while she'd tried to force her to eat something with protein in it—an egg from the chickens she wasn't raising, or a bowl of yogurt—but Marianna put up such a fuss, and really, who cared? How terrible was it to eat frozen waffles for breakfast every morning? Elise caught herself going down this train of thought all the time. In the grand scheme of life, who cared if Tommy wore a stained shirt to school (the teachers in his private school, apparently)? In the grand scheme of life, who cared if Piper wouldn't eat any vegetables (truly not a single one, unless you counted pickles as a vegetable, which Elise did)? Her pantry was filled with jars of the sodium-ridden sandwich accessory. In the grand scheme of life, who cared if she was drinking too much coffee (even if it did mean she had to use the bathroom far more often than a woman her age should, and that it occasionally gave her heart palpations)? At least it was Fairtrade.

She poured herself another cup before hollering up the stairs.

"Come on, kids, hurry up. We've got to get going." No one responded. It was only the first warning anyway, and they all knew the first warning didn't mean anything. It wasn't till Elise was red-faced and frantic that anyone actually stopped what they were doing—texting, *always texting*—and got in the car. As usual Brad had already left for work, leaving Elise with the joy of getting everyone fed and out the door. Actually, he'd left for the gym, where he went before work each morning. Elise knew she should be glad her husband was exercising, but she suspected part of the reason he went before work was to escape the mayhem of the morning routine.

Elise flipped open the iPad again, scrolling through her Facebook feed. She'd already gotten several "likes" on her post about the weekend away, mostly from other college friends. Acquaintances really, since none of the others were friends in the way Ada, Ivy, and Libby were.

She took a sip of coffee and opened the document she'd created for the weekend, scanning the list for last-minute items she needed to pick up. She hoped Ada remembered everyone's dietary restrictions. These days Ada was sleepy and preoccupied, and Elise got it, she *did*—she'd been sleepy and preoccupied for several years when the children were little—but Ada wasn't the only woman ever to have had a baby. Lately when they spoke on the phone, it was like Ada was just waiting till Elise stopped talking so she could tell Elise how many times Sam had woken up the previous night.

The last time they'd seen each other, two years ago at Ada's wedding, there'd been too much going on for the four of them to spend any quality time together. They barely had a chance to talk with all of the wedding events. Ada had sat them all together, but between the toasts and the dancing, there was hardly any time to really talk. Then there were all those other people from Ada's adult life—new friends Elise didn't know, colleagues of Tyler's, and multiple siblings and cousins. Ada was one of her oldest and dearest friends, but Elise felt like she, Ivy, and Libby were out of place the whole time, interlopers.

This weekend would be different. This weekend was just about the four of them, her BFFs as Piper would have said, followed by little heart emojis. Ivy would fly in from San Francisco in just a few hours, and Elise had promised to pick her up at the airport, even though Ivy insisted she could take an Uber. Why take an Uber when Elise was only a half-hour away and more than happy to get her? That way they could drive to the Cape together. Besides, Elise needed the extra time alone with Ivy. The last few times they'd seen each other, Elise got the sense she was grating on Ivy's nerves. In fact, she was pretty certain Ivy had rolled her eyes at her during Ada's wedding—and not in a chummy BFF way, in an annoyed you're-driving-me-nuts way. No, Elise needed some time with Ivy to remind her why they were friends.

"Kids, come on, let's get going," Elise called up the stairs, her voice a little shriller this time. She wished she could just stick them on a bus like her mother had done when Elise was a kid, but they each needed to be carted off to different places—Tommy to his private school in Brookline, Piper to the public school just a few blocks away, and Marianna to the school on the other side of town which she'd school-choiced because it had the best special ed program in the district. She dropped Marianna last, not because her school started later, but because Elise loved having a few extra minutes alone with her youngest and sweetest child. At six, Marianna was the only one of the three of them who actually talked to her anyway. Tommy had stopped several years ago when he entered middle school. Elise used to be able to count on Piper for a few minutes of conversation, until she made the mistake of buying her an iPhone at the beginning of fifth grade. Now Piper spent most of their time together with her earbuds plugged in, her face slack and empty, illuminated by the blue glare of the screen. Piper stared at it so intently it was like she was praying. *Thou shalt not worship false idols*, she often thought watching Piper, her own Catholic upbringing rearing its head. She really should take the children to church more often.

"We need to be in the car in two minutes," Elise yelled up the stairs. "Do you hear me? Two minutes!" Surely, they sensed her frustration this time. If they heard her at all—those foolish earbuds were like an extra body part, something they weren't born with but sprouted as they neared adolescence, like pubic hair and breasts.

Brad was just as bad, constantly checking his email covertly at the dinner table, his phone in his lap like a teenage girl trying to text in class. He was on it more than ever these days, but Elise knew that was partly to avoid having to converse with her. For the past two months their interactions had been curt and chilly, and Elise couldn't help but worry what it was he was doing on his phone all that time—emailing a lawyer? Looking for a new apartment across town? She hoped he was only playing video games or checking on sporting stats, annoying yet less significant pastimes. Then again, Elise could feel the pull of her iPad like a magnetic current across the room. How many "likes" did she have now? They were all addicted to the machines, itching for their next fix of data and affirmation. Was there a program to dry out from technology? A cold turkey approach in the name of raising better-adjusted children? She'd google it later today while she waited for Ivy.

ADA

When Ada Clark first opened her eyes, she remembered. Today was the day.

It was dark, barely morning by most people's standards, but Sam was babbling in his crib across the hall. At nine months old he still wasn't sleeping through the night, and insisted on getting up before five. In her previous life, on a weekend Ada lounged in bed till nine. Tyler brought coffee, and then she'd sit in bed for another hour, reading or browsing online.

Not anymore.

Beside her, Tyler slept deeply, "like a baby" Ada would have once said, until she actually had one and learned how wholly inaccurate that phrase was. Sleeping like a baby actually meant eyes popping open every hour and a half, as if caffeine coursed through Sam's veins and not blood. Sleeping like a baby meant only sleeping if someone held you for an hour before you were lowered carefully, slowly, into the bed. No, Tyler slept like a man who was very tired, who missed sleeping soundly night after night.

Ada wasn't going to let the four thirty wake-up call get her down—not today, with three luxurious days of napping and freedom in front of her. She slid from the warmth of bed and pushed open Sam's door. He had a habit of pooping first thing in the morning, and the ripe smell hit her as she entered his room. *Three days*, she reminded herself. Despite the soiled diaper, Sam gave her the toothless smile of an old man that always won her over, even before dawn had broken.

"Hey, big boy." She lifted him from the crib and brought him over to the changing table, undoing the snaps of his onesie and unsticking the tabs on his diaper. She cringed at the mess inside. It was sometimes shocking the amount of poop one tiny person could produce, not to mention the rainbow of colors the waste came in. Forget brown. Sam pooped in shades of yellow, orange, beige, and green. Every day his diaper was a surprise. She pulled out extra wipes.

There were four of them going to Elise's house on the Cape this weekend—Ada, Elise, Libby, and Ivy. They'd been friends for twenty years, since they met freshman year at Harper College in Newton, Massachusetts. For four years, they did everything together—gorged on frozen yogurt in the dining hall, crammed for finals in the library, did keg stands on homecoming weekend, watched Lifetime movies on TV. For four years, they were a unit. Now they were scattered about the country. It was impossible to believe twenty years had passed.

Ada knew the others were looking forward to the weekend, but she was the only one with an infant at home. The rest of them had children who ranged from six to eighteen, and it seemed they'd long forgotten the ravages of sleep deprivation, the way it could consume you and tear you down bit by bit. They complained that they couldn't drag their kids out of bed in the morning in time for school, while Ada would have given her engagement ring to sleep till seven, just one morning. Whenever she complained, she got the typical, "been there, done that," reaction that made her grit her teeth and shut up.

Ada brought Sam into the living room and settled on the couch to nurse. He was a round cherub of a baby with the appetite of a teenage boy. He drank lustily, and while he ate he fidgeted, grabbing at her hair, the hem of her tee shirt, her cell phone, before finally settling into a comfortable spot. She'd been looking forward to the weekend for months, one of the few things she'd mustered up enthusiasm for. Part of her wished Ivy wasn't able to come. Seeing her always brought out a toxic combination of emotions. First the insecurity she'd had around Ivy in college, followed by the guilt she felt later.

There were several texts from the night before about how excited everyone was for the weekend, attached to an endless thread that had been looping for weeks. Ada had finally started turning on the do-not-disturb at night, after the incessant chime on her phone kept waking her and Tyler up in the middle of the night. Just as she'd be dozing off into a fitful sleep, the phone would ding, sending her heart racing. Who stayed up till eleven anymore? By eight o'clock, Ada's eyes were so heavy it was like monkeys were hanging from her eyelashes.

There was an email from Elise about food. Until Marianna was born, Elise had been a first-grade teacher, and she conducted her life with the same efficiency and organization that she must have brought to her classroom.

Of course the grocery list was color-coded. The message to Ada was in pink:

Ada, you volunteered to bring breakfast items for all three days. Fruit salad? Oatmeal? Omelets? I'll get a few things just in case. I've already picked up coffee and half and half!! Xo

It had been two years since they'd all been together at Ada's wedding. Ada had been thrilled to have them there, but she'd hardly had any time to be with them between all of the wedding events. Ada had seen Elise and Libby several times since then, but being with them was always easier, in part because they lived closer and saw each other more frequently, but also because things with Ivy were rarely easy and never had been. Ivy had always brought out the worst in her, all of her insecurities and self-doubt bubbling to the surface. Even when she was being nice, Ada always felt judged by Ivy. In addition to whatever snarky drama Ivy brought with her, time spent with her always left Ada with an uncomfortable twang of guilt. She wondered if the others felt the same way or if it was just her.

Ada gazed down at Sam who was drifting off to sleep, his lips still moving though his eyes were closed. She hadn't married Tyler till she was thirty-nine, hadn't had Sam till she was forty. She'd worried about every possible diagnosis. For weeks, she'd stressed about the mojitos she'd drunk at a retirement party she'd gone to before she realized she was pregnant. Autism, cerebral palsy, cystic fibrosis, trisomy—just about every common and uncommon diagnosis out there, Ada had imagined. Ada was older than most of her friends had been when they'd had their last children, and she knew the risks were higher. Elise had proved that. Every ultrasound, scan and amnio had come back clear, but Ada spent sleepless nights imagining what might be wrong with her unborn baby.

And then Sam arrived, ten fingers and ten toes, a full head of wheat-colored hair, and long curling lashes. His perfection was a shock. Every time Ada looked at him, even now, nine months later, she felt like she'd had the wind knocked out of her.

She hadn't realized motherhood would be like having her body cleaved open and her heart removed. No one had told her. The days passed in a blur of soiled diapers, nursing, fatigue, spit-up, and the endless quest for sleep. Sam was a finicky napper, and he preferred to sleep with his head resting against Ada's chest. She loved the feeling of his cheek on her skin, but instead of sleeping, she gazed down at him with gritty-eyed adoration. During the rare moments when Tyler took Sam out and she had a half-hour to read a book or have a cup of coffee, Ada found herself wandering aimlessly around the house, folding tiny onesies still warm from the dryer, pressing the lightly scented fabric to her face and inhaling his intoxicating smell. On the few evenings when she'd gone out to meet a friend, Ada missed Sam intensely, the familiar weight of him in her arms, even though she spent much of her day with a sore and aching back. There was no returning to the way life was before, or who she was before. Her body and heart had been permanently altered.

She suspected her friends had learned this long ago. Ivy's kids were teenagers now, which was crazy, since Ada sometimes felt like a teenager herself. Though not so much lately. These days she felt more like an old woman, her body protesting all the time, bones aching from the awkward bulk of a squirming Sam, his mouth and hands constantly reaching for her. There was a reason people did this in their twenties.

Ada wished she'd met Tyler at twenty-five. Things would be different now if they'd met earlier, if she'd had a chance to become a mother the way she'd imagined—overcome only with happiness, not racked by grief and sadness. If she'd met Tyler earlier, her mother would have had a chance to know Sam, and Ada wouldn't have felt so alone. This was also why she needed the weekend—to see her oldest friends and to feel connected to someone other than Sam.

Sam snored lightly, his lips parted, her nipple only halfway in his mouth. He reminded her of Tyler, so easily satiated: a beer, an orgasm, and a nap, and he was good as new. Though Ada couldn't imagine ever wanting to have sex again. Her body was too depleted to give anything more.

She adjusted the pillow and slowly lowered herself till she was lying on the couch with Sam against her chest, his wet mouth spilling a pool of drool onto her skin. Fatigue circled just around her consciousness, and when she closed her eyes, it was a relief to give in to the heaviness of her lids. Sam sighed in his dreams, and

Ada's eyes snapped alert, locking on his long lashes and creamy skin. No matter how tired she was, sleep continued to elude her, a slippery dark beast that she couldn't quite catch. She focused instead on the rise and fall of his breath, the faint milky smell that hovered between them. This would have to be enough.

IVY

Facebook status update: See you later, SF! Here I come, Cape Cod!

Ivy adjusted her sunglasses and stepped onto the moving walkway at San Francisco International Airport. Her head pounded, and she knew she'd be hungover for the better part of the day. She hoped she didn't get sick on the plane.

Around her the airport bustled with life, all that coming and going, people heading out on business trips and vacations. She hadn't been on a plane since she flew to Boston for Ada's wedding two years earlier. She hadn't seen any of them since, not even Libby, and she knew she was supposed to be excited about the weekend, but she was having trouble mustering the enthusiasm.

She couldn't afford the trip, first of all. She knew Elise would have happily bought her ticket, but there was no way Ivy was going to plead poverty. Easier to put the ticket on a credit card and deal with it later. It was Elise who'd insisted on the weekend, desperate to hold the group together, when the rest of them would have happily drifted off into their separate corners of adulthood, forming new and more compatible friendships with people they actually had things in common with. Still, she couldn't imagine not going and watching the weekend unfold through their text messages and social media posts. Being with them was like coming home, with all of the complications that came with family.

She stepped off the walkway and trudged toward her gate. She'd take some Tylenol once she boarded. She hadn't meant to drink so much but the kids were both out for the night, and she'd spread a stack of paperwork and bills across the table, and poured herself a tall glass of wine in order to face the terrifying pile. After opening only a few overdue notices, she ended up shoving the pile in a drawer and drinking most of the bottle, trying to calm the panic that always hovered around the edges lately. Her head pounded this morning, and she felt sick about it as she always did when she ended up drinking too much, her father's phantom rising up to remind her of the cost of her self-destructive impulses.

Settling into one of the cushioned chairs in the waiting area, she pulled up the hood of her coat, seeking a moment of quiet. There would be no quiet once she got to the Cape. She loved Elise, but she was one of those people who hated silence and worked hard to fill every moment with an unceasing prattle. Talk, talk, talk—the woman didn't shut up. It didn't matter where they were or what the conversation was about, Elise could talk endlessly on a subject as mundane as the gravel in her driveway.

They still didn't know about Sebastian. It had been seven months since he and Ivy separated, and last week the divorce papers had arrived. They were amongst the pile of papers spread on her table last night, and she'd stared at the places where her signature was required, unable to pick up the pen to sign. All of Ivy's friends from San Francisco knew about the separation and looming divorce, but she hadn't told any of her Harper friends, not even Libby. Part of it was shame, which she knew was stupid. It wasn't her fault Sebastian had an affair with a twenty-two-year-old student from his Introduction to Oil Painting class. Ivy had met Fauna at a student art show just once before she found out about the affair, and she practically smelled the pheromones in the air between them. Fauna, only four years older than Ivy's son Jax, who ogled his almost-stepmom in a way that they all pretended to ignore.

Fauna... Ivy couldn't even think the name without feeling like she might vomit. Fauna, a cross between a deer and a flower, a made up hippy dippy California name. Not that Ivy could really throw stones with children named Trina and Jax, but Trina was shortened from Katrina, Sebastian's grandmother's name. In some places a name like Jax might have been unique, but there were three others in his high school class—Jacques, Jacks, and Jaxe. Fauna, on the other hand, was just ridiculous.

Ivy didn't know whether the relationship would have continued if Fauna hadn't gotten pregnant. Sebastian never did like condoms, and apparently, Fauna was too preoccupied with artistic theory to bother with something as mundane as birth control. The girl actually had the nerve to show up at the apartment with Sebastian last week when he came to pick up Trina and Jax. She was practically glowing, her belly round and tight under an empire-waist sundress, hair falling in curls around her shoulders, all soft curves and fertility. Ivy certainly didn't look like that when she was pregnant. She was nauseous for nine months, her skin more green than glowing, and her ass had nearly doubled in size.

The real reason she hadn't told her friends about Sebastian was because she was humiliated. The young student turned lover, the unplanned pregnancy, it was all such a cliché, like something out of one of those terrible Lifetime movies they used to watch together. Ivy couldn't bear to think that her life had become as predictable and trite as one of the characters in those overacted dramas.

She also didn't want them to know about the other strains the divorce was putting on her. Despite rent control, they'd always struggled to make the payments on their San Francisco apartment each month. The city was on a swift upward climb. It had become a city of entrepreneurs, venture capitalists, and techies, not a place for adjunct art professors and massage therapists/jewelry makers. So when Sebastian moved into Fauna's apartment in the East Bay, Ivy was left to pay the entire rent, which she couldn't afford. It was hard not to be bitter, and she wasn't looking forward to the reminder of how her life could have been.

It didn't help that Sebastian had dropped the Fauna bombshell just months after he'd encouraged Ivy to quit her job as a massage therapist to focus on making jewelry full-time. So full of ambition she'd been, and then she was suddenly responsible for paying the rent on her own. The child support payments barely covered food, electricity, and Trina's dance classes, not to mention the rent, and there was no way she was making Trina give up her dance classes just because her father was an asshole. But she couldn't squeeze blood from a stone. Which was why she was considering her friend Samantha's suggestion.

Samantha had a friend who worked for an upscale escort service in Pacific Heights. When Ivy googled the website, the company proclaimed that they were a boutique agency servicing wealthy educated men in the Bay Area. Most of their clients were middle-aged or older, though there were a handful of "younger gentlemen whose careers leave them too busy to focus on finding the right date for important work functions and social galas." Samantha's friend swore that, though sex was usually an option, most of these men just needed a pretty woman for a date, and it would be up to Ivy how far she was willing to go.

She'd gone on her first trial date the other night as part of the agency's hiring process. Marshall was in finance, and Ivy accompanied him to a dinner function at a downtown hotel that must have cost at least five hundred a plate. He looked to be about fifty, balding but handsome in the fit and tailored way of the wealthy. He smelled of expensive aftershave and held the door for her, making easy small talk. When he introduced Ivy, he called her "my friend Ivy," and she wondered if any of his coworkers knew she'd been hired. It was possible that the event was filled with paid escorts.

The dinner was over by ten. In the lobby of the hotel, Marshall put his arm around her waist and asked if she'd like to come back to his apartment for a drink. It had taken Ivy a moment to understand what he was asking, and another before she lied and said she had an early morning. In the Uber home, though, she wondered if she'd made the wrong call. The amount she was paid for the dinner was more than she made in an entire day of massage work. She could only imagine how much she could ask for if she were willing to go further. And would it be so wrong? She'd had plenty of impersonal sex with guys she didn't care about in college, and that was for free. By the time the car dropped her off at her apartment, she was certain she'd made a mistake.

Ivy had a meeting scheduled with the owner of the agency the week she got back. And while she was a little sick to her stomach that she was really resorting to this, the possibility of lifting herself out of debt filled her with a small blossom of hope.

The ticket agent called her row, and Ivy rose sluggishly from her seat, dragging the carry-on suitcase behind her. She'd sleep on the plane, maybe watch a movie. When they landed, Elise would be waiting. She'd have her giant minivan neatly packed with everything they could possibly need over the next three days, including a whole bunch of stuff they wouldn't even touch. Three days away from her worries which seemed to take up all the space in the apartment, away from Sebastian and his glowing new girlfriend, three days away from a city she'd once loved but that was quietly turning toxic. Three days away from who she was becoming.

As Ivy stowed her suitcase in the overhead compartment and settled into her seat, she felt a loosening in her chest, the lifting of something heavy as a lightness returned at the idea of seeing her friends again. They would cook and drink wine and catch up. They would laugh. Ivy couldn't remember the last time she'd really laughed, so hard that tears came out of her eyes. It was only ever with them.

She pulled out her phone to switch it to airplane mode. There was an unfamiliar 800 number along with a message which she didn't listen to. Instead she took a quick stop on Facebook to see Ada and Elise's recent posts. She liked them and then tapped out a quick text message to the three of them, finally looking forward to the weekend for the first time since she'd booked the ticket.

LIBBY

Group text: Ivy to Libby, Elise, and Ada
There better be a mojito waiting for me the minute my plane
touches the ground. Or a G&T? What are we drinking these
days?

Text message: Adam to Libby
Have a great weekend with your friends. Give me a call if you
get bored.

"Caitlin, stop dragging your bag on the ground. You're getting the bottom filthy," Libby Green scolded her thirteen-year-old daughter. Caitlin rewarded her with a half-hearted eye roll, lifting the bag less than an inch from the ground. Her eyes were lined with thick black makeup that took forever each morning, though she emerged from the bathroom looking like she was dressed for Halloween. Libby thought she looked like a goth clown. Every morning they argued about the makeup and every morning Libby lost.

"I don't want to stay at Grandma and Grandpa's house," Bethany whined. At eight, she was clingier than Caitlin had been at her age, always hovering around Libby, reaching for her. She clutched Libby's hand tightly. It was greasy with something—likely butter from the toast she'd barely eaten.

"It's only for a few days. You'll have fun with Grandma and Grandpa."

Caitlin let herself into her grandparents' house without holding the door for her mother and sister, and the screen door banged behind her. Libby tamped down the irritation that prickled at the back of her neck. Three days away from Caitlin would be good for both of them.

"Their house smells funny," Bethany said softly, hovering on the front steps.

"It does?" Libby asked, automatically sniffing the air even though they were still outside.

Bethany nodded. "Like stuff burning."

"That's just the wood stove." Libby loved the smell of the wood stove in her parents' house. Some of her fondest memories from childhood took place in the warmth of that living room. Bethany pressed herself into Libby's hip.

"I don't like it," she whined, her pale blonde hair slipping from its ponytail. There was a patch of eczema on her cheek the size of a dime. Libby knew if she held up Bethany's arm, her elbows would be a flaky pink mess. She'd have to remind her mother to put the cream on twice a day and to check Bethany's nails at night, so she didn't claw herself bloody and raw.

"Well, it's going to be warm for the weekend, so they probably won't even use the stove." Libby peeled Bethany from her and tried to guide her into the house, but Bethany remained where she was.

"Why do you have to go?" She planted her feet hip-width apart and crossed her arms over her chest. Libby took a deep breath and willed herself to be patient. She knew as soon as she buckled her seat belt and got on the highway, she'd miss the thin frame of Bethany's arms around her waist.

"I haven't seen my friends in a long time," she answered.

"Are they your best friends? Like me and Sophie?" Bethany asked.

Libby thought for a moment. Yes and no. At one point, but not now, but also forever. The real answer was too complicated, certainly for Bethany, and certainly for this particular moment. Libby needed straightforward and quick. Best friends were something Bethany could understand.

"Yes, like you and Sophie. Can you imagine if you didn't see Sophie for two whole years? Wouldn't you be excited to see her?"

Bethany nodded reluctantly, and Libby took the opportunity to pull her through the front door of her parents' house.

"Hello! We're here!" she called, stepping inside.

Bethany was right, the house did smell like stuff burning. Until her daughter mentioned it, she'd never given the wood stove much thought, but it really did permeate every corner of the house. Had she been one of those kids with a distinct smell, the kind that made others wrinkle their nose in displeasure when they were assigned as partners? How had she never noticed it before?

"Hi, sweetheart." Libby's mother Anne-Marie greeted them in the hall, arms outstretched for Bethany. Libby gave her daughter a little push, and Bethany stepped forward into Anne-Marie's arms. Her mother wore a pair of faded jeans and an old flannel shirt. Her gray hair was clipped neatly around her face, which was clear of any makeup. Anne-Marie never wore makeup, except for the occasional dab of Vaseline on her lips for a night out. On her feet were thick wool socks and Birkenstocks. Libby's father had an identical pair. Anne-Marie released Bethany who wandered into the kitchen in search of a snack, though they both knew all she was likely to find was dried fruit and raw nuts. "Hi, Libs. You ready for your trip?" her mother asked.

"I think so." Libby tilted her head in Bethany's direction. "She's a little clingy. She doesn't want me to go."

"She'll be fine," Anne-Marie said lightly.

"I hate to leave them," Libby said, the familiar guilt re-emerging from its hiding place.

"You never do anything for yourself. Stop worrying," her mother ordered.

"I know. I just feel bad about leaving them."

Anne-Marie shook her head, catching Libby's chin in her hand. "You need to take care of yourself too. Life has to go on."

"Yeah, Mom, I know. Obviously I know that," Libby said. It wasn't fair to get irritated with her mother, especially since she'd so readily agreed to babysit the girls for the weekend. She heard her phone beep from her pocket and pulled it out to see the message from Ivy and the one from Adam. Libby felt a smile snake across her face and her mother's expectant eyes on her, and she put the phone back in her pocket without replying. Anne-Marie was always encouraging Libby to "get back out there," and Libby was always telling her mother she wasn't ready. She hadn't told her about Adam yet, but she knew how happy it would make Anne-Marie. Libby wished her own feelings could be as uncomplicated.

"You'd better get going. You don't want to have to drive in the dark," Anne-Marie said.

"It's not even noon, Mom," Libby pointed out.

"Aren't you anxious to see your friends? You're on vacation," Anne-Marie urged.

"Okay, okay." Libby threw up her hands in surrender. "I'm going. Let me just say goodbye to the girls."

"Fine, but don't get Bethany all worked up. You're only leaving for three days." Libby swallowed her response. It might only be three days, but what if it wasn't? What if Libby's car broke down on the side of the road and she was mowed down by a passing truck? What if her heart stopped beating, just ceased to pump blood through her veins any longer? It could happen. She understood that now. None of them were invincible.

Libby found her daughters in the kitchen hunched over Caitlin's phone, watching music videos on YouTube. She was surprised it worked as the cell service at her parents' house was spotty. A familiar pop song played through the tinny speakers, and Libby cringed at the sight of the singer in her spangled shorts that barely covered her ass cheeks. A lace bustier shoved the girl's breasts into an unnatural position. Did Caitlin want breasts like that? Good luck to her. Libby had extra room in her B-cups, and Anne-Marie's were so small she rarely bothered with a bra.

"What are you watching?" Libby asked.

"Just some music," Caitlin mumbled, without looking up from the screen.

"That's not appropriate for your sister." Bethany stared at the phone with a glazed expression of indifference, her cheek pressed against Caitlin's arm so she could see better.

"So she doesn't have to watch." Caitlin shifted her body away from Bethany.

"Hey! I can't see!" Bethany squealed.

"Mom said you can't watch," Caitlin said.

"Caitlin, come on." Libby wasn't even certain what she was asking. For Caitlin to show the video to Bethany? To find something less disgusting to watch that wouldn't lead both girls to feeling inadequate in all areas? To not blame Libby for everything?

"*What?*" Caitlin cut her eyes at Libby, her mouth an unsmiling pink stripe across her face.

"Phones away." Anne-Marie appeared behind Libby in the doorway of the kitchen. She held her hand out for Caitlin's phone. Libby stood between her mother and daughter, waiting for all hell to erupt. Bethany watched wide-eyed, waiting to see what would happen.

"I'm not giving you my phone," Caitlin snapped.

"Don't sass your grandma," Libby said automatically.

"What? I'm not giving her my phone." Caitlin's eyes widened under the thick black makeup. "Mom, tell her I don't have to give her my phone."

Libby turned to Anne-Marie. "Mom. Please."

"What?" Anne-Marie's face looked free of guile, but Libby had a feeling her mother knew exactly what she was doing. "I'm just asking for her phone. Is that so crazy?"

Yes. What she was asking was completely crazy, considering that Caitlin was like a feral animal with her phone, or like a mother bear ready to draw blood in order to protect her cub. Libby didn't tell her mother this though, because Anne-Marie's cell phone was one of those flip ones with the giant buttons that you only used in an emergency. In the kitchen, they still had a rotary phone. *A rotary phone*, for God's sake. It was like an artifact from another time. She'd felt like a historian as she explained to her children how it worked, and it had taken Caitlin three tries to finally make a phone call.

"How about she just puts it away?" Libby implored. "You guys can agree on some ground rules for when she can use it." *After I'm gone*, she wanted to add.

Anne-Marie crossed her arms and looked at Caitlin. Libby watched in disbelief as Caitlin slipped the phone into the back pocket of her jeans. For a moment, peace seemed to reign. Then Bethany turned to Libby, her chin quivering in the way it did when tears were imminent.

"Please don't go, Mommy," she said, a single tear falling, followed quickly by another one.

"Drama queen," Caitlin muttered under her breath.

"Shut up," Bethany whined.

"Everybody outside," Anne-Marie ordered. "Grandpa's working in the garden and we're all going to help him. There's plenty of mulching to be done."

"Great. Sounds thrilling," Caitlin muttered. Libby had to work hard to recall the time in Caitlin's life when every word she uttered wasn't a sarcastic quip.

"Kisses for Mom, then outside," Anne-Marie said firmly.

Bethany threw herself upon Libby, until Anne-Marie enticed her outside with promises of her own pair of gardening gloves and a spade. Caitlin remained in the kitchen, hands in her back pockets, likely just for the smooth reassuring feel of her phone's metal case. Like a little Xanax against her palm.

"Be nice to your sister, please," Libby began. Caitlin stared at the tiled floor. "And listen to your grandma."

"Does she have to be such a bitch?" Caitlin asked quietly.

Libby had wondered the same thing on more than one occasion. "Don't call her that. She's just stricter than I am," she said instead.

"Yeah, no shit."

"Lose the attitude and the curse words. It will get you nowhere fast in this house," Libby warned. Caitlin grunted, and Libby pulled Caitlin into her arms and attempted to hug her. Caitlin remained rigid and sullen. "I love you," Libby murmured into Caitlin's hair. She'd recently dyed it a shocking shade of red, and it had taken everything Libby had in her to tell Caitlin how nice it looked. Now there was so much product in it that it was stiff and brittle under her palm, but Libby stroked it anyway.

"I love you too," Caitlin finally said, so softly that Libby almost wondered if the words were in her own head.

ADA

Group text: Ada to Libby, Ivy, and Elise
Hello? I'm still nursing. Did we pack anything nonalcoholic?
I'll pick up some seltzer for me and anyone else who wants it.

Ada backed her car out of the driveway and waved to Tyler, who stood on the front lawn with Sam in his arms. Tyler held Sam's chubby hand up and made him wave back, and Ada forced a smile. She'd nursed Sam less than an hour ago, but her breasts already felt full, and she'd probably have to pull over at a rest stop to pump in the car.

Flipping on the radio, she tried to find a station to lighten her mood. This was supposed to be a good thing, three days with her best friends and no baby to care for. Yet, despite the excitement that had been building for the past several weeks, Ada just felt weepy and far away from Tyler and Sam. She was only a few blocks away, close enough to turn back and bail on the weekend. Then she pictured Elise's face, the confusion and disappointment that would quickly color her features, and she kept driving.

Ada sighed, settling on a classical station, mentally scanning for anything she might have forgotten to tell Tyler about Sam's schedule. It wasn't that she didn't trust Tyler. He just didn't *know* Sam like she did. When the baby let out a wail, Tyler assumed he was fussing, while Ada could identify each particular cry—the one that signaled hunger, discomfort, fatigue, or just the desire to be held. She and Sam spent all day every day together, not to mention the many silent hours in the fuzzy black night, whereas Tyler only saw him before and after work, when neither of them were at their best, both man and baby fussy, tired, and hungry.

Last weekend Tyler insisted on going out, just the two of them. Ada's friend Sarah from work had been hounding her to babysit, and she was thrilled when Ada called to ask if she could come over for a few hours. Ada had spent the entire meal preoccupied and worried that Sam wouldn't settle for the night. When they returned home, he was sleeping peacefully in his bed, but Ada had scooped him up and nursed him anyway. Nestling her face into the damp space of his neck, the spot that usually held his intoxicating sweet-sour scent of powder and milk, Ada smelled Sarah's perfume. It wasn't that the perfume smelled bad, it was just the scent of someone else on her baby that made her feel so sad. Later in bed, Tyler circled his hand around her hips, pressing himself against her back in an obvious initiation of sex, but he must have felt how Ada's whole body tensed up, and a moment later he rolled back over. Ada had squeezed her eyes tight to contain the tears.

In just four months her maternity leave would end, and she'd return to her job as a high school English teacher. She needed to figure out childcare for September, but every time she sat down to make a list of possible daycares, her chest grew tight, her heart beating so fast she wondered if she needed to see a doctor. It scared her a little, the suffocating feeling she had more and more often, when she thought about being away from Sam but also in the morning when the nine-hour day, just her and Sam, loomed emptily before them. None of her friends had babies and none of them were home. Sometimes she took Sam for aimless drives through the backroads of Western Massachusetts, just for something to do. He'd sleep and Ada would listen to music, and for those hours in the car, she felt calm. Then she'd pull into their parking spot and Sam's eyes would snap open, and the rest of the interminable day would stretch out before her.

It would all have been more manageable if her mother were still alive. She had succumbed to pancreatic cancer just two weeks before Ada discovered she was pregnant with Sam. She and Tyler had been trying to get pregnant since they married, but still the timing felt like a cruel joke as Ada tried to muster up excitement for the baby through a hazy cloud of grief. Between the horrible morning sickness that lasted all day and the clutch of grief came the realization that her mother would never get to see or hold the baby. On these days, Ada struggled to get out of bed. She went through all of her sick days, personal days, and anything else that was left in the weeks and months after her mother's death. Tyler would return home from work to find Ada still in bed, wearing an old pair of his sweatpants and an oversized tee shirt to accommodate her growing belly. Some days she felt sorry for him. They were still practically newlyweds, after all. This wasn't what he'd signed up for when he married her. But she'd been a different person back then—an aspiring writer, an amateur chef, a hiker, someone in the workforce. Much as she tried, she didn't seem able to resurrect the earlier version of herself he'd fallen in love with. Sometimes she wondered if her sadness had damaged Sam somehow, if his fussy nature and sleeplessness was due to the black hole that opened up inside of her just as his cells were fusing together and he was becoming himself.

Something was on the verge of consuming her. Sorrow or anger or terror, she wasn't entirely certain which one, but she felt as if she were barely above the water level. She kept swallowing cold and briny mouthfuls, thrashing her arms wildly in an effort to stay afloat, but one of these days her lungs were going to fill.

She put on her signal and took the turnoff for the freeway.

ELISE

Group text: Elise to Ada, Libby, and Ivy
I have a new favorite cocktail I'm making—grapefruit-infused
vodka with a splash of lemonade, club soda, and mint. So
yummy! We can always make yours virgin, Ada. Can't wait to
see everyone. xo

Text message: Elise to Brad
There's a lasagna in the fridge for tonight. Make sure you check
the calendar for info about the weekend. See you Monday.

Elise's car idled in the cell phone parking lot of Logan Airport. She was a half-hour early, which left just enough time to send a few emails and double-check her to-do list before Ivy arrived. She'd already done most of the shopping for the weekend and the back seat of her minivan was overflowing with bags from Whole Foods and Trader Joe's, not to mention another whole box from the liquor store.

She scrolled through her emails. There was a message from the head of the PTO about the upcoming auction at Piper's school, including a reminder that Elise had volunteered to donate a week's vacation at the Cape house. There was another message about Marianna's field trip to the zoo that Elise had agreed to chaperone, and yet another reminder that it was her turn to bring snacks to Piper's soccer game this weekend. She'd need to send a message to

Brad because there was no way he'd remember on his own, even though it was marked on their calendar in bright pink Sharpie. She shot off a quick text to Brad, grateful to be spared one of their awkward conversations, punctuated by tension and silence.

Sometimes she wished that she'd betrayed her husband in the traditional way. How hard would it have been to have a fling with one of his colleagues or the father of one of the children's friends? She'd had opportunities, but she'd never allowed herself to contemplate being unfaithful. Instead she'd deceived him in a way that neither of them had ever expected, and both of them had been blindsided by its aftermath.

Elise was sixteen weeks pregnant with Marianna when she had the amnio. Because she was over thirty-five, the procedure was standard, yet Elise had watched in horror as they inserted the needle into her round belly. She hadn't spent much time catastrophizing the pregnancy, having had two smooth ones with Piper and Tommy, so when the genetic counselor sat her and Brad down in the office and told her the amnio indicated that the fetus had Down syndrome, Elise had been stunned. She'd glanced over at Brad who looked equally shell-shocked and felt the bottom of her world fall out.

Keeping the baby was the only option. Elise had sat through too many catechism classes and Sunday masses to ever really consider terminating a pregnancy, and she was still haunted by the time she'd accompanied her sister Missy to get an abortion. Missy never talked about it, but Elise sometimes imagined the shadow niece or nephew she would have had. So Elise got ready for Marianna's birth the way she did for everything. She researched and planned and organized, all in a futile effort to prepare.

Marianna was born, and she was just as amazing as Tommy and Piper when they first came into the world. She had bright blue eyes and a pink bow of a mouth and smooth skin, and she was beautiful. There were the distinguishing facial differences, the upward slanting eyes, the flatter features, but she was just a baby like any other. Elise watched as the rest of her family crowded around the bed to meet Marianna, Piper offering up a pinky, Tommy cooing in a soft and gentle voice Elise didn't recognize. She had looked at Brad, whose eyes shined with wonder, and knew they were going to be okay.

And they were, to a point. But there was no guidebook for your heart when raising a child like Marianna. Not that there was a guidebook for any kid, but all of her careful research and planning could never have prepared her for all the things websites and books couldn't explain. At six months old, Marianna underwent heart surgery to correct a congenital defect. Elise had accompanied her into the operating room. When the anesthesia kicked in, Marianna's whole body went limp, and for a moment Elise thought she was dead. She'd felt her legs go weak before a nurse assured her everything was fine and ushered her out of the OR. The surgery was a success, but the ever-present fear never left Elise, an even deeper and more urgent fear than she'd previously had as a mother.

No one told you that having a child with disabilities impacted every area of your life. No one told Elise about the appointments—with doctors and physical therapists and occupational therapists, the audiologist and optometrist and cardiologist, with teachers and counselors and all of the other well-meaning people there to help Marianna succeed—it all took time. And not just time. It took energy. Emotional energy to think about all of the ways her child wasn't matching up with everyone else, all of the ways Marianna was different, and while everybody loved to say they valued differences, no one really wanted to be different. No one told her how much it would hurt when your child didn't have real friends, when the kids were kind because they'd been taught to be but didn't invite your child over for a playdate or sleepover. No one told her that you worried over every milestone—sitting, standing, walking, saying a word and then another one, then another. No one told her that she'd celebrate these successes while equally mourning the limitations they highlighted. No one told Elise about the fear that Marianna would live with her and Brad forever, and the even stronger terror about what would happen when they were both gone.

Elise was the oldest of four. Her father was a good man, especially when he wasn't drinking. He was an electrician, but he wasn't a very good one, and he was constantly out of work. The family survived on Elise's mother's job as a nurse at Mass General. Elise's mother was a strong and determined woman, and she taught her children the importance of charity and self-sufficiency. She made Elise, Jackie, Missy, and John spend weekends volunteering at their church, serving watery chicken soup to the elderly and babysitting the toddlers during mass. She pushed them to do every free extracurricular offered; she prepped them for the exams required to get into Boston Latin, and when Elise was the first of her siblings to get in, her mother made certain that her grades never dipped below an A minus.

Her parents had been married for forty years. They lived in Florida now, where her father only had a few beers every night, and spent his days reading automotive magazines and playing cards with a group of men in their retirement community. Despite what Elise suspected was a bucketful of disappointment and resentment, her mother still loved her father fiercely. Elise and Brad, on the other hand, had been married for fourteen years, and she wasn't sure they would make it to fifteen.

As a child in a family that never had enough, Elise had been a hoarder. Not one of those people you saw on TV nowadays who saved newspapers from the early seventies and had a whole cabinet designated for extra shoelaces. Hoarder was the word her siblings used before it was trendy. Elise preferred to think of herself as a saver.

It started with candy. When she was little, Elise had a special shoebox under her bed that she used to store the candy she received on holidays. It was filled with rock-hard marshmallow Peeps and candy canes so old they crumbled in the plastic wrappers, chocolate kisses gone waxy in their silvery skin. Elise didn't even like candy that much, but knowing that the stash was there was a comfort when things at home were bad. If her father never found another job or if her mother's hours got cut again, at least Elise would be able to offer up a month's worth of candy. It didn't make any sense, and even as a child she recognized this, but it didn't stop her from plastic-wrapping her hollow chocolate bunny so it would stay fresh. Some nights she'd sit on the floor by her bed and count out how many pieces of candy she had, all that extra in case she ever needed it.

As she got older, she realized her candy reserve was meaningless, and so she switched to money. Every ten-dollar bill she received for a birthday, every weekly allowance, every quarter she found stuck between the cushions of the couch was saved. This too was hidden under her bed, first in a glittery pencil case, and then when she ran out of room, in an old coffee can.

Sometime around then, the saving took a slippery turn. On Sunday mornings, her mother would hand each of the children a dollar bill to put in the collection basket at church, and each week, Elise would lower her hand in but hang on to the bill, snatching a quarter or two in the process, which she'd pin between her thumb and palm. When everyone closed their eyes, and knelt to pray, Elise slipped the dollar and coins into the elastic of her ankle socks. On the school bus each morning, Elise removed the quarter at the bottom of her lunch box, the one meant for a carton of milk. She'd drink water with her peanut butter and jelly sandwich, and when her stomach growled during last period, she'd place her hand in her pocket and rub the shiny quarter between her fingers. Once, at a sleepover, she'd stolen a five-dollar bill from the dining room mantel when her friend was in the bathroom. Elise had felt jumpy and guilty for the rest of the night, but when she tucked the bill into her secret stash the next morning, there was a wash of relief.

Her family knew about Elise's savings. Once her brother John stole thirty dollars from the coffee can to pay for a new baseball mitt. Elise punched him in the mouth when she found out, a sharp and nasty swing that resulted in a fat purple lip. What he didn't understand was that she wasn't saving just for herself, she was saving for an *emergency*. Her siblings might have joked about what a tightwad Elise was, but it was no joke when Missy was a senior in high school and their mother asked for help paying for her college applications. Elise had handed over three hundred dollars without blinking an eye.

By college the coffee can had been upgraded to a checking account, but even with the financial aid and scholarships and part-time job, there were always so many expenses that it was hard to put much aside.

And then she married Brad.

He was nine years older than Elise, and when she met him at twenty-five, he was already comfortable. That was the word she quickly learned to use, more socially appropriate than wealthy, or just rich, the word that first came to mind. Elise was working as a first-grade teacher at Sunny Acres, a private school in Brookline, the type of school that trained the next generation of lawyers, doctors, and engineers. She met Brad at a donor dinner to which the staff were all invited. Brad was a corporate lawyer and a graduate of Sunny Acres, and he quickly introduced Elise to a world she'd never known.

She had expected a corporate lawyer to be buttoned up and boring, but Brad was neither. He was funny and kind and generous. Despite his money, he was warm and unpretentious, eager to meet her family who all fell in love with him, neither because of nor in spite of his money. They married after just a year, and Elise settled into the relationship and all that came with it, confident for the first time ever that there was enough money to take care of her parents and siblings if she should have to.

Elise paid the bills. She didn't actually make the money to pay them, but she was the one responsible for making sure each one was paid on time. It was one of those divisions of labor in marriage, like how he took care of all the car and house maintenance, and she made all the doctor's appointments. Feminism be damned, she had no interest in being in charge when the house needed to be re-shingled. They had a savings account and money for retirement, but there was so much money going out every month that it was hard to find the time to keep track of it all. There was enough for a second house and a little boat, for private school and new laptops and an addition on the kitchen and new clothes whenever she wanted them. But there were so many expenses too—landscaping of the backyard and a new washing machine and a new rug in the living room to match the new couch. The bounty of it was almost overwhelming. Sometimes she had the urge to grasp one of her children by the chin and make them look around, to really see everything they had. "Look at this," she would hiss. "Do you understand what you have? Do you see how blessed you are?" But of course, she didn't and they couldn't, knowing only what they had had all along.

When Marianna was born, Elise quit her job. She had been thinking of it anyway, even before she found out about the diagnosis. She loved teaching first grade, but three kids were a lot with two working parents, and they didn't need Elise's income. Once they knew that Marianna had Down syndrome, Elise knew there was no way she would go back to work, at least not full-time. She needed to be home, first to care for the baby and then to navigate this new world.

Marianna's birth awoke something that had been sleeping inside Elise, a primal fear, a desire to contain the uncontainable chaos. As a child it was the fear that not having enough money brought—the embarrassment of having to tell her teacher she couldn't pay for the field trip, the sick feeling she'd get when she noticed her shoes were too small, knowing she'd be stuck in the same sneakers for the rest of the school year unless her mother stumbled across a secondhand pair, the tension that hung in the house when her father lost a job and the burden lay solely upon their mother again. Every month, every day, they were always so close to the edge, there was always the fear that there wouldn't be enough to go around. And what then? What would happen then?

She was the opposite of poor now, with 401Ks and college accounts and savings accounts and credit cards and life insurance and health insurance, a seemingly endless abundance. There was no need to steal. Yet around the time that Marianna entered preschool, Elise began to hear that niggling voice. *What if there's not enough?* It didn't even make sense, because of course there was enough, there was more than Elise had ever been able to imagine as a child. She thought of all the health issues Marianna was at risk for in addition to the ones they managed now. What if they lost their health insurance? What if Brad made a bad investment? The trouble with money, she had learned, was that there was always someone with more, and it was always possible to lose it.

For the first time since she was a child, Elise felt the tug of dread begin to pull her under. There were too many unknowns in Marianna's future, too many ifs and maybes. It seemed like a good idea to tuck aside a little extra, for whatever the future might bring.

*

Elise still had her old bank account from college, the one she'd opened all those years back. She began to deposit a little whenever she could, just a bit of extra savings to tide them over in case the worst happened—death, divorce, illness, who knew what the future might bring?

It wasn't hard to do. A hundred here. Two hundred there. All of it deposited into her own private account in a different bank, over the course of two years. She cut corners where no one would notice, stretched her haircuts from every two months to every four, skipped the spa day she liked to do, bought generic granola bars instead of the pricier organic ones. When Brad suggested a dinner out, she cheerily countered with a quiet night in, picking up the ingredients for his favorite scallop dish. She'd take the extra money left over and deposit it in the bank.

She didn't think of it as stealing, although she never told Brad what she was doing. How would she explain it? There was no way he would understand. But with every deposit, no matter how small, she felt a little calmer. The unknown felt a little less terrifying, in this tiny corner that she could control.

What she hadn't expected was for the money to grow so quickly. Within two years she had over twenty-five thousand dollars. The more money there was in the account, the more deceitful Elise felt. She considered donating the whole lump sum to a charity, but every time she thought about dumping the money, she'd hear a little nagging voice in the back of her mind. *What if there's not enough?*

It turned out Brad was more attuned to their finances than Elise realized. One afternoon in February, she returned from school pick up. She bustled Marianna, Piper, and Tommy into the house, a whirl of duffel coats, wet boots, enormous backpacks, and lunchboxes. Brad's car was already in the driveway, which was unusual for a Wednesday. When she got inside, he was sitting at the kitchen counter with an open beer, which was also unusual as it wasn't even four. Piper and Tommy grunted a surprised greeting at him before attacking the pantry and going upstairs to do homework. Marianna curled into his lap for a cuddle.

"You're home early. What's going on?" Elise asked. She put away the peanut butter and crackers that Piper had left on the countertop, sweeping the crumbs into the trash.

"That's a good question, Elise. What *is* going on?" The ice in his voice startled her. Brad pushed several printed pages forward on the counter. They were bank statements for her account. She'd worried about him seeing the statements, so she'd opened a PO box where they were delivered. She kept the statements in a file folder in her nightstand. It had never occurred to her that Brad might go snooping.

"Daddy?" Marianna leaned back to look at her father's face, also shaken by the unfamiliar tone. Brad pushed Marianna's hair from her face and kissed her lightly on the cheek.

"Go play upstairs for a little bit, honey. I need to talk to Mommy." She uncoiled herself from his lap and slumped from the room.

"You were digging through my drawers?" Elise asked, though clearly this was the least of the indiscretions here. Brad flashed her a look of disgust.

"I told you I was bringing the lawnmower into the shop today. I came home early to look for the warranty. I thought it might be in your nightstand. Instead I found this." He held up the bank statement. "What is this?" When she didn't answer, he asked again. "Just what the hell is this, Elise?"

"It looks like a bank statement." She wasn't sure how she was able to keep her voice so calm when her heart banged away in her chest.

"I know that." Brad's face was an unhealthy shade of red, his lips pulled taut in an angry line. "But it's not an account that I ever opened and my name's not on it. And yet there's nearly thirty thousand dollars in it. Do you want to tell me what the hell's going on?"

"It's for Marianna," she began. Brad frowned, alarm flickering across his features.

"Why? Is something wrong? Is she sick?" he asked. As if Elise would ever keep something like that from him.

"No, no. She's fine, it's nothing like that," Elise hurried to reassure him.

"So what then?" he asked.

"For her future. For when we're gone," Elise tried to explain.

The concern was replaced with confusion. "Are *you* sick?"

"No!" Elise said. "I just… I can't explain it. The money makes me feel better. Just knowing it's there."

"The money. Where did it come from?" He pushed the statement toward her, and she glanced at the balance. The sum was close to her starting salary as a teacher.

Elise swallowed the lump that had risen up in the back of her throat. "I just deposited a little bit here and there."

"From our other accounts?"

She nodded.

Brad frowned. "Without telling me? All that money? You took all that money and never told me about it? I don't understand."

Neither did Elise. She chewed her thumbnail, searching for the words. "I feel better knowing it's there. Just in case."

"Are you leaving me?" Brad asked. His expression had gone from anger to confusion and now had rearranged itself into hurt. His sandy eyebrows arched upward.

"No, of course not," she said quickly.

"So what do you need the money for?" Brad asked.

Elise sank beside him onto one of the kitchen stools. "It's just in case. In case something were to happen. If we lost our money. Or one of us wasn't around anymore. If I was suddenly on my own with the kids."

"I don't understand. Are you cheating on me?" He was back to confused.

"No!" And then, softer, "*No.*"

He didn't look relieved. Brad pinched the bridge of his nose between his thumb and forefinger. "So why do you need this money?" he asked again. She could hear the effort it was taking to keep his voice calm.

Elise bit her lip and tried to find the words. How to explain the anxiety that financial worry created to someone who had never experienced it? How did she explain that Elise and all of her siblings started working as soon as they were old enough, and there was never any question that they would hand over at least a portion of their paycheck at the end of the week? Elise took a job as a checkout girl at the grocery store because she knew she'd get a discount on food, and would be allowed to bring home the dinged cans and bruised fruit that no one else wanted to buy. Her brother John got a job at the drugstore for reduced Tylenol and bars of soap. And they were all appalled when Jackie got a job at the Gap, intent on using her paycheck to buy the faded jeans and button-down shirts that all her friends wore. Growing up, there was always food and heat and love, *always* love, but Elise had often wondered if these were enough. Like when she looked at the deep lines etched across her mother's fair freckled skin and wondered what the toll had been. How much had it cost her to unsuccessfully shield her children from the ravages of financial stress?

How did she explain that, even though they were nowhere near the brink she'd grown up on, she was on another brink? She loved Marianna with a ferocity that sometimes scared her, but the foggy future scared her more. Children with Down syndrome were at an increased risk of leukemia, a disease that had haunted Elise since her sister Jackie had been diagnosed in high school. There were a whole host of other medical complications that Marianna was at risk for. Then there were the less urgent questions but ones that still mattered. Would she ever have a best friend? A boyfriend? A job?

Would her life ever expand beyond the walls of the house she lived in now? Would Piper and Tommy look after her, and if they did, would they resent the burden of having to care for her? On and on it went.

Brad was looking into the bottom of his beer bottle. He clutched it tightly in his fist and his knuckles bulged white. "I'm sorry," Elise tried. "I know it doesn't make sense, but I just got scared. What if you're not around? What if *we're* not around?"

Brad digested this, draining the last of his beer in one long swallow. He strode across the kitchen and opened the door that led to the deck. A sharp gust of cold air cut through the house, but Brad was already down the three steps of the deck and on the lawn. Elise followed him, pulling the door closed behind her. The sun was setting, and the motion-activated lights in the garden switched on. Brad stood on the far end of the lawn where the trampoline was. Elise had been trying to get rid of that trampoline for years, ever since she found out how much it raised their homeowner's insurance to have it, but it was Tommy's favorite thing in the world in the warmer months, and she loved to watch Piper flip through the air, her long legs unfolding like a sleek colt. Brad leaned against the trampoline's frame, his chin pressed into the black vinyl fabric. Elise hurried to where he stood, rubbing her arms to keep warm in the raw New England air.

"What's going on in your head?" he asked, without looking at her.

Elise blinked, trying to make sense of his words. "Nothing. I don't know. It's fine, Brad, really, it's fine." When he didn't answer, she took a step closer to him and put her palm upon his back. His sweater was soft and emerald green. Cashmere. She'd bought it for him last Christmas. "Honey, I'm sorry. We'll put the money back in the savings account. Or even better, we'll use it for a vacation. Take the kids to Disney? Or just the two of us. We could go someplace warm, get out of here for a week. Leave the kids with Missy." She still thought she could make him understand, or if not understand, forget the whole thing. Someday they would laugh about this.

When he whirled around to face her, his face was tight with rage. "Goddammit, Elise, you really don't get it, do you?"

Elise shivered in the sharp winter air. "Get what?"

His chest heaved in the expensive sweater, as if he'd been out for a run. "You don't talk to me. You don't let me in. You never let me in." His voice rose and he clutched the empty bottle in his hand. "I don't understand what's going on in your head because you never tell me! Is this about Marianna or you or me? I have no idea. You organize our life so it runs like a fucking machine, but I have no idea what's going on in your head." Tears glittered in his eyes, but his face was set in anger. "You're my wife. I thought we were in this together. And you're hiding everything from me. Not just the money, but how you're actually feeling. For *years*. You have your own *PO box*? What the hell, Elise?"

Brad took a step away from the trampoline and pulled his arm back. For a moment, Elise thought he was going to hit her. He'd never laid a hand on her in all their years of marriage, but his fury was so uncharacteristic, so palpable in the air between them. It wasn't until she held up a hand to fend off the blow that she realized he was just throwing the empty beer bottle across the yard, but by then he'd already seen her reaction, taken in her fear and doubt.

The bottle hit the stone wall that lined the patio, breaking the suburban quiet with the shatter of glass. The shards would be on the pavement for months, even come summer, and Elise would need to make the children wear shoes when they played in the yard at night, forever fearful of an invisible fragment piercing the tender skin of their feet. When Brad met Elise's eyes, his were full of contempt.

"Fuck you, Elise." He spat the words at her, more hurtful than if he had actually hit her. "Fuck you."

That was the first night Brad slept in the guest room.

*

An alert came on her phone that Ivy's plane had landed. Elise checked her hair in the rearview mirror and applied another coat of lipstick.

IVY

Ivy looked out the window and saw the sun glinting off Boston Harbor. The roar of the engine rose as they got ready for landing, and then they were cruising lower and lower, the water getting closer and closer. Ivy gripped the plastic armrests and tried not to think about it diving nose first into the tarmac. But as always, the wheels hit the asphalt and then bounced a few times, racing forward before slowing. They'd made it.

Ivy took out her phone and switched it back on. It lit up with several missed calls: one from Trina, another from Sebastian, and two more of the 800 numbers. She read Ada's text with familiar irritation. It was just like her to gripe about the weekend before they'd even arrived. Ada was one of those people who'd been born with something to complain about. She'd probably come out of the womb whining about the close quarters of her mother's uterus.

Beside her, a young woman just a few years older than Trina zipped up her backpack. She'd been watching Netflix the whole flight, but now Ivy noticed the blue and yellow backpack with the Harper logo on it.

"Do you go to Harper?" Ivy asked.

The young woman nodded. "I'm a freshman. I was home in Berkeley for spring break."

Ivy thought about telling her that she'd gone there too, but thought better of it. She didn't need to hear about Harper now, or describe what it had been like twenty years ago. "Good school," was all she said, then packed up her own stack of magazines and snacks.

Ivy remembered returning to Harper after her first trip home over Christmas break her freshman year. It was always just Ivy and her mother for Christmas, and her mother didn't see the point of cooking an elaborate meal, so they spent the day in their pajamas and had spaghetti and meatballs for dinner. Ivy gave her mother a Harper sweatshirt and a new coffee mug, and her mother gave Ivy an empty photo album, a bulky winter coat, and new sheets. Ivy spent the rest of the month-long break doing Sudoku puzzles and reading. At night, she and her mother settled on the couch to watch whatever movie her mother had picked up from the library, and then Ivy slept till the morning sun was high in the sky and her bedroom a hot little cave.

None of this was unusual for Ivy—the solitude, the quiet of their home, the smallness of it all. In high school, she hadn't had many friends. She didn't fit in with the other girls, though she could never figure out what it was she wasn't doing right, whether it was her choppy dyed hair or her odd clothes, the way her head was always in a book or plugged into a headset. It wasn't until she'd spent four months living with Libby, Ada, and Elise that she recognized her former world as one saturated with loneliness. She didn't talk with her college friends over the endless month, though she was certain that each of them was having a better time, reconnecting with old friends and family, finding comfort in the rituals of home. Sometimes, lying on the overstuffed couch with her mother or sitting in the backyard on a plastic beach chair, Ivy wondered if her life at Harper actually existed.

January finally rolled around. Ivy's suitcase was packed three days before her flight, and she spent hours poring over her new schedule, relishing the time spent imagining the new semester's routine—when she'd study at the library, which classes had enough time between them for a cup of coffee at The Nut or lunch at the student union. When it was time to board the plane, Ivy practically ran up the stairs, only feeling guilty after she settled in her seat and realized how sad her mother looked when saying goodbye.

When she arrived back at Harper, the rest of them were already there, and they greeted Ivy with shrieks and hugs. After dinner that night, squeezed into her twin bed with Libby and watching reruns of *Seinfeld*, Ivy felt more at peace, more at *home*, than she'd felt in her whole life.

LIBBY

Group text: Libby to Ivy, Ada, and Elise
Dropped the girls with my parents and hoping my mom and
Caitlin don't kill each other over the next few days. See you
all soon! xxxxxxxx

Libby focused on the highway and tried not to worry about the girls. Her mother was right, they would be fine. She allowed herself to look forward to the weekend, to no responsibilities and time with her friends. How young they'd been all those years ago when they first met, yet they'd thought themselves so mature, so certain of the future. Libby's thoughts drifted to Steven, who was inextricably tied to those Harper years and her friendships with Elise, Ada, and Ivy.

They met the first week of college. He lived in the dorm room directly below the one she and Ivy shared. Wickingham Hall was where all of the education majors lived. They met when Libby accidentally walked up three flights of stairs instead of four, and found herself trying to put her key in a door that wouldn't unlock. Normally she would have noticed that the whiteboard on Steven's door was a different shape and color than the one on her door, but Libby was preoccupied. Her high school boyfriend had just broken up with her.

Bobby was a nice guy. He was funny and smart, and he was the first guy Libby ever slept with, but she wasn't in love with him.

The letter took her off guard, during the sensitive early days of college when everything still felt scary and unfamiliar, and home so far away. Libby burst into tears in the hot mailroom, stuffing the letter into her bag, and then hurrying across the campus to her dorm. It was late August, and the sun beat down relentlessly. By the time she arrived at the dorm, her shirt was sticky with sweat, her hair stuck to her forehead. All Libby wanted to do was crawl into bed and cry, but it was her pale yellow bedroom in Vermont that she dreamed of, the one with the white patchwork quilt and pine floors, not this concrete dorm full of strangers.

She struggled with the key, fiddling it this way and that unsuccessfully before banging on it with her fist and calling for Ivy. A stocky blond guy with a face full of freckles opened the door.

"Who are you?" Libby asked, blinking back tears.

He cracked a grin, nonplussed by her aggressive tone. "Steven Green. Who are you?" He extended his hand. When she shook it, his grip was strong, like a man more than a boy. Bobby had the long slender fingers of a piano player. Steven's hands looked used to manual labor and throwing footballs.

"I'm Libby. This is my room." She peered over his shoulder, looking for Ivy, wondering if her roommate had picked up this big beefy guy on her way home from freshman comp. Where Libby's tie-dye tapestry normally hung, the walls were decorated with Red Sox posters and Patriots flags. Libby took a step back, noticing the number on the door for the first time. 301. Libby lived in 401. "I think I'm on the wrong floor."

"Are you sure? I wouldn't mind a new roommate." Steven cocked his head, eyes crinkling with his smile. Bobby's letter, stuffed in the pocket of her shorts, suddenly didn't feel so dire. Steven's smile was enough to remind her how happy she was to be at Harper.

"What's wrong with your roommate?" Libby asked, playing along.

"Not a fan of his music." He stepped back and gestured to the wall on one side of the room, covered in posters of heavy metal bands.

Libby wiped her eyes, suddenly aware of how disheveled she must look.

"Are you okay?" he asked. Libby flushed and tightened her grip on her bag.

She pulled out the letter. "My boyfriend just broke up with me." Already Bobby was fading into her past. No longer was she looking for comfort or sympathy. Now she just wanted to convey the information to Steven that she was single.

"Dumb guy. His loss, right?"

"I guess."

"I was just about to go over to the dining hall for some dinner. Do you want to come?"

And that was that. It was college, and you could meet the people who would change your life just by skipping a set of stairs or getting assigned as roommates.

It had been nearly three years since Steven died of a heart attack. Three years that felt like an eternity and also just yesterday. She often thought about the adage, *It's better to have loved and lost than never to have loved at all*. Sometimes she thought this was a load of bull, because no one's love could compare to Steven's. His love was the bright beacon she had followed for so many years. She couldn't bask in the memory of it. All she felt, even still, was the cold blackness of his absence. And she wasn't sure that she was any better off knowing that such love was possible.

The narrow back roads of Vermont unwound before her, an endless black thread looping and uncoiling as it led to the highway. She always thought about Steven, but lately she'd been thinking about him with the tender bruise of guilt, grieving for him anew because she feared she might be falling in love again.

   She hadn't told anyone about Adam, instead holding the secret close, something that both terrified and excited her, a tangled web of emotions that needed to be sorted out. She hoped her friends might be able to help her, that over the weekend they might give her the absolution she needed to try again.

ADA

Text message: Ada to Tyler
Give Sam one more kiss for me. And make sure you put him
down for his nap on time. He'll be a monster if he misses it.
Love you.

In the car on the way to the Cape, Ada listened to a podcast on sleep training. She'd been unsuccessfully trying to get Sam to sleep through the night for several months. It had gotten desperate. Last week she'd spent several torturous nights letting him cry it out, but Sam's stamina for misery was higher than hers, and Ada broke down after just twenty minutes. When Tyler pressed her to give it longer, Sam worked himself into such a tizzy that he threw up. Then both Sam and Ada were in tears, while Tyler changed the sheets and cleaned puke from between the wooden slats of the crib.

For the first few months after Sam was born, Ada tried a mom and baby group. She knew she needed to be around other mothers and to meet women going through the same thing as she was. They gathered in the children's area of the community center, a dusty room of secondhand couches and plastic toys that always smelled of hot dogs and macaroni and cheese. The first time Ada went, there were five other mothers, the oldest other than Ada just pushing thirty-five and on her second baby. The women gathered in a circle, and each went around the group and shared a high and a low of their week.

"Sophie smiled for the first time yesterday!" proclaimed a bouncy blonde woman who looked like she could be on the cheerleading team at the school where Ada taught. Though little Sophie was only three months old, her mother looked to be back in her pre-pregnancy jeans while Ada was considering ordering new maternity clothes. "I don't have any lows right now. It's been a really great week," she beamed.

"Evette and I are co-sleeping," a woman with waist-length hair and dewy skin shared. "When she wakes up to eat, she just cuddles into me and then falls back to sleep when she's done. I feel so close to her." She smiled beatifically at the group. "My low this week was when I ate some broccoli and Evette was gassy for a bit. Poor little peanut had an upset tummy." She cooed down at the dark-haired infant sleeping soundly in her arms.

When it was Ada's turn, the group waited expectantly for her high of the week. "I… Um…" She looked at Sam who was fast asleep in his car seat, though she knew he'd wake up squalling as soon as they were back in the car. Ada blinked at the women and stifled the urge to yawn. A bottle of unfiltered apple juice and a sleeve of graham crackers sat on the table, but not a single cup of coffee, as if this were snack time for a group of toddlers.

There were many highs she could have confided. The feel of Sam's breath on her neck, the smell of his bedroom in the late afternoon (after the vomit had been scrubbed off the crib) like milk and baby wipes, and some unnamable scent that brought her to her knees. The way he looked at her, his eyes still that indeterminate shade of bottomless midnight blue, and Ada felt like he was reaching inside of her, like the umbilical cord hadn't actually been cut. These moments were the highs of her days, but they were too intimate and intangible to share.

"I got to take a shower yesterday," she finally said. The others waited for the rest, the enchanted maternal moment. "In the morning. Before my husband left for work," she added. Sam opened his eyes and let out a cry. "That was nice."

Debbie, the facilitator, was a white-haired woman in her fifties who looked like she was also still wearing maternity clothes. She smiled encouragingly at Ada. "And why was that a high for you this week?"

"Because usually I don't shower all day, and I smell like spit-up by the time my husband gets home. And these days taking a shower is about the only time I get to myself." Ada blinked back hot tears that were suddenly threatening to spill forth. None of it was coming out right. She sounded so bitter, so joyless, when that wasn't how she felt, or at least not all of it. "So yeah. That was the high."

The facilitator nodded. "Have you been getting any time to yourself since the baby was born?" she asked.

Ada let out a harsh laugh. "When exactly? My husband's at work all day and then Sam's up half the night. When am I supposed to squeeze in some time to myself?" She glanced down at her lap, seeing again the extra flesh around her waistband. When she looked up, the rest of the women were staring at her with concern. "Sorry," she added.

"It's important to get some time to ourselves. That's one of the hardest things about having a baby. Maybe you can find a sitter for a few hours a week so you can go for a walk or have coffee with a friend?" Debbie suggested. Ada didn't try to explain that sitters cost money and she didn't have a family member close enough to drop Sam off with each week.

"Maybe," was all she said.

"And your low?" Debbie asked.

All day, every day, Ada thought. *The minute the door closes behind Tyler. The middle of the night when my heart won't stop racing. When Sam cries, and I feel it in the pit of my stomach, and I'd do anything*

*to make it stop. When he sleeps and all I can do is clean the house,
scrub the toilet, sanitize the bottles. When I wake up in the morning
and know I have to do it all over again.*

"Nothing this week. Everything's great." Ada picked up Sam
and buried her face in his sour-smelling neck. She'd bathe him
when they got home.

It wasn't that the other women didn't have lows or weren't struggling with the huge transition of life after a baby. They fretted over
nursing and napping, sleep deprivation and allergic reactions. It
was just that their concerns seemed so small compared to their joy.

She returned the next week and the week after that, wanting
to feel connected to the other women. It took an hour to get
Sam ready to go, and he screamed when she bundled him into
his snowsuit. By the time she packed diapers and wipes and burp
cloths and binkies, it was time to nurse again, and she had to
undress him so he didn't overheat in the giant fleece suit. It was
too much trouble, though the babies' group was the one scheduled
activity in the whole week, the only time she ever made it out of the
house to socialize, not that it could even be considered socializing.
Pre-Sam, socializing meant makeup and cocktails, not plastic cups
of juice and sweatpants.

Ada didn't know how Elise managed. *Three kids.* How did
anyone do this more than once? Ada's whole being was ravaged by
Sam. She was a lumpy, leaky, exhausted mess, and she didn't see
an end in sight, though Elise was proof that there was life on the
other side of motherhood. Elise in her cigarette pants and ballet
flats, her makeup perfectly understated, her hair nicely styled, and
that was being superficial because Elise was more than that. She
was also the first one to bring a lasagna after a major life event,
the first to send a birthday card, the first to offer to take Sam
overnight. If Elise could do this then so could Ada.

But of course that wasn't true, because Elise was a different breed
than Ada. Elise effortlessly got straight As all through Harper, while

Ada killed herself to scrape by with Bs. In college Elise wrote for the student newspaper, she played intramural field hockey, and she went to church every Sunday. Church! Who went to church in college? Elise Kelly did.

Ada had tried to confide in Elise about her worries. She tried to explain how spent she felt, how the relentless monologue in her mind wouldn't shut down, like the ticker tape running along the bottom of the TV screen during an emergency. It just kept going and going and going, and Ada couldn't stop reading the headlines.

"The first baby rocks your world," Elise had told her confidently when Ada tried to get the words out. What had she said? How had she tried to express it? *I just don't feel like myself.* This was true and also the biggest understatement of all time. Ada felt as if her life had been flipped upside down while she was taking a nap and that her whole body, inside and out, had been rearranged without her consent. Everything from her breasts to her tender inner organs were bigger or in a different place or stitched up while she wasn't looking.

At her first postnatal visits, the doctor had asked how she was feeling. *Tired,* she'd said. *Okay, I guess.* And it was true, sometimes. There were moments when Ada would catch herself holding Sam, her cheek pressed against his damp head, and think, *This is all I need.* And then there were moments when she missed her old life terribly—having a job to go to every day, clothes that fit, her mother always just a phone call or short drive away. She and Tyler used to go hiking in the woods near their home every weekend, and she missed how she felt after those walks—refreshed and strong. She'd slipped out of her old life and into this new and unfamiliar one as suddenly as a snake shedding its skin.

One evening a few weeks ago Sam wouldn't go down for his afternoon nap, the only time of the day that Ada could count on to get a few minutes' peace. He'd spent the later part of the day fidgeting restlessly in her arms, making that fussy little "eh, eh, eh" whine that drove her mad. She'd finally put him in his crib and locked herself in the bathroom, and the two of them had cried separately behind closed doors. When Tyler finally came home, they were both red-faced and spent.

It was just a bad day, she'd reassured him. Nothing she couldn't handle. She wasn't one of those women who was about to drive off a cliff with the baby in the car. Even if, for a moment, a tiny part of her had wanted to throw Sam against the wall, she *never* would have done it. It had scared her though, the trembling rage that flickered through her muscles, the way she felt as if she'd exited her body and was watching herself from above, an angry and unhinged woman falling apart over something as small as a fussing baby. She could almost see her mother's face, brow furrowed in concern, reminding Ada that if she had done this four times, surely Ada could do it *once*. She'd always managed to talk Ada out of her self-pity and neediness, both building Ada up and comforting her at the same time. *Pull it together and put your big girl pants on*, her mother would have said with a light kiss on the cheek.

She loved Sam. Even in the depth of her grief for her mother, even at her most exhausted, even when he called out in the middle of the night for the fifth time and she felt like she was losing her mind, she loved him. She just needed him to sleep.

Over the car radio's speakers, a woman spoke in a clipped British accent about the importance of a bedtime routine, books, a warm soapy bath, followed by a gentle massage with lavender-scented lotion, all for baby to begin to associate relaxation with bedtime. Ada turned off the podcast, turning on the radio instead. What a load of bullshit.

This weekend she would relax. She would remember who she had been before Sam came along, someone smart and funny, and maybe not sexy, but at least a little pretty when she spent a few extra minutes on herself. Maybe at some point over the weekend she'd be able to pull Elise aside, or even Ivy or Libby, and ask the questions she'd been wondering for the past nine months, since Sam had been born.

Is this normal? Is there something wrong with me?

And maybe one of them would be able to tell her the truth.

ELISE

Elise waited in her car for Ivy. Fifteen minutes later, Ivy stepped through the automatic doors and into the late April sunshine. Since Elise had last seen her, Ivy had cut her dark hair into a short pixie style that would have aged Elise by ten years but made Ivy look closer to thirty. She was tall and thin as ever, dressed in tight jeans, boots, and a knee-length cardigan. She pulled a small black suitcase behind her, and an oversized leather bag dangled from her arm as she scanned the busy terminal. Elise stepped from the car and waved.

"Ivy! Over here!"

Ivy waved back, and Elise hurried around the front of the car and caught her in a quick hug, mindful of the endless traffic guards just waiting to give out tickets to anyone who dared leave their car unattended for more than fifteen seconds. Once she'd stowed Ivy's suitcase in the trunk, nestled behind a bag of organic kale chips and mangoes, she turned back to Ivy.

"You're here!" Elise exclaimed, exhaling a sigh of relief. She'd been waiting for Ivy to bail. Every time Elise checked her email for the past week, there had been a tiny part of her that expected a message from Ivy saying she wouldn't be able to make it. It was only now that Elise realized she'd both been dreading that email and hoping for it. The weekend wouldn't be the same if Ivy weren't there. But also, the weekend wouldn't be the same if Ivy *were* there. Much as Elise loved her, things were always a little harder with Ivy, partly because Ivy had a way of making things more difficult, but also because of the events that occurred their senior year that the four of them always tiptoed around. Either way, she was here now.

"I made it!" Ivy's face loosened into a smile and Elise pulled her in for another hug.

"I'm so glad." All around them, cars were pulling out into the ring road that circled the airport. The screech of horns and tires was magnified by the overhead ramps. Heading in their direction was a police officer in an electric orange vest, notebook in hand.

"Let's hit the road," Elise said, releasing Ivy and jumping in the driver's seat. Once they were out of the terminal, she turned to Ivy. "We're just going to swing by my place first and then we'll head to the Cape. I need to grab a few things and then we can get going."

"No problem," Ivy said, fiddling with the radio.

"There wasn't enough room in the car with the kids this morning. I made some food, and I didn't want it to sit in the back any longer than it has to," she added. Already she was nervous about Ivy's judgment, knowing how extravagant both her homes would appear to Ivy who was quietly struggling to stay afloat in the city. Ivy had stayed at Elise's house in Newton for Ada's wedding, but they'd only purchased the Cape house the previous summer, and it would be the first time her friends saw it.

Elise and Ivy had both been on scholarships at Harper. They had always quietly taken work-study jobs, and though they never discussed their lack of money, it had always silently bound them together. Now, the disparity between their situations was jarring, and while Elise loved both her homes and the life that she and Brad had, she felt uncomfortable about it in Ivy's presence.

Elise navigated the complicated airport roads. Thank God for the GPS on her dashboard, which patiently recited the directions aloud in a crisp calm voice, although it was difficult to hear over the music. Ivy had settled on one of the stations Piper had programmed into the car. One of her daughter's favorite pop songs was playing, the one Elise hated even while she'd find herself humming bars as she went about her day.

"Let me just…" Elise reached to turn down the volume just as the GPS instructed her to take the next turnoff. The exit flashed by her window. "Crap!"

"What's wrong?" Ivy asked, unconcerned. She'd pulled down the mirror on the visor and was reapplying lipstick.

"That was our exit. *Crap*."

"Can't we just take the next one?" Ivy asked.

"This is *Boston*. You can't just take the next exit. Who knows where we'll end up?"

She immediately felt guilty for snapping at Ivy, but she didn't have time to think about that now. Cars flew past them on either side and Elise clutched the steering wheel. Maybe she *should* have let Ivy take an Uber back to the house. Elise hated driving in the city, especially to the airport. She'd always been a nervous driver. She was confident navigating the familiar streets of Newton, but finding her way through the intricate maze of Logan was another story.

"Are we getting on Ninety-three?" Ivy asked.

"What? I don't know." She looked at the screen of the GPS. *Rerouting. Rerouting.* The little wheel kept spinning around.

"I think we are. Take the exit coming up for the Ted Williams Tunnel," Ivy instructed.

"Are you sure?" Elise asked, merging across a row of traffic. A car honked at her. Ivy gripped the armrest.

"I think so. Right here."

Elise took the turn, and when she looked back at the GPS, the screen had reconfigured itself and the voice was politely telling her the next direction. Elise's palms were sweaty against the wheel.

"How did you know where we were going?" she asked.

Ivy shrugged. "I remembered from Ada's wedding, I guess."

Elise had forgotten that Ivy, despite her occasional flakiness and unreliability, was one of the smartest people she knew. Not that you needed to be brilliant to navigate Boston traffic (well, you kind of did), but Ivy had a memory that bordered on photographic. Once, when Elise had left a textbook in class, Ivy had recited all of the important points in a chapter on special education. Elise had actually taken notes from Ivy's impromptu lecture.

They drove in silence until Elise got closer to the familiar roads of Newton.

"Oh," Ivy said softly.

"What? Did you forget something?" It would be just like Ivy to forget a bag at the airport. Photographic memory or not, she had a mind like a sieve. Elise didn't care—she would replace everything in Ivy's missing suitcase. There was no way in hell she was driving back to the airport.

Ivy shook her head. "It's just… Harper."

Elise hadn't even noticed they were passing the campus. The buildings of Harper were part of the scenery of her adulthood now, and she drove past them almost every day. Last year Tommy had taken an enrichment math class in the building where she'd had freshman composition. She no longer thought about her time here whenever she drove by the campus, but it was where they'd met all those years ago, during their first week of freshman orientation when they snuck into an off-campus party. Elise remembered drinking flat beer from a plastic cup, smooshed on a couch with Libby, Ada, and Ivy, and then stumbling back to the dorm in a giggly buzzed huddle. She didn't remember what they talked about or what they'd discovered they had in common. What she did remember was that from then on, the four of them were a unit. One night together and an illicit trip off-campus had cemented the future of their friendship.

Driving through the Harper campus now, nearly twenty years after that night, it was hard to believe they were ever that young. Elise slowed to let a group of young women cross. They looked barely older than the girls in Tommy's class. Their hair hung in shiny flat-ironed curtains down their backs, and they each wore the standard uniform of skinny jeans and boots. They looked far more glamorous than Elise remembered being in college. Elise spent most of her four years at Harper in sweatpants and flip-flops. At that point, she still hadn't figured out how to properly wield the hair dryer, and so her hair usually air-dried into a frizzy mane. And they all were fat. Well, not fat, but each of them gained the requisite freshman fifteen, and in pictures from those early years, their cheeks were round and soft. When Elise looked at those pictures now, she was surprised by how pretty they all looked, despite the extra pounds. Their faces were open, like they still expected good things around every corner. In the pictures of her Harper friends that Elise saw on Facebook these days, they were all leaner and more sculpted (except for Ada who still battled her pregnancy weight gain), but there was a hollowness to each of them, something brittle and hard, their smiles tight and for show, gone the second the camera disappeared.

"I haven't seen the campus in years," Ivy said.

"When was the last time you were back?" Elise asked. She wondered if maybe she should have taken the long route home, the one that didn't wind past the campus.

They'd gone to their fifteenth reunion four years earlier, all of them except Ivy, who was the only one who hadn't graduated from Harper.

"God, I can't even remember. I don't think I've been here since college." Ivy stared out the window at the manicured grounds and stately buildings.

"They shouldn't have kicked you out like that. They should have given you another chance," Elise said softly. It was the thing they all tried not to talk about when they got together. Elise didn't think Ivy had ever fully recovered from it. She wasn't sure any of them had. She braced herself for Ivy's reaction.

"Well, they didn't. I'm sure things would be a whole lot different now if they had," Ivy said. Her voice had the rasp of emotion in it, but she kept her face toward the window so Elise couldn't see her expression.

"I'm sorry," Elise said, knowing the words didn't mean much.

Ivy let out a gruff laugh, and turned toward the window so Elise couldn't see her face. "Don't be. It was all a long time ago," she said. They passed Wickingham, red brick with turrets and creeping vines, the dormitory for the teachers' college, where the four of them had first met. Elise pressed her foot down on the gas just a little harder. Neither of them spoke as Wickingham disappeared behind them.

IVY

Group text: Ivy to Elise, Ada, and Libby
I hope you're all hungry and thirsty. Elise packed enough food
for the rest of the month.

Ivy fell asleep on the drive to the Cape. She awoke to the crackle
of oyster shells under the wheels of Elise's minivan. When she
opened her eyes, they were pulling into the driveway of a newly
shingled modern-style home overlooking the ocean. The house
was boxy and square with windows on all sides. If possible, it was
even larger than Elise's other house.

"Holy shit, Elise. This is your house?" Ivy asked.

Elise let out a nervous trill of laughter. "We bought it last summer."

"Well, you've certainly moved up in the world. This place is
amazing," Ivy said.

Elise gave a tight smile as she put the car in park and unsnapped
her seat belt. "Thank you. We love it here. Let's get unpacked, and
I'll give you a tour."

Ivy stepped out of the car and stood for a moment staring at
the house. With its geometric shape and the wraparound glass
railing that bordered the upper-level deck, it was not in the style
of most of the houses in the area, but it was nestled at the end
of a quiet road and didn't need to fit in with any neighbors. Just
beyond the house, the ocean glittered a deep blue. The air held
the sharp tang of the sea. When Ivy turned back toward the car,

Elise was already hauling out cloth bags full of groceries, lining them up on the edge of the walkway. It was difficult to reconcile this version of Elise with the girl she'd once known, the one who ordered hot water and lemon at the coffee shop, who stuffed her purse full of granola bars and apples from the dining hall instead of buying snacks from the grocery store to keep in her dorm room.

Ivy followed Elise around to the trunk of the car. She looked at the abundance of food and alcohol. "You realize we're only here for three days, right?"

"I know. I just wanted the weekend to be perfect. I'm so glad you're here." She put her arm around Ivy's shoulders and gave her a quick squeeze. "Thank you for coming. I know how far it is."

"I'm glad I could." If Ivy had realized just how loaded Elise was, maybe she *would* have let her pay for the plane ticket. Her pride only stretched so far. She followed Elise up the walkway and inside. The house smelled like dried lavender and fresh paint.

"Let's put the groceries away first," Elise said. The kitchen was bright and full of windows overlooking the ocean, big enough that Ivy's San Francisco apartment would have fit in it with a few feet to spare.

"God, Elise. This place is amazing. Seriously."

"Oh. Thank you. I know it's a little… extravagant." She bit her lip and glanced around the room. Ivy knew how much Elise enjoyed playing host, but she sensed the discomfort that rippled just below the surface, pride and embarrassment rubbing up against each other. It wasn't envy that Ivy felt as much as disbelief. The chasm between Elise's current life and her own was so vast it was hard to believe they'd started in the same place.

"Hey, if you can afford it, why not?" Ivy said, breaking the cardinal rule of talking about money. It was only taboo to discuss money if you had it.

Elise busied herself fixing a tray of snacks. She laid out a cutting board with a bowl of olives, a soft creamy cheese, and a box of rosemary crackers. "So what are we drinking? Cocktails? Champagne?" she asked.

"You know me. I'll drink anything." Ivy slathered a cracker with cheese and popped it in her mouth.

"Let's do champagne! Or should we wait for Libby and Ada? Oh, there's plenty. Let's have a glass." She fluttered back into the open kitchen.

"Works for me," Ivy said, reaching for an olive.

Elise pulled out a pair of tall flutes and removed a bottle of champagne from the fridge. With practiced ease, she popped the cork with a deep thunk and poured them each a glass.

"Should we save the toast till the others are here?" she asked, after Ivy had already taken a sip. "Just a cheers, then." Elise clinked her glass against Ivy's. They settled into the white couch, and Ivy felt her body begin to relax until Elise started to pepper her with questions.

"So, what's going on with you? How are the kids and Sebastian? How's work? What's new in your world? I feel like we haven't talked in ages. Tell me everything." Elise leaned in closer in that way she had, like she really didn't want to be anywhere other than right here, listening to Ivy.

As much as Elise drove Ivy nuts with her micromanagement and ridiculous cheer, she cared so much about everyone else that it was hard to hold the annoying bits against her for very long.

"Oh, not much," Ivy said evasively. "The kids are good. I mean, they're teenagers, so they kind of suck. But they're fine."

Elise nodded in agreement. "I'm dreading the teenage years. Already Tommy doesn't talk to me anymore, he just grunts at me. But Piper's even worse and she's only ten. Some days I want to remove her eyeballs from her head because she rolls them at me every time I open my mouth. It's like my voice and her eyes are connected. Everything I do annoys her."

Ivy laughed and drank more champagne. "Well, Trina just got her lip pierced. And then it got infected, so she had all this crusty yellow puss coming out of it. I'm no prude, but what is attractive about that?"

"Ugh." Elise gave an exaggerated shudder and refilled their glasses even though Ivy's was still half full. "How's Sebastian?"

"Oh, fine. He's fine." This was her chance to admit the truth, that while he might be fine, *she* wasn't. At some point, she would have to tell them. That was what friends did after all, confide in each other.

Ivy knew if she met Libby, Ada, or Elise now, they wouldn't be friends. The three of them led such stable, traditional lives in respectable suburbs and small towns. They owned houses and cars, had the careers they'd set out for way back in college (except for Elise, but her two massive houses certainly made up for the teaching career she'd given up), and steady routinized lives. Ivy's life, on the other hand, was an unpredictable bohemian mess, which it had been even when she was with Sebastian. She lived in one of the most expensive cities in the country in an apartment meant for a couple, not a family with two teenage children. Her friends were artists and dancers and non-profit workers. In her circle at home, they were *all* on the edge of poverty, and while that didn't make it any less stressful, it did make it less shameful. Once upon a time, she was a student at Harper and wanted to be a science teacher. Some days she wasn't sure which was the real Ivy, the girl back then who envisioned the kind of life her friends now had, or the one she'd been before and after, flighty and brash, always landing herself or someone else in hot water.

"How are *you*?" Ivy asked, deciding to save the topic of Sebastian for later in the weekend. Elise focused on the tiny bubbles rising to the surface of her drink.

"Fine, fine. Nothing new with us really. Just the same old, same old."

Ivy gestured around the kitchen to the granite countertop and ocean view. "Well, that's not so bad."

Elise gave a quick smile. "No, it's not. It's great," she said unconvincingly. Ivy sensed she was holding something back, but it might have just been the embarrassment of her obvious wealth colliding with Ivy's thrift store sweater and worn out boots. All of Ivy's friends shopped in consignment and secondhand stores; it only occurred to her now that not everyone her age still did this.

"Hello?" a voice called from the entrance of the house.

Elise leapt from her seat, nearly knocking over her glass. "We're in here!"

Ada appeared in the doorway looking tired and fat, which was unkind, but also true. Over her shoulder, she carried an oversized messenger bag with clear plastic tubes dangling to the floor, which Ivy recognized as a breast pump. Ada's hair hung in a limp ponytail and the front of her shapeless top was soaked. She looked close to tears.

"Honey, are you okay?" Elise hurried over to her.

"I need to pump," Ada nearly yelled. "I tried to do it at a rest stop but there were too many people around. And the bathroom was so filthy that I couldn't even put the bag down on the floor. I'm about to explode." Ada held her hand to her breasts, as if they might actually volcanically erupt.

Ivy pinched her lips together to keep from laughing.

"It's not funny," Ada barked.

"Sorry," Ivy said, swallowing a bubble of laughter. Elise shot her a look, and Ivy tipped her face into the champagne glass.

"Come on." Elise held Ada firmly by the arm, taking the breast pump from her. "We'll get you settled upstairs. You can relax and take a shower when you're finished. Then come down and have a drink." Elise hustled Ada out of the room and up the softly carpeted stairs.

Left alone, Ivy wandered around the spacious house. Unlike her own cramped apartment, which was overflowing with the detritus of two teenagers and the scraps of life, not a thing in

Elise's house seemed out of order. Ivy assumed there was some kind of hired help to assist with this, because every item in both of Elise's homes seemed to be intentionally in place. There were decorative dish towels with seashells embroidered on them, hanging neatly from the stove. A corkboard with a calendar and several postcards was mounted to the wall. Framed photographs of Elise's family lined a bookcase. There were no kicked off shoes by the doorway or stray sweaters draped on the arm of a chair, no tangled phone chargers or crumpled receipts. Only clean lines and natural light.

Ivy was staring at a professional portrait of Elise's three children, marveling at how Elise had gotten all of them to wear matching white and navy blue outfits, when she heard Libby calling from the front hall.

"In here!" Ivy turned away from the photo and hurried toward her most beloved friend.

Libby looked so much like her former self that it took Ivy's breath away, bringing her back to being eighteen-year-old freshman roommates all over again. Libby was small and compact with a round open face, and shiny brown hair cut into the same simple bob she'd had for as long as Ivy had known her.

Ivy nearly pitched herself into Libby's arms. "You're here!"

Libby kissed her lightly on the cheek and then released her. "Look at you! I love the new haircut." She ruffled Ivy's messy hair. "Where is everyone?"

"Ada just arrived and she's having a nursing situation. Elise is upstairs helping her get sorted out," Ivy said.

"Everything okay?" Libby left her bag in the hallway and followed Ivy into the kitchen, where she plopped herself down at the counter and helped herself to a cracker with cheese. Ivy sat down beside her.

"I guess. Apparently, her breasts might explode." She poured Libby some champagne and handed the glass to her. Libby reached for the glass and gulped down a sip, leaning back in her chair with a contented sigh.

"Oh, you remember that, don't you? Nursing. How hard it was?"

Ivy shrugged. She barely remembered nursing either Jax or Trina. It was another lifetime, though in some dusty crevice of memory she could summon up the sour-sweet scent of breast milk and the gentle tug of Trina's lips against her nipple, insistent and surprisingly strong.

"God, look at this place," Libby marveled, glancing around the room.

"I know, right?" Ivy said, glad that Libby shared her disbelief.

"How lucky are we? I feel like we're in a hotel. Or in the pages of *Architectural Digest*," Libby said, taking another sip of champagne. Ivy watched her relax into the cushioned barstool.

"The girls got off okay?" Ivy asked.

"I guess. I left them with my mom. I should probably call." Libby stayed where she was, making no move for her phone. She reached for an olive.

"Hello, hello! We're all here!" Elise came back into the kitchen, pulling a slightly less disheveled-looking Ada with her. Her hair was damp and she'd changed out of her dumpy wet shirt. The new shirt was also large and formless as a trash bag, but at least it was clean and in a pretty shade of purple.

There were hugs and exclamations and a general rundown of everyone's travel schedule.

"What are we all drinking?" Elise asked, lifting the empty champagne bottle.

"How about making some of that cocktail you were telling us about," Ivy suggested.

"I told you, I'm nursing. I can't drink," Ada reminded them.

"Don't even give me that. You're not nursing for the next three days. You can have a few drinks," Elise said, with the authority of someone who had wrestled with this before. She pulled out her ingredients, including an actual mortar and pestle, which she used to pulverize a handful of mint leaves.

"I was planning on keeping the milk and freezing it. I brought bags. And a thermos," Ada said.

"You're kidding, right?" Ivy asked. "You're planning on not drinking for the next three days and driving home with a trunkful of frozen breast milk? *Seriously?*"

Ivy waited for Ada to snap and tell her to shut the hell up. She loved Ada, but somehow they always managed to bring out the worst in each other. Instead, Ada let out a sigh. "Forget it. Just make me a drink."

"Woo hoo! Atta girl." Ivy reached out a hand and high-fived a reluctant Ada.

"Shall we have a toast?" Elise handed out drinks that looked like they would cost fifteen dollars apiece in a bar in San Francisco. They held up their glasses, pink and green shimmering in frosted glasses. "To my three best friends in the whole world, yesterday, today, and tomorrow. Cheers."

"Cheers," they echoed and clinked glasses. Ivy took a sip, and the smooth tang of vodka and grapefruit slid down her throat easily. *Let the fun begin.*

LIBBY

Libby poured herself a second cocktail from the pitcher Elise had made. At home she rarely drank more than a glass of wine, always aware that she was the person in charge, the one to pick Caitlin up at a friend's house at ten or who'd need to drive to the hospital if someone spiked a fever in the middle of the night. But no one needed her now, and even if they did, she was hours away. She was tempted to turn off her cell phone but knew her mother wouldn't call unless there was a real emergency. Something involving blood and broken bones. Otherwise her mother would hold things together with her iron grip, even if Libby would pay the consequences for weeks when she returned. Caitlin would just ignore her, which wasn't so different from a usual day, but Bethany would become even clingier and needier, sidling up to her like a cat, slipping into Libby's bed in the middle of the night, pressing her hot little body against Libby, making it impossible to sleep soundly. She hoped the three-day break would be worth it.

"Should we go over the weekend?" Elise asked.

Of the four of them, Elise looked the best, Libby decided. Ivy still had her punk-rock look going, but it didn't look as good at forty-two as it had at twenty. Still, she was tall and thin as ever, sexy in a careless rumpled way. Ada just looked tired and worn out from the early days of motherhood, her normally slender body still doughy and soft. Libby was pretty sure she herself looked like an older, less patient version of the girl she'd once been. Elise, on the other hand, appeared energetic and stylish. Her sandy blonde hair looked natural, although Libby suspected it was the result of regular visits to an expensive salon. In college Elise rotated through a collection of sweatshirts and jeans, giving her the look of a gym teacher or middle school boy, but sometime in the last twenty years she'd found her style, a kind of preppy bohemian look that suited her. Her makeup was artfully applied so as to make her look cheerful and well rested.

Elise went on. "I made a little itinerary. Nothing set in stone, but let's just do a quick run through." She opened a pink folder and handed everyone a document. Elise began to read like a tour guide, and Libby wondered whether it would be Ada or Ivy who would make the first biting remark. "So tonight we'll just relax. Cocktails and an easy dinner. Just a salad and some appetizers. Tomorrow morning we'll make breakfast and then maybe go for a walk along the beach. I've booked us all in for massages in the morning—my treat, no arguments! Afterwards we'll have lunch at the Seastar. They have the best lobster rolls in town." Elise looked up from the paper and beamed at them, flashing a surprisingly white smile, the result of professional whitening treatments, no doubt. Libby had trouble remembering to floss. "For dinner tomorrow night we can either cook, family style, or we can head into town for dinner. And then Sunday—" Elise began, but Ada cut her off.

"You're tiring me out. Is there any time in this weekend for naps? Or just relaxing? Watching mindless movies on Netflix?"

Elise looked stricken, but she recovered quickly. "Of course! We don't have to do any of this. I just wanted to make a plan, so we wouldn't have to waste our time together trying to figure out what to do. But we can do anything. Really!" She smiled kindly at Ada who glanced back down at the schedule.

"It all looks great, El. Sorry, I'm just tired. Sam was up three times last night." Ada forced a smile.

"You can take a rest now if you want. That way you'll be all fresh for dinner," Elise said.

Ada looked down at her barely half-finished cocktail. "Maybe I will. I'll probably feel better for it." She pushed herself up with what looked like an enormous amount of effort. When Libby looked closer, she noticed that Ada was pale but there were blotchy dried patches here and there on her face, similar to the eczema Bethany suffered from. Her eyes were red-rimmed and her lips chapped. She looked like she might tip over if someone brushed against her.

"Are you okay?" Libby asked. Ada blinked a few times rapidly, and her eyes locked on Libby's for a fleeting moment before she ran her fingers through her messy ponytail.

"I'm fine. Just tired."

"We know. You mentioned it," Ivy said.

"Oh, fuck off, Ivy," Ada snapped. Libby's heart jumped and Elise's eyes widened, her mouth forming a little O. Ivy glanced at Ada in surprise, though she appeared unruffled. Of the foursome, it was Ivy and Ada's relationship that had threatened to undo the group on more than one occasion. Ada was too neurotic and sensitive for Ivy, and Ivy was too loud and bullish for Ada. They gave each other a wide berth for the sake of the others. Yet Libby had hoped it would be at least twenty-four hours before they started sniping at each other.

"I'm sorry," Ada said quickly, and looked like she might burst into tears. "I'm such a mess. I'm all hormonal and exhausted." Both Libby and Elise cut their eyes at Ivy, to stop her from pointing out that Ada had already made it quite clear she was tired.

"Of course you are," Elise murmured, standing and putting a protective arm around Ada. "These first months are so hard. Let's get you upstairs where you can take a nice rest. You have no responsibilities for the next three days."

Ada nodded miserably, and Elise led her away for the second time so far. Ivy looked at Libby with a conspiratorial smirk on her face.

"*Don't*," Libby said, as soon as Ada was out of earshot.

"What?" Ivy asked innocently.

"Give her a break, will you? She's having a hard time. With her mother dying and having a new baby, all in such a short time span. It's a lot." She and Ada spoke on the phone every few weeks and Libby knew how difficult it had been for her, even if seeing it up close made it that much more apparent.

"Let's go in the other room," Libby suggested, changing the subject. They gathered their drinks and Elise's artful snacks, and headed into the living room. It was huge, with three white couches set in a horseshoe around a coffee table. Home improvement and lifestyle magazines were spread in a fan on the table. One entire wall was made of glass and led to a deck that overlooked the beach. The dark water glittered in the thin April sun.

"Can you believe this place?" Ivy asked.

"I know. It's another world."

"Makes you rethink that school counselor major, huh? You'd have been better off going into private practice," Ivy said.

"Yeah, you're telling me. Or corporate law. Or whatever it is that Brad does," Libby added.

Sometimes Libby wondered what her life would be like if she'd gone into private practice instead of working as a school counselor. The girls who came to sit in the big flowered chair in her office at Wolf Mountain High School talked about boyfriends who yelled at them. They talked of parents who didn't understand, teachers who hated them. They showed her the angry red marks on their arms from where they'd held a razor blade until blood pricked to the surface.

Some days it was too much. There was the afternoon Milo Jenkins got sent to her instead of the principal, after he tore up a test in science class and proceeded to eat the scraps of paper one by one. And the day Samantha Brown was found puking up her meager lunch in the bathroom for the third day in a row. Or the morning when the principal called her into the office to tell her that Jeffery Badger had been arrested for building a bomb in his parents' garage. He'd sat in her office the previous day and told her that he didn't have a single friend in the school, and even his parents didn't like him very much.

These were days when Libby wanted to go home, put her weary head down on a pillow, and weep for the tragedies visited upon these children, but also for her own, because wasn't a healthy thirty-nine-year-old father of two dropping dead while mowing his lawn a tragedy? Where was her comfortable flowered chair and box of tissues? But self-pity didn't accomplish anything, so instead Libby cooked dinner for the girls, called her mother, and went to bed early with a book, the queen-size bed spreading endlessly on Steven's side, because even though he'd been dead for two years, Libby couldn't bring herself to sleep in the middle of the bed.

"Do you think she's happy? Elise?" Ivy asked.

"What?" Libby startled out of her reverie and returned to Ivy who cast her eyes about critically, taking in the sparkling wood floors and sun-washed room. "I guess. Probably. Why wouldn't she be?"

Ivy shrugged. "I don't know. Everything just seems a little too perfect, don't you think?"

"God, Ivy, you really can find a problem with everything, can't you?" Libby said. Ivy just shrugged and refilled her drink. Ivy's snarky criticism was funny when they were twenty. She just sounded bitter and jealous now.

"So what's going on with you?" Ivy asked, and Libby softened. She looked into her drink glass, gathering the courage to say the words aloud.

"I've met someone," she finally said.

"Really? You didn't say. Tell me everything." Ivy's eyes lit up with genuine excitement, and Libby felt guilty for thinking poorly of her oldest and dearest friend.

"I feel weird about it." Libby tucked her legs beneath her on the couch and got comfortable.

"Why? Is he fat and bald? Is he old? Not old like us but *really* old?" Ivy asked, eyes gleaming.

"No, none of those!" Libby tried to explain. "It's just weird that he's not Steven," she finally said.

Ivy nodded. "Where did you meet him?"

"At Bethany's tennis class. His younger son was in the same class," Libby said. They'd started chatting while watching the children run around the court, missing every ball that was lobbed to them. Libby had been surprised when Adam asked for her number at the end of the lesson. She'd been even more surprised when she gave it to him.

"So... What's the story?" Ivy pressed.

"He's nice." Libby felt tongue-tied. The whole thing with Adam felt so new and unfamiliar that she didn't know how to begin.

"Nice?" Ivy waited. "Libby, come on! Tell me about him."

Trying to talk about this with Ivy, she couldn't help but wonder what Steven would think. She thought about him every day and his absence crept in at unexpected times. She'd be feeling like things were going okay, and then Bethany would come home in tears because they were making Father's Day projects in art class. Or stupid things, like when she was taking the garbage out the other night for what felt like the hundredth time that week. As she lugged the bag to the shed outside, she looked up at the starry sky with tears in her eyes. Until Steven died, she had no idea how often the trash needed to be taken out because it was one of those things he always did without a word of complaint. It wasn't just chores and holidays that were hard. It was everything and nothing and all the moments in between that she missed him.

She knew that Steven would want her to meet someone new and to have another chance at a relationship, marriage even, but knowing this didn't make her feel any less guilty about being with Adam. It still felt like a betrayal. She was certain that Caitlin would feel the same way, which was why she'd been careful to keep their few dates a secret. The idea of telling Caitlin about Adam—or any new relationship, for that matter—filled Libby with a sticky dread.

"His name is Adam. We've gone out a few times," Libby began.

Ivy kicked off her cowboy boots and left them splayed across Elise's cream-colored carpet. "Go on."

Elise came into the living room with a fresh pitcher of drinks. "I think I've got her settled," she said, as if Ada were a fussy toddler. "What's happening here?"

"Libby was just telling me about her new boyfriend," Ivy said with a grin.

"Boyfriend? You didn't tell me you have a boyfriend!" Elise's eyebrows shot up, though her forehead was suspiciously still. Libby wondered if she was getting Botox injections. Did people their age actually do that? Probably, though she doubted the women in Wolf Mountain went for that sort of thing. Most of the women there were like her mother, letting their hair fade to gray naturally and wearing their dressy sneakers for special occasions. Libby still hadn't decided which type of woman she wanted to be, though she suspected neither.

"He's not my boyfriend," Libby corrected, though this was not quite true. "We've just gone out on a few dates."

"Tell us!" Elise prompted.

Libby stalled. She'd started the conversation, but she wasn't ready to divulge all the details. They'd only just sat down, seeing each other for the first time in so long. She needed to ease into spilling her guts. "He's an architect. He lives in the next town over from us."

"Any kids? Has he been married?" Elise asked. The coffee table was already strewn with the remains of their snacks, nearly empty cocktails, and balled up napkins cluttering the table.

"He's been divorced for two years. He has two boys—one is ten, the other's fifteen. They go back and forth between his house and their mother's. His older son actually goes to the high school where I work." She didn't add how odd it had been to bump into Adam at a basketball game, just a week after their first date, her personal and professional worlds crashing into each other in the chilly gymnasium.

"What have your dates been like?" Ivy asked. She looked relaxed, stretched out on the couch in her bare feet. Her toes were painted bright red, the vine tattoo she'd gotten senior year creeping up her foot and disappearing into the leg of her jeans.

"We went for coffee the first time. And then a few dinners."

What she didn't tell Ivy and Elise was that their first coffee had turned into lunch. They had dinner a few days later, which ended with a make out session in Adam's car, and Libby had gone home feeling giddy and guilty as a teenager. There had been a few more dinners. Their last date was just the previous weekend, and while she hadn't intended on sleeping with him, she'd known it was a possibility, digging out her nicest underwear from the back of the drawer. Her mother had babysat (she'd told Anne-Marie she was meeting a friend), and Libby had stumbled in bleary-eyed and flaming with what she was certain was the obvious afterglow of sex for the first time in over two years. Two years! Her mother hadn't looked suspicious, only asked if she had a nice time, and informed her that Caitlin had argued with her because she wouldn't let her stay up till eleven. Libby was so stunned by the sex that she couldn't even get mad at Caitlin.

"Do you like him, Lib?" Elise asked, leaning forward, her face so open and hopeful.

"I do," she said, reaching down to the wedding ring she still wore and spinning it around her finger.

"I'm so glad. You deserve someone. Steven would want you to be happy," Ivy said, watching Libby fiddle with the silver band.

Libby nodded, and swallowed down the lump that always formed at the back of her throat when someone mentioned Steven. She wondered if there would ever come a day when she could think about all of the good memories without the tinge of sadness. She tried to talk about him for the girls' sake. Bethany loved to hear stories about her father. She'd been almost six when he died, but her memories of him were fuzzier than Caitlin's. When Libby tried to talk about him, Caitlin's face closed up tight, a dark cast coloring her features, her eyes going hooded and blank. The pain practically radiated from her in waves of heat, and all Libby wanted to do was hold her close, but Caitlin didn't ever want to be held these days. The only thing she hugged was her phone, the little piece of plastic that kept her separate from the rest of them, alone on a tiny digital island where all that existed were YouTube videos, and the selfies she and her friends posted to sites no one Libby's age used.

Libby knew she needed to get Caitlin some help, for her lingering grief and for whatever threatened to overtake her. She'd seen enough girls like Caitlin in her office to know that her daughter was on the edge of something dark and dangerous. Libby even had the number for a private therapist in town who treated many of her students. Both girls had gone to a therapist for a short period of time after Steven's death, but then they'd sold the house and moved back to Vermont, and Libby hadn't gotten another therapist. She knew she needed to make an appointment for Caitlin, she just couldn't face the conversation, knowing Caitlin would scream at her and tell her she didn't need a stupid therapist. If Caitlin refused to go, Libby wasn't sure what the next option was.

She sighed, pushing away thoughts of Caitlin. "I think I might lie down myself, if you guys don't mind."

"I'm with you. I think the flight is catching up with me," Ivy said.

"Of course!" Elise hopped up from the couch. "Relax, make yourselves comfortable. We'll figure out dinner when you guys are up. Or we can just have snacks. It doesn't matter. Whatever!" She drained the last sip of her drink and carried the tray of snacks back into the kitchen.

Ivy linked her arm through Libby's. "Glad you're here," Ivy whispered, her head dropping to Libby's shoulder.

"Me too," Libby said, and she was.

ELISE

Facebook status update: Champagne and cocktails — girls' weekend off to a great start!

Elise wiped down the counter one last time and carried a glass of water back into the living room. Upstairs it was quiet, except for the soft sounds of someone's footfalls in the second master bedroom. It wasn't as large or ornate as the other master, with its massive picture window facing the sea and its plush cream-colored carpeting. The second master was smaller, with a tiny balcony just big enough for a chair and table, but it was Elise's favorite room in the house, the one she'd slept in the last time they'd come for the weekend—not that anyone needed to know that.

At home, Brad slept in the third-floor guest room, though last week she'd heard him tiptoe down the stairs to her (their?) room. She saw the shadow of his feet under the door and could practically hear his breath and hesitation, unsure whether to knock or just come in. Elise had lain in bed, breathless, hoping he would knock or open the door. Instead, she watched the shadow of his feet disappear from under the door and the slant of yellow go dark as he flicked off the hall light. She lay awake, her chest tight with disappointment, wondering why she hadn't jumped out of bed and opened the door for him.

Elise opened her phone and tapped on the Facebook icon. She scrolled along the feed, eyeing pictures of friends and family and people she barely knew. She took a quick photo of her near empty cocktail glass and quickly uploaded it, typing a quick cheerful post and then tagging Ivy, Libby, and Ada. It sounded better than *Everyone's taking a nap but me*, even if the second was more accurate. The cocktails had gone to her head, and she was suddenly overcome with sleepiness. She needed to review the ingredients in her fridge and make an appetizer, but she could rest her eyes for just a few minutes. There was nothing that needed to get done immediately. She lay down and felt herself falling slowly backwards into sleep.

When she opened her eyes, the sky outside had softened to a pale pink blush and the ocean had taken on the dark blue tint of evening. Elise pushed herself to sitting, aware of the pounding in her head, the result of the afternoon cocktails. Stupid Martha Stewart recipe. None of the others had come back down, but Elise heard movement upstairs and murmurs of conversation. She picked up her phone and noticed two texts from Brad, and a voicemail from Marianna's teacher. She looked at Brad's texts first. They communicated better digitally than in person these days. He had a question about Piper's dance class, and there was some trouble with Tommy. The voicemail was from Ms. Munroe, Marianna's kindergarten teacher, asking Elise to call at her earliest convenience to set up a time for their next parent-teacher conference. Elise responded to Brad's text with information about Piper's pick up from dance class, and told him she'd call him later to talk about Tommy.

She ignored the message from Ms. Munroe. It was a Friday evening, and what teacher actually wanted to hear from parents then? Possibly Ms. Munroe. She was a surly presence in the classroom, with her red bifocals on a chain and her shapeless cardigans that Elise was certain she got at the Goodwill in town, not because she couldn't afford something nicer but as an overt snub to the wealthy families in town. *Look at me, I can't even afford proper sweaters*, she seemed to say, which Elise knew was ridiculous as she'd seen the latest teachers' contract, and Ms. Munroe had been working at the school for about a hundred years and was on the top end of the salary scale. She was always peering down at the children with a dour expression. She looked like she was frowning, even when she wasn't, like she'd actually frozen in the mean face. Elise wished Marianna had gotten Ms. Poplova, or Miss Annie as the kids called her. Miss Annie was young and freckled, always smiling or laughing, a child nearly always draped across her or clutching her hand tightly. Ms. Munroe made the children walk in a line with their hands clasped in front of them, no hand holding or touching of any kind. "Hands, feet, and all objects to yourself," Elise had heard Ms. Munroe bark on more than one occasion when she volunteered in the classroom.

Marianna did have an aide, Miss Jenny, a fresh-faced recent college graduate who accompanied Marianna to most of her classes and activities. Miss Jenny had long hair that she tied up in complicated braids, and each week her fingernails were painted a different color. During recess, she'd fix Marianna's hair, or whip out a bottle of polish and give her a manicure. Marianna often came home from school with her stubby little fingers painted a dazzling shade of blue, her hair done in intricate French braids. Marianna adored Miss Jenny, but Elise worried how much the aide was helping her with the academic demands of the curriculum. Elise remembered the endless cycle of teachers' aides from her own days in the classroom. The jobs were ludicrously underpaid, a stepping stone to gaining one's own classroom, and so were often filled with the youngest and most inexperienced workers. Despite her college education, Elise doubted Miss Jenny knew much about the complexities of development with a learning-disabled child, much less the specifics of how Marianna learned best, and Elise feared that Miss Jenny's work was that of a babysitter or big sister more than a teacher.

Elise wasn't looking forward to the conference with Ms. Munroe, uncertain how she would get her concerns across in a way that didn't throw poor Jenny under the bus. The phone call to Ms. Munroe could wait.

Last week she'd seen the name Josh Parker flash across Brad's phone. He'd left the phone on the counter while he ran to the store for milk, and Elise had been tempted to pick up the phone and ask Josh why he was calling. Josh Parker was the lawyer who'd handled the divorce of two different friends, and he was known for being ruthless. Elise's friend Noelle had walked away from her divorce with the house and a custody arrangement that gave her every holiday with the kids except the Fourth of July. When Brad returned with the milk, he'd checked the phone and gone into another room to return the call. He hadn't said a thing about the conversation to Elise, but her mind couldn't help going to worst-case scenarios involving divorce and custody disputes.

In the downstairs bathroom, Elise rinsed her face with water and drank several gulps to clear the stale taste in her mouth. She reapplied blush and smoothed down her hair. She smiled at herself until the expression came naturally. Then she headed upstairs to check on the others.

ADA

Text message: Tyler to Ada
Hope you're having a great time. Call me when you get a chance.

Ada lay under the heavy down comforter and inhaled the fresh scent of laundry detergent. She kept her eyes shut, clinging to the last blessed remnants of the nap. Sleep normally eluded her during Sam's rests, but she'd slipped into a quiet blissful darkness. It was probably the sheets. They were softer than any Ada had ever slept on, which wasn't surprising considering that her own sheets came from Target, like most everything else in her house. Ada wondered if Elise ever shopped at Target anymore.

When she finally opened her eyes, only an hour had passed, but she felt like a new person. Thank God, because she'd been so obnoxious to everyone when she first walked in the door, a weepy, angry mess. She'd apologize later. Just a few more minutes in these sheets wouldn't hurt anyone.

Ada finally pushed herself to sitting and took a moment to look around the room. It was decorated in pale pink, and she suspected it was Piper's bedroom, despite that there were hardly any signs of a child living here. No posters of boy bands or stacks of magazines. Just a photo booth roll of Piper and another girl tucked into the mirror, and a few middle grade paperbacks on the bookcase.

Like most of the other bedrooms in the house, this one also had a private balcony. Ada slid her legs from the warm cocoon of the bed and unlatched the sliding door that led outside. There was an Adirondack chair, and a table just big enough for a cup of coffee and a plate, but in April it was far too cold to sit outside for long. The waves crashed along the empty beach with a violent force, and Ada shivered in her cotton shirt but didn't return to the warmth of the bedroom. Instead she closed her eyes and gripped the rough wood of the railing, enjoying the feel of the sharp salty air.

It had been such a hard year. The weight of it hit her as she stood on the balcony, alone for the first time in months. She had been single for so long before she finally met Tyler, cycling through a series of short-term relationships with men she wasn't in love with, even as she tried to convince herself that maybe it was time to settle. Maybe she'd reached a stage in her life when the romantic dreams she'd once had were unrealistic. Maybe it was enough just to find someone she could share a home with, a bed, a family. And then she met Tyler and she was fourteen years old again, blushing and heart pounding, disbelieving that she'd really fallen in love so hard so fast. For a little while, it seemed like her whole life was falling into place.

And then her mother was diagnosed with cancer and died so quickly, followed by Ada's pregnancy and Sam's birth. On top of that was the added financial stress of trying to survive on one salary. What should have been the happiest time in her life was woven tightly with the worst, the close proximity of grief and joy leaving her raw. She missed her job and her friends from school, even while she dreaded the end of her maternity leave.

She tried to remember back to what her life was like less than two years ago, when she and Tyler were first married. She'd recently been made head of the English department, an accomplishment that had both surprised and thrilled her. Tyler loved her cooking, and every night she'd return home from work with a new meal in mind—Thai or Indian or Korean recipes—excited to experiment with different spices and unfamiliar ingredients. When Tyler got home, the kitchen smelled of lemongrass and basil, and they'd sit down to dinner and talk about the day. Or they'd talk about the future, the places they'd travel to someday soon, the next vacation they'd take together, the baby they hoped to someday have. Sam.

Tyler tried to be a good father, but Ada knew she didn't make it easy for him. When he offered to get up with Sam in the middle of the night, Ada insisted she do it. When he tried to feed Sam, she told him she'd prefer he didn't drink formula unless absolutely necessary. When he changed Sam's diapers, she criticized the way he'd mis-stuck the tabs, allowing the diaper to leak more easily. At Tyler's every attempt to parent, Ada snatched Sam back into her arms, then grew frustrated by how alone she felt.

She'd seen women like this before, the ones who spoke of their husbands' parenting as if they were hired babysitters who swooped in for a few hours' respite here and there. Ones who didn't leave the children alone with their husbands, for no good reason other than that they assumed they could do it better. Ada had quietly pitied these women, so certain she would never become one. Until Sam came along, and it seemed that every day offered a million ways to fail him, a million things that Ada could do just a tiny bit better than Tyler. Caring for Sam made the loss of her mother slightly more bearable. But the burden of doing everything had a high price tag.

She took another breath of the salty air as a shiver rushed through her. Away from the smallness of their condo that over-flowed with plastic baby paraphernalia, without Sam in her arms or fussing in his crib, she felt stronger. For a moment, she could see her way through it all. Staring out at the crashing waves, she had a glimmer of clarity, a view through the haze of sadness and love and exhaustion and worry to the other side, where things weren't bathed in a perpetual grayness. Perhaps it was being here with her oldest friends, the ones who had known her before she was a mother or a wife or a middle-aged woman, when her biggest worry was getting through finals week. Life had ground them down too, yet here they all were, still intact, still some version of themselves, even if not entirely who they'd once been.

From inside the bedroom came the trill of her phone ringing. She wanted to ignore it, but it would be Tyler, calling with a report on Sam. She wished she could put the baby out of her mind for just a few days, even an hour or two, yet he was never far from her thoughts, always pushing in along the edges when he wasn't at the center. She stepped back into the bedroom.

"Everything okay?" Ada answered, instead of hello.

"Yeah, hi. How is it? How's the house?" Tyler asked.

"It's amazing. I just took a nap. A nap!" she declared, as if it were a great accomplishment.

"That's great, babe." There was reluctance in his voice. He was holding something back.

"What's wrong? Did something happen?" She felt a flurry of panic imagining all the things that could have happened to Sam since she'd left—he'd choked on an oversized piece of banana, he'd found a stray button on the floor and ate it, he'd had an allergic reaction to a new food and was covered in hives. "Is Sam okay?"

"No, nothing happened. Sam's fine. He's right here with me. Want to say hi?"

There was a shuffle, and then a few giggles and gurgles that made Ada's heart flip. She cooed to him for a moment and then Tyler was back on the phone. Ada peppered him with questions.

"Did he take the bottle? He doesn't always like the powdered kind of milk, so I got you a few cans of the liquid stuff if he gives you any trouble. Did he nap this afternoon?"

"Yup, he napped fine. And he's been eating like a champ. Right, buddy?"

"Okay." Ada waited. There was something more, she knew it.

"The thing is…" Tyler began.

Down the hall, one of the doors opened and Ada heard someone heading downstairs. She wanted to hang up, to join her friends, to actually sit and relax and enjoy one of those beautiful cocktails Elise had made. She wanted to get a massage tomorrow, and eat out at a restaurant, and catch up and be nice, be patient, be *happy*. She wanted to feel like herself again, even if just for three days.

Tyler continued. "You know the job Tim bid on? The one for that summer house they're remodeling? He got the job."

Ada forced herself to focus on the conversation. In her mind, she was already downstairs having a drink with some of that lovely soft cheese. "That's great."

"The thing is, he needs to get started right away. He's called some of the other guys to give him a hand but no one else is available." Tyler worked for a high-end carpenter. His boss Tim was a decent guy but always short-staffed, and Tyler often ended up shouldering the slack. He was terrible at saying no.

"And neither are you. You've got Sam." The panic began to swirl inside her, hot and electric.

"I know. But Tim's willing to pay. Not just time and a half, but double. And he's going to give me something extra at the end of the week." Tyler spoke in the patient voice Ada used with her students.

"Tyler, I'm away this weekend," Ada said, as if maybe he'd forgotten, as if that wasn't the purpose of the phone call.

"We need the money," Tyler added. He paused, letting Ada digest this. She sat on the bed, the phone pressed against her cheek so hard she felt its heat. "It's probably just for tomorrow. Tim hardly ever works Sundays. I was thinking I could get a sitter for the day if it's okay with you."

"We don't have a sitter." Ada had been meaning to ask around for someone to watch Sam for a few hours here and there, but hadn't gotten around to it yet. Every time she thought about someone else staying with the baby, she put it off. Tyler's parents adored Sam, but they lived in New Jersey and were in their late seventies. She was suddenly near tears, all of the calm from just a few minutes earlier gone. She wanted to beat her fists against Tyler's chest.

"What about a friend? What about Sarah who watched him a few weeks ago. You could ask her?" Tyler asked.

"I can't ask her to watch Sam all day, that's crazy." Tyler would be gone at least ten hours.

"What about one of those babysitting services you can find online?"

"There's no way you're leaving him with some stranger you found on a website," Ada snapped.

"Is there anyone else?" His voice was smaller.

"No! You know there's not. There's just me." She felt the weekend slipping away. She tried again. "Tyler, I've been planning this for months. Do you know how much I've been looking forward to this?"

"Yeah, I do," he said quietly. He knew what he was asking. "You know I wouldn't ask if we didn't need the money. I can't turn this down. I'm really sorry, babe."

It was true, he wouldn't ask if it wasn't necessary. That was what made the whole thing so frustrating. There were still months till the end of her maternity leave, and while Ada had pushed the money worries out of her mind, too fixated on sleep and dirty diapers and Sam's milestones, Tyler was the one paying the bills each month out of their dwindling account. But that didn't make what he was asking any easier. Her anger flared, little prickles that broke out on her skin. She hated Tyler for calling, for knowing she'd cave. She hated Tim for asking Tyler to work on a weekend, she hated herself for not having found a sitter. She even hated Sam a little, just a tiny bit, for the way her love for him sometimes felt like pain. It was this hatred, unnatural, unwarranted, that made her relent.

Ada took a deep breath and tried to compose herself. "I can come home."

When he spoke, she heard the relief in his voice that she wasn't going to make this hard for him. "Well, I was thinking maybe I could drop Sam off tomorrow morning and then pick him up after work. Even if Tim is working on Sunday, I'll tell him I can't. That way you'll still get to see your friends and the whole weekend won't be ruined." It would, but Ada didn't say it. She thought about what he was proposing. Their house was an hour from the Cape, and Tyler usually left for work by seven. He'd need to be out of the house before five in order to make it back on time.

"It's okay," she forced herself to say, even though it wasn't. It wasn't okay at all. "You can bring him tonight. That way you can sleep till six, and you won't have to get up with him in the middle of the night." Hot tears pushed themselves out of her eyes and rolled down her cheeks, the cost of getting out the words he wanted to hear.

"Are you sure? I don't mind bringing him in the morning," Tyler said.

"It's fine."

"Ada, I promise, I'll make this up to you. We'll get you another weekend away, or at least a night really soon. Maybe you can book a massage when you get back."

Ada pressed her lips together. She rubbed her fingers against her temple. "Sure."

She listened while Tyler went over the logistics of the drop-off, interrupting to remind him of things he'd need to pack for Sam and giving him Elise's address. "If I leave in the next hour, we should be there by eight," Tyler said. Ada nodded, considering how she'd spend those final two hours. "I'll see you soon, okay? I love you."

"Love you too," Ada mumbled and hung up the phone.

She lay back down in the bed. Its softness and lavender-scented sheets seemed to mock her now, as she imagined how often Sam would wake up in an unfamiliar bedroom, the added stress of trying to keep him from waking the others.

First world problems, she imagined her mother saying. She'd heard it on a talk show program once, and was known to drop the quip into daily conversations in an effort to gently remind Ada that life was good. Her mother had always been incredibly practical, reminding her children of all the reasons they should be grateful. If her mother were here, she would have picked Sam up and brought him home with her for the weekend. She would have reassured Ada that she had nothing to worry about, that everything was under control.

She tried to think about all of the other people in the world who had real problems. Mothers in refugee camps, children without clean water, single parents holding down two jobs and trying to get by. It only made her feel worse about her own self-pity. She lay down on the bed and let the tears overtake her.

IVY

Sometimes Ivy wondered why her Harper friends had let her be part of their group. Even back then, she'd been so different from them. While Libby, Ada, and Elise were all East Coast girls, Ivy was raised by her mother in Butler, a hot dusty town in Southern California. After he left when Ivy was three, her father was a volatile and sporadic presence in her life, dropping in every few months, only long enough to send her mother into a tailspin and let Ivy down all over again. He died of cirrhosis of the liver when Ivy was a sophomore at Harper, leaving only a trail of unpaid bills and disappointment. Ivy's mother was a waitress at a local restaurant in town, and at sixty-two, she still worked three shifts a week, skinny and quick on the floor as she refilled beer glasses and cleared dirty dishes.

As a child, Ivy had longed to escape Butler. In the neighborhood, she hung with the boys who liked climbing trees and burning up bugs with a magnifying glass rather than the girls, who spent their afternoons sunbathing in baking backyards and painting each other's nails garish shades of orange and green. There was something about Ivy that made them look away when they saw her coming. She couldn't figure out just what she was doing wrong in order to change herself.

The town was far enough inland that a trip to the beach took hours. In the summer, the only places to swim were the overcrowded public pool or the tiny swimming hole cradled in a quarry. Jagged rocks lined the floor, and everyone had heard about the boy who died after attempting a dive in the shallow area, not that it stopped them from sneaking in for a dip when the weather was sweltering. Summer afternoons were usually spent under the cold beam of a sprinkler, seeking shade as the sun swanned its way across the sky.

Despite her father's absence, despite the lack of female friends, there were good moments in her childhood. Sunday afternoon movie fests, curled up in bed beside her mother, a bowl of Jiffy Pop cradled between them as they watched back-to-back horror movies; the annual Fourth of July celebration when the whole town convened in the park for hot dogs and watermelon, and watched the fireworks; her next-door neighbor and best friend Gene, a chubby freckled boy who metamorphosed into a lithe muscular crush their sophomore year, the first one to kiss Ivy, the first one to tell her she was beautiful.

But she never belonged in Butler.

There was no money for college. Ivy knew this from an early age, knew also that the only way out of Butler would be of her own making. In high school, she signed up for every honors class offered at her tiny school. Butler High didn't offer AP classes, but Ivy was the only student in her class to take summer courses at the community college three towns over, spending an hour on a sweaty bus each way in order to take a freshman anatomy class. Most of the college-bound students in her graduating class would go there in the fall, but Ivy had her sights set higher. She wanted to go as far away from Butler as possible, and with the help of a guidance counselor who'd seen Ivy's potential, she was able to get a full scholarship to Harper College in Newton, Massachusetts.

When Ivy arrived at Harper, it was so different from Butler that it might as well have been another country. Ornate brick buildings towered over the campus. Massive oaks shaded the sprawling green grounds, and the sun shone through the thick leaves, casting shadowy patterns on the grass. Even the heat was different. In Butler, it got into your pores, wormed its way inside your ears, lay thick and fetid upon your tongue. In Massachusetts, on that late August day, it brushed her skin and hovered around her head, glittery and yellow with expectation.

The students dressed more conservatively than the kids in Butler, the girls in khaki shorts and tank tops, the boys in plaid or madras shirts. In her sleeveless baby doll dress and purple Doc Martens, Ivy stuck out like a sore thumb. Everyone looked tanned and healthy, with shiny ponytails and bodies lean from seasons of high school sports. Ivy was both awed and terrified.

When she dragged her enormous duffel bag into room 401 of Wickingham Hall, Libby was already there. Her parents were with her, Anne-Marie clucking over the length of the bed, worrying that the standard twin sheets wouldn't fit the extra-long mattress. Despite the grand exterior of Wickingham, the dorm room was simple and sparse with Sheetrock walls and sky blue office carpeting. Over the summer, Ivy had received Libby's name and phone number in the mail, yet she hadn't mustered the courage to call her. A week before leaving for school, a postcard addressed to Ivy arrived in the mail. On one side was a picture of Eddie Vedder screaming into a microphone. On the other side, just two sentences in neat curling script. *I hope you like Pearl Jam because I'm obsessed. Looking forward to meeting you soon, roomie!* Libby signed her name with a little star beside it. Ivy hated Pearl Jam, but she'd been thinking about Libby ever since.

Libby had brown hair cut just below her chin, and a light dusting of freckles along the bridge of her nose. She was compact and athletic in a pair of navy running shorts and a high school track tee shirt. She was plain looking, certainly more cute than pretty, but when she saw Ivy, her face cracked open in a smile that transformed her features and instantly made Ivy want to be her friend. Libby carried a confidence and surety about her place in the world that Ivy wanted to possess for herself.

"Ivy!" Libby jumped up off the bed and came closer. Ivy gave a tentative smile, not sure if they were supposed to shake hands or just say hello. Instead, Libby surprised her by throwing her arms around Ivy's shoulders and giving her a quick tight squeeze. "I'm so happy you're here. We're going to have so much fun."

In that one moment, all of Ivy's fears and insecurities evaporated. Her clothing, where she was from, the subpar high school education she had compared to the other students—none of that mattered. Libby wanted to be Ivy's friend.

Ivy stood outside the bedroom where Libby was sleeping and mulled over that first afternoon they met. What if she had graduated from Harper? How different the trajectory of her life might have been. She might have her own classroom, a closet full of beakers and test tubes and her own white lab coat. Maybe she would have decided to go for her PhD, and settled in as a professor at some small college like Harper or a bigger university. Maybe she'd be working for one of the research firms in San Francisco, spending her days peering through a microscope and discovering the cure for cancer instead of the mess she was in now.

There was no point to this thinking. It just left her bitter and resentful. Her life had been diverted dramatically that early spring day her senior year, and she had no one to blame but herself. She knocked on Libby's door.

"Come in," Libby called.

Ivy opened the door. Libby lay on the bed atop the flowered comforter, looking at her phone.

"Hi. What are you doing?" Ivy asked.

"Just checking in with my mom." She heard the sigh Libby held back.

"Everything okay?"

"Yeah, I guess." Libby shook her head in exasperation. "Caitlin's being a pain in the ass, but what else is new?" Libby scooted over and patted the thick down comforter. Ivy lowered herself to the bed, stretching out beside Libby. "I feel like we haven't talked in ages."

It was true, they hadn't talked much recently. It was unbelievable to Ivy that, of all of them, she hadn't told Libby about Sebastian. Ivy knew she would—she knew she *had* to—but getting the words out was impossible. She'd felt herself pulling away this past year, taking longer to return Libby's phone calls, cutting them short when she finally did call back. She couldn't talk to Libby because she didn't want to tell her how things really were. It wasn't just Butler she'd wanted to leave behind all those years ago. It was the crush of financial worry she'd witnessed her entire childhood that she hoped to shed. The four different credit cards her mother juggled, each for a different time in the month as she paid off the minimum on one, freeing up a little space for groceries or gas. All those years with Sebastian they'd been tight, but they were in it together, and at the end of the month there was usually a tiny cushion, enough for a night at the movies or a dinner at their favorite Thai place. Since he'd left, Ivy felt the chronic nag of dread that came with money worries, the way they seeped into everything else—the decision of what to make for dinner, the way Saturday afternoon was spent, the thrill of seeing Trina dance in her upcoming ballet recital overshadowed by how she would pay for the costume.

She rested her head on Libby's shoulder. At Harper, Libby had paid Ivy's share whenever they ran out of Mountain Dew or Twizzlers or ramen noodles, the staples of their college diet. More than once, Libby picked up a bill for Ivy when her financial aid and the paycheck from her work-study job at the library didn't stretch far enough. Libby was Ivy's guardian angel.

It was Libby who was always certain of Ivy's abilities, her limitless potential and bright future. Ivy could still picture her best friend's face when she heard that Ivy was getting kicked out of Harper. The disbelief. The disappointment. All of it unfamiliar on Libby, who typically greeted both Ivy and the world with an unconditional smile. How horrified she would be now if she knew about Ivy's new escort job. What had felt practical and almost amusing in San Francisco felt shameful and dirty in Libby's presence, thrust into the harsh light of day.

"How's the jewelry making business going?" Libby asked.

"It's okay. Still figuring things out," Ivy said vaguely. She eased herself back onto the plush feather pillows.

"Your website looks great," Libby said.

"Oh, thanks." Sebastian had done the website for her in the pre-Fauna days, and Ivy hadn't touched it since he left.

"Are you thinking of setting up a storefront?" Libby asked.

"I have a little place just south of the city," Ivy said, aware how outrageous this exaggeration was. Libby was likely picturing a trendy boutique in Noe Valley, not a wheelie cart at a mall off a highway. Opening a store in San Francisco was about as likely as a bag of gold falling from the sky and landing in Ivy's lap. Rent for business space was even more outrageous than residential.

"That's so great, Ivy!" Libby said, and she looked so happy for Ivy that she felt even worse about the lie. She'd been so optimistic when she decided to start up the business for real. Ivy had been making jewelry for years, in a corner of their apartment where she squeezed a small table and all of her supplies. For a while she had a booth at the Treasure Island Flea Market. Once a month, she'd spend the afternoon sitting in an uncomfortable folding chair, selling her mosaic glass necklaces and silver-hammered cuff bracelets. Over the course of the day, she'd be lucky if she cleared a couple of hundred dollars, minus the vendor fee, but it was better than nothing. Then one night, after too many glasses of red wine with Sebastian, she decided to really make a go of it. They had a little saved, enough to cover a few months' rent, and Sebastian, always a champion for the arts, even at the cost of everything and everyone else, convinced Ivy to quit her massage job and focus on her jewelry full-time.

She'd been so excited about it, ordering business cards and getting Sebastian to start the website. There was no way she could afford an actual retail shop. Instead she rented a tiny kiosk at the mall just south of the city. Now she spent her days watching college girls from San Francisco State prance right past her and into Abercrombie & Fitch. Occasionally they might stop at her booth to try on a ring or hold a pair of earrings up in the mirror. Then they'd look at the price tag and put it down, heading into Forever 21 where they could find factory-made jewelry that might fall apart after a month or leave a green ring around their finger, but was only a fraction of the price. After eight hours in the mall, Ivy felt dirty and square-eyed, like she'd been watching TV in the dark for too long.

She wanted to blame Sebastian—for his dreaminess, his encouragement of the business even while he was betraying her at the same time, sleeping with Fauna and preparing for his new life. But she knew, deep down, that she couldn't blame him for her failed business or any of her other failures. Each of those belonged to her alone.

This was not the artist's life she'd envisioned, and now that Sebastian was gone, it was even worse because the small amount of money she cleared each month barely covered the expenses. It was what made becoming an escort sound so practical, a few hundred for an evening spent at a black-tie fundraiser. Ivy wasn't sure how she'd become forty-two with a list of marketable skills small enough to fit on a Post-it note.

She shifted on the bed beside Libby, wishing she could unburden herself of all that had happened. But for the twenty years of their friendship, Ivy had tried so hard not to disappoint Libby. She'd spent four years molding herself into the person Libby believed her to be, just to avoid that disappointment. Ivy became someone smart and funny and good, a version of herself that Libby created, and it was so real and true that for nearly four years, this was who Ivy was. Libby made Ivy want to be a better person, and she made Ivy believe that deep down, beneath it all, she *was* a better person. Even if it hadn't lasted, she was still trying to be that person in Libby's presence.

"This guy that you've gone out with," Ivy said, changing the subject. "It sounds like you really like him."

Libby let out a little sigh that held so much. Steven's death still seemed like a cruel joke all these years later. "I do. I like him a lot. It just still feels wrong somehow."

Ivy found Libby's hand and laced her fingers through hers, giving them a little squeeze. "It's not. You deserve to be happy. Steven would want that. You know he would."

"Would he?" Libby asked. When Libby looked at her, Ivy saw how unsure she was.

"Yes," Ivy said firmly. "Yes, he most definitely would."

"Well, maybe Steven would, but I don't think Caitlin or Bethany will feel the same way. I haven't told them, partly because it's still so early, but also because I'm afraid of their reaction," Libby said. Ivy thought about this. How would Trina and Jax feel about her remarrying someday? But, of course, this was completely different because Libby's children were much younger, not to mention the fact that Steven was dead, unlike Sebastian who was very much still alive—and preparing a nursery for his new baby. Both of the kids were furious about it, a quiet and long-simmering anger that would take years of therapy to untangle.

"The girls will come around," Ivy said, even though she wasn't sure this was true.

Both women startled at the sound of a scream from down the hall. Not of fear or pain, but the raging yell of frustration. Scrambling from the bed, they met Elise in the hall, her eyes wide with concern.

They found Ada on the bed in her room, her hair limp around her face. Her eyes were closed, and it looked like she was making an effort to breathe deeply.

"Are you okay? What's wrong? Ada, what's going on?" Elise asked, sitting on the bed beside Ada.

Finally, Ada opened her eyes. The emptiness behind them was unnerving. There was something seriously wrong with Ada, and Ivy wondered if either of the other women saw it as plainly as she did, or if maybe she was just better attuned to the appearance of sheer desperation when she saw it.

Ada mumbled something indecipherable.

"What did you say?" Libby asked.

"I said Tyler's on his way. He has to work this weekend. He's bringing Sam." The words finally out, Ada crumpled up into a little ball, tears coming afresh.

Ivy didn't know Tyler, other than the one time they'd met at the wedding, but Ivy felt pissed off at him anyway. "Seriously? He can't watch the baby for one weekend?" Even Sebastian had been capable of that.

"He has to work. We need the money," Ada said softly, and Ivy shut her mouth.

"It's no problem! It will be great to have Sam," Elise said brightly. "Why are you so upset?"

Ada glared at Elise through the slits of her eyes. "All I wanted was a few days to myself. I just wanted to sleep through the night, and have some cocktails, and maybe even take a nap. Is that too much to ask?"

Ivy might not have remembered her children as babies all that well, but she certainly remembered the mind-numbing exhaustion she'd felt in those early days, especially with Jax, when the weight of parenthood had hit her like a shovel to the back of the head. Sebastian was always useless during those days, sleeping through every nighttime feed, hardly ever offering to take over for even a few hours so she could take a nap, though somehow still finding time to go paint in his studio. She should have known then what a self-centered jerk he actually was.

Ivy sat down on the bed, rubbing Ada's heaving shoulders.

"We'll take care of him. We'll take turns with Sam, and you can have your cocktails and naps and sleep through the night." Ada sometimes drove Ivy nuts, but clearly the woman needed a break. Elise and Libby watched her with surprise before echoing her words.

"Of course, we'll babysit all weekend!"

"You won't even know Sam's here!"

"It will be fun. I haven't taken care of a baby in ages."

"You just relax and let us handle everything."

Ivy rubbed Ada's back until she'd calmed down. Then they all followed Elise downstairs to find out what she had planned for dinner.

ELISE

Facebook status update: Take a look at the cheeks on our surprise visitor! So glad to be able to spend time with baby Sam.

"Who wants more wine?" Elise held up a fresh bottle of chilled chardonnay. Despite the elegant spread of gourmet salads and appetizers that she'd put out, they'd all changed into pajamas except for Elise. The room resembled an adult slumber party.

Libby raised her glass and Elise filled it, looking expectantly at Ada and Ivy.

"I'll have just a little. I'm on baby duty tonight, so I'll keep my wits about me," Ivy said, and Elise gave her a little top-up.

"Ada?" Elise held up the bottle and waggled it at Ada.

Since learning that Tyler would be arriving with the baby, after her mini meltdown, Ada had perked up and recalibrated. It had taken a great deal of comforting and reassurance that the rest of them would take care of Sam before Ada finally began to relax again. But with Tyler's imminent arrival, Elise saw her tensing back up.

"I probably shouldn't. Tyler will be here soon with Sam." She looked longingly at her empty glass.

"You only had a tiny bit. A little more will be fine," Elise said with authority, filling Ada's glass. She'd been down this road with three kids of her own. "You can always give Sam a bottle if you're really worried about your milk."

Ada looked at the glass guiltily for a moment before taking a sip. Elise was scooping another serving of grape leaves onto her plate when the doorbell rang.

"The baby's here," she crooned, putting down her plate and wiping her hands on a napkin.

Elise had met Sam before. When he was first born, Libby came down from Vermont and the two of them drove to Ada's hometown in Providence, Elise's car loaded with onesies, diapers, wipes, and board books. Elise had held the infant Sam in her arms, marveling at his tiny features, the smudgy pink skin, hair smooth and shiny as a pelt. Since then she'd only seen Ada one other time, although they spoke on the phone every few weeks. Their conversations tended to revolve around Sam's sleep schedule, and Ada's worry over finding childcare for the fall. Every now and then Ada would ask about Elise's life, but it didn't come naturally, at least not at this point in Ada's life. Normally their friendship was two-sided, even if Ada was the one who confided more and Elise was the one who comforted. This wasn't because Ada was unwilling to listen, but because Elise rarely confided in anyone, uncomfortable with the tsunami of emotion that accompanied such baring of her soul. As a child, she'd had a tendency to burst into tears during her weekly confession at mass, even when her sins had been minor ones like calling her brother John a fathead. She kept her real sins to herself, and could never admit to the priest that she was skimming from the collection basket. Still, she was left a teary and emotional mess after each encounter, and so after a while, learned it was easier not to share. These days, though, Elise found herself wishing Ada would probe and force her to open up. There was so much in there that Elise didn't know what to do with. Yet she knew Ada was incapable of this at the moment, too stunned by how motherhood had consumed her in one great big swallow.

Elise hurried to the hall with Ada, Ivy, and Libby right behind her. When she opened the door, Tyler stood on the front step.

He was a big and cheerful man, dressed in Carhartts and work boots, a baseball cap on his head. In one arm he carried a blue and white flowered diaper bag. In the other hung the plastic bucket seat with Sam tucked inside. He was bundled in a snuggly, just his face peeking out. He blinked in the brightness of the house.

"Hello, ladies," Tyler said as Elise ushered him inside. "Sorry to crash your weekend."

"It's no problem at all," Elise said, even if it was a lie. It was a problem, especially for Ada, but they would manage. "I'm glad to get a chance to see this little guy again. He's gotten so big since the last time I saw him."

Libby and Ivy crowded around the car seat, cooing at the baby. "Oh, Ada, he's so beautiful," Ivy said. This was the first time Ivy had seen Sam, other than in the photos Ada posted online. Ada had already taken Sam's car seat and was crouched over it, unsnapping the buckles of his seat belt. She scooped the baby up, holding him to her chest. He whimpered softly in her arms.

Ivy sidled up to Ada and held out her arms for the baby. "Hand him over, Ada. Remember, he's all mine tonight."

Ada looked reluctant but she handed the baby to Ivy. Libby reached for the diaper bag that Tyler held.

"Is that all you brought for him?" Ada asked, pointing at the bag.

"Everything should be in there. Clothes, pajamas, there's an empty bottle and a package of formula at the bottom of the bag," Tyler said.

"Did you remember the overnight diapers?" Ada asked.

"Oh, shoot, sorry," Tyler said with a shrug. From the look on Ada's face, it was clear he didn't understand the magnitude of the diaper situation.

"You know he always leaks through the regular ones," Ada said. "He'll be soaked by the morning. Or else he'll wake up."

"It sounds like he already wakes up," Ivy murmured. She bounced from side to side with Sam on her hip.

"Don't worry about it, we can run to the store to grab some if we need them," Elise said.

"When did he last eat?" Ada asked.

"Just before we left, but he didn't have much. Just a little rice cereal and some milk," Tyler said.

"He's tired. It's past his bedtime," Ada said, looking over at Ivy, and Elise knew she wanted to reach out and take Sam from her.

"Do you want to come in and have a drink or a bite to eat?" Elise asked Tyler. They were still standing in the open doorway. The sky was an inky purple as it plunged headfirst into night. The streetlights on the road glowed orange. He gave her an easy grin but shook his head.

"No, thanks. I should probably get back on the road. I'm going to have an early morning tomorrow." He looked to Ada and reached out a hand, pulling her close. "Thanks for this, hon. I'm sorry again." Ada nodded and let him wrap his arm around her shoulder and kiss her on the cheek, but it was clear she was still annoyed. Looking up at Elise, he added, "And thank you ladies for helping Ada with this guy. I know she needs a break."

"Of course," Elise said, and the others murmured in agreement.

After a moment, he released Ada and kissed her once more on the mouth. "Love you, babe," he said. When Elise looked at Libby and Ivy, she knew they were both struck by Tyler's tenderness, even if Ada appeared unmoved. Elise couldn't remember the last time Brad had kissed her, much less publicly declared his love for her. He reached for Sam, palming the baby's skull in his large hand. He planted a kiss on Sam's cheek. "Bye, little buddy," he whispered. He straightened up and turned toward Ada. "I'll call you tomorrow, okay?"

"Okay," Ada said.

He gave a sheepish wave and headed back out to his car.

"Let's get this guy inside," Elise said, trying to rally the good mood of just a few minutes earlier. She knew it wasn't Ada's fault, but she was terrified the baby was going to ruin the rest of the weekend.

"God, I haven't held a baby in so long," Ivy said. She breathed in his scalp. "I forgot how good they smell. What is it that smells so good on a baby's head?"

"Baby shampoo?" Libby suggested.

Ivy shook her head. "No, it's more than that. It's that weird sweet milky smell too. You could bottle it and sell it in drugstores. Like catnip for moms."

"I'm going to put him to bed," Ada said, reaching for him.

"I'll do it," Ivy offered.

"It will be easier if I nurse him," Ada said, and Elise understood, she did, but she wished Ada would let Ivy give him a bottle. She'd nursed both Tommy and Piper, but Marianna had refused to latch on. Elise had been amazed at the freedom giving her a bottle had allowed. Suddenly she wasn't the only one responsible for the nighttime feedings, and she could leave the house for more than a two-hour stretch of time.

"Ivy, you're sure it's okay if he sleeps in your room? He's probably going to wake up," Ada warned.

"It's fine. I'm sure you'll give me a million and one instructions about how to get him back to sleep," Ivy said.

The rest of them gathered around the table while Ada brought Sam upstairs. Ivy reached for her wineglass and fought back a yawn. "I think all the travel is catching up with me. I'm beat." She glanced up the stairs at where Ada and Sam had disappeared. "Something tells me this might be a long night."

"It's good of you to take care of him. I think she could use a night to rest. Me too," Libby added, rubbing her eyes.

It was barely eight o'clock, and Elise wasn't ready for everyone to turn in. "Oh, I almost forgot!" she said, jumping up. She headed over to the cupboard where they kept the kids' board games, withdrawing a small box with a deck of cards inside. "Look what I have."

"Is that Truth or Dare?" Ivy asked.

"Yes! I saw it the other day when I was at the toy store picking up a birthday present for a friend of Piper's. I thought it would be fun to play."

In college they played it all the time. It was how they had passed most Sunday nights at Harper, after the glut of the weekend, trying to stave off the inevitability of Monday. Truth or Dare was how they learned that Ivy's father was an alcoholic. It was how they learned that Ada had a phobia of public restrooms, and that Libby lost her virginity junior year in high school on a smushed couch that smelled of mothballs. It was Truth or Dare that got Elise to admit that she had accompanied her sister Missy for an abortion, and that now she was scared they were both going to hell. Each truth had been whispered in the hush of their campus apartment, and though the secrets had been carefully guarded for years, speaking them aloud was like confession in church, a sacred and holy forgiveness.

And then there were the dares.

The dares weren't as intimate as the truths, but they were exciting. There was the time Ivy dared Elise to sneak into the dorm room of a boy and steal a pair of underwear. It had taken six attempts before Elise found an unlocked door and empty room, but she returned triumphant with a pair of blue cotton boxers. They'd laughed all night over the skid marks left on the seat, and none of them could pass the owner in the halls without stifling a giggle. Another time Ada dared Libby to sneak into the dining hall after hours. Libby had returned victorious with an industrial-size jar of pickles that languished in their refrigerator for months. Not to mention the time when Elise was dared to borrow a condom from their resident advisor. For the rest of the year, every time Elise passed her in the hallway, she was embarrassed.

She held the box up hopefully but neither Libby nor Ivy looked enticed. In fact, both of them looked very tired, and Elise was beginning to worry that Ada had fallen asleep with Sam. "Come on. What do you say?" she asked.

"I don't think I'm up for it tonight, El. But tomorrow for sure," Libby said.

Ada appeared looking bleary-eyed. "I think he's down," she announced with a yawn.

"I was just trying to get these guys to play Truth or Dare," Elise said.

"Oh God no," Ada said, collapsing into her chair.

"Tomorrow, Elise. Promise," Libby said, absently spinning the wedding ring on her finger. Elise wondered if she would continue to wear it forever, even though she was no longer married, at least not in the way the ring implied to someone first meeting her. Libby gestured to the table covered in dishes. "Should we clean up here?"

They rose and began to stack the dishes and bring them to the kitchen. When they were all loaded in the dishwasher and the counters had been wiped, Elise offered more wine. She wasn't the least bit tired.

"I think I'm going to turn in pretty soon," Ivy said.

"You can't yet," Ada said quickly. "Sam will wake up if you go in now. You need to give him at least a half-hour to settle."

"If everyone's tired, we could just throw on a movie," Elise said. It wasn't what she'd envisioned for their first night, but it was better than bed.

"Sure, that sounds good," Libby said.

"I doubt I'll last," Ivy said.

"Why are you so tired? Isn't it three hours earlier in California? So it's only, like, five thirty?" Elise pointed out.

"I had a late night. And I've had a hangover all day," Ivy said.

"Anything fun? Date night?" Elise asked. She and Brad used to have a weekly date night. Somehow they'd fallen out of the routine in the past few years, and now date nights were every few months or on a special occasion. In June it would be their fifteenth anniversary. She wondered if they'd do anything to celebrate or if they'd even acknowledge the day.

Ivy shook her head without meeting anyone's eyes. "Not really. Just too much to drink. So what movies do we have?" she asked.

They relocated to the living room, carrying their wineglasses with them. It took a while, but they finally settled on a cheesy romance on Netflix. They arranged themselves on one of the couches, wineglasses lined up on the coffee table, the four of them sandwiched together, much as they'd spent many evenings at Harper. Elise let herself be lulled into the predictability of the film, able to anticipate where it was going even while she became absorbed. At one point, she tore her eyes from the TV and glanced at her friends. Libby and Ada were slumped on either side of her, and Ivy's legs were spread across their laps. All three of them were fast asleep. Elise smiled to herself and let out a sigh, watching the rest of the film alone.

LIBBY

Text message: Adam to Libby
Hope you're having a great weekend with friends. Can I see you when you get home?

Text message: Caitlin to Libby
Grandma's a psycho. And I had that dream again last night.

When Libby checked her phone first thing the next morning, her heart fluttered to read Adam's text and quickly sank when she read Caitlin's. Not about Grandma being a psycho, which she expected of Caitlin and wasn't really true—though it kind of was, at least by the standards of the new millennium. No, it was Caitlin's nightmare that upset her, the one she'd had so often the year she lost her father.

Steven died on a sunny day in June while Libby was at the grocery store and Steven was in the backyard doing yard work with the girls. He was on his knees in the garden pulling out weeds when the heart attack struck him. According to ten-year-old Caitlin, he toppled sideways and went unconscious. Caitlin ran across the street to a neighbor who called 911. When Libby arrived home with a trunkful of food, the ambulance had already taken Steven to the hospital, too late, and Caitlin and Bethany were crying on the neighbor's couch.

It wasn't that Bethany was okay, but Libby suspected her age had helped her to recover more easily. At five and a half, her memory was more slippery, and while Libby knew she remembered her father, he wasn't fully formed in her mind as he was for Caitlin. For Caitlin, both the loss of her father and seeing it happen was a trauma that Libby wondered if she'd ever recover from.

In the dream, Caitlin was out in the backyard playing and then Steven died. It wasn't even a dream, it was the reality of what she'd seen that day, but Libby hated that her daughter had to relive the worst moment of her life every night. For months after Steven died, Caitlin was afraid to go to sleep, always worried about the dream, a returning monster, except in this case the boogeyman was her own father. Libby let her stay up late, waiting till Caitlin's eyes were droopy and rimmed by purplish circles. She began putting her to sleep on Steven's side of the bed, though she'd wake Libby nightly with her thrashing cries. Some nights Bethany woke up too, and she'd sandwich into the bed on the other side of Libby.

The psychiatrist prescribed a sleeping pill, which allowed Caitlin to sleep more easily but left her sluggish and fragile in the morning. Over time, the nightmare subsided, and the length of time between each occurrence grew. She hadn't had it for over a year now. Finally, she was sleeping through the night in her own bed, and Libby had managed to ease her off the sleeping pills, though she kept a bottle in the medicine cabinet just in case. The nightmare was a step backward, a direct result of Libby daring to leave her children in order to have a few days on her own, and she was reminded of the dark days that followed Steven's death, the year in which it was all she could do to keep her head above water, and not roll over and die with him.

The sun filtered through the parted curtains of Elise's guest room, revealing a clear blue sky. It was close to ten, later than Libby had slept in years. Yet last night's cocktails, coupled with travel and the emotional exhaustion of being with her three oldest friends, had clearly wrung her out. She wondered how Ivy had fared last night with Sam.

They'd come up with a schedule for the baby. Ivy slept with him last night, Libby would take the first half of today and Elise would take the second half, including nighttime, if Ada's prediction that Tyler would call about working on Sunday proved to be true. She hoped Ada had slept as well as she had.

She tapped out a message to Caitlin.

Are you okay? It was only a moment before Caitlin's response came through.

Yeah. I had a hard time falling back to sleep though.

I'm sorry, Libby wrote. It was hard not to feel directly responsible for the dream, even though it was possible Caitlin could have had it even if she was home. Libby tapped out another message.

What are you doing today?

Sleeping and watching Netflix.

Libby thought, *Yeah right,* considering the likelihood of Anne-Marie letting Caitlin spend the day in bed watching TV.

Have fun! she wrote instead, putting the phone back on the nightstand.

Libby pushed herself out of bed, padding barefoot along the soft wall-to-wall carpeting and down the stairs. The kitchen was empty, but there was a full pot of coffee and Elise had left out a bowl of fruit salad. Libby fixed herself a plate and a cup of coffee, and went to search for the others.

She found Ivy and Elise on the back deck that overlooked the ocean. Ivy lay on a wicker couch with a blanket over her lap, and Elise sat on the weathered wood floor playing with Sam.

"Morning." Libby motioned for Ivy to move her legs, which she did with a reluctant grunt, and Libby settled on the couch beside her. It was chilly on the deck, the cool of the water coming off the air, but the sun was out and it gave off a hint of warmth. The beach was an empty expanse, the brightness of summer's colors muted in the early spring light. It was far too cold for swimming, but Libby felt the pull of the ocean.

"Morning. How did you sleep?" Elise looked up from Sam to give Libby a smile.

"So good."

Ivy let out a noisy yawn. "Well, I'm glad someone did. This little stinker woke up three times. No wonder Ada looks like she's ready to lose her mind. I hope he does better for you tonight, Elise, otherwise you're screwed." She reached for Libby's coffee and took a sip.

"You're off duty now! You can nap whenever you want," Elise said. She turned back to Sam who chewed on a rubber elephant. "Besides, look how sweet he is. I miss this age, don't you?"

Both Libby and Ivy murmured noncommittally.

"Ada's still asleep," Elise noted.

"I'm sure she's tired. And we told her she didn't have to do anything with Sam," Libby said.

"Oh, I know. She left plenty of bottles. I don't mind hanging with this little chunk all day." She squeezed Sam's round thigh. "It's just... Does she seem a little... I don't know... *off* to you?" She pursed her lips together, as if trying to keep any other words from spilling forth.

"Off?" Ivy barked. "That's a nice way of putting it. She's like a walking talking zombie. I'm afraid she's going to take a bite out of my face."

"Let's see how she seems today," Libby said, just as the sliding door to the deck opened and Ada stepped out, bleary-eyed in flannel pajamas, holding a cup of coffee.

"Good morning! How did you sleep?" Elise asked.

"Okay, I guess. My head is killing me. What was in those drinks, Elise?" Ada sank down beside Sam, planting a kiss along the soft skin of his temple. "How did he do last night?"

"Fine," Ivy said, and Libby was proud of her for how much effort she knew the lie took. Ada pulled Sam into her lap.

"We have our massages booked for the morning. I've already called someone to come over to babysit," Elise said before Ada could ask.

Ada frowned and looked down at Sam. "I don't know. He's never really been with a sitter before."

"It's fine. She's a young woman I know from the neighborhood who used to babysit my kids all the time when they were younger. It's all arranged, so don't argue about it," Elise said firmly.

"Okay. That sounds all right, I guess," Ada relented.

"Lib, tell us more about this guy you're seeing. You didn't say much about him yesterday," Elise urged.

"Well, his name is Adam," Libby said. She felt herself blushing just saying his name.

"Yeah, we know. You told us that much," Elise said.

"He's nice," Libby stalled.

"Well, I hope so, but what else?" Elise waited patiently. Even Ada leaned forward expectantly. Libby took a sip of coffee and tried to find a way to begin, wondering why it was so hard to talk about this with them. When she and Steven had sex for the first time, Libby had gone back to her dorm room and told Ivy every moment in such shocking detail that there might as well have been a videotape of it.

It wasn't just sex they talked about. The four of them confided in each other about *everything*. When Ivy's father died, and she was paralyzed by a grief that was complicated by rage, they had taken turns sitting in the bedroom with her, not talking, just keeping her company when she didn't have the will to get up. When Ada was dumped by her boyfriend sophomore year, they all listened when she told them she feared no one would ever love her again. And when Elise's little sister Jackie was diagnosed with leukemia, Elise came home and sobbed every Sunday night after visiting her. They'd crowd around Elise on one of their twin beds, and listen as she told them how afraid she was of Jackie dying.

Libby didn't talk like that with anyone anymore. All of her relationships seemed to consist of small talk and pleasantries—

conversation about the children, a rundown of the previous weekend's events, comparing dinner recipes. She knew that no adult life could maintain the highs and lows of college, the tumult and tangle of all that insecurity and desire. But when had they stopped talking about the things that mattered? When did they stop sharing their fears and hopes and the shameful things they'd like to forget? Even now, when Libby wanted to tell her friends about Adam, she had trouble finding the words. She was out of practice, but determined to try.

"He's so different from Steven, and I know I shouldn't compare them, but I can't help it," Libby finally said.

"Different how?" Elise asked.

She tried to explain. "Well, looks, first of all. He's really tall and thin. And he has a shaved head, but I think it's one of those haircuts guys get when they're going bald." Steven had been stocky and solid with a full head of hair.

"Steven could have gone bald too," Ivy reminded her.

"I know, but it's not just looks. He's quiet and sort of intense—but not in a weird way," she added quickly.

"Steven definitely wasn't quiet." Elise smiled, remembering.

"No, he wasn't." Steven had a voice that could carry across a football field, and he needed it too, as head coach at the high school where he worked. Steven's voice filled their small house, and he was constantly in motion. Weekends were spent re-sanding the floors or finishing the basement. When he fell asleep at night, he crashed into bed, passing out like a rumpled toddler after a day of hard play. Adam had a quiet calm about him that was unfamiliar.

"Have you slept with him yet?" Ivy asked with a wicked grin.

"That's not our business," Elise said, though she turned to Libby, waiting to see if she'd answer. Libby pinched her lips to keep the smile from overtaking her face, but Ivy had already seen it.

"You did!" Ivy said, lighting up.

"Ooh, how was it?" Elise asked. Her eyes shined with excitement and Libby was touched by how happy they all seemed for her, even if her own feelings were more complicated.

"Good." Libby ducked her head so they wouldn't see how pink her cheeks were.

"Good? How good?" Ivy asked.

"I don't know. Good. A little weird, it being the first time and all."

She had so little to compare it to. She'd slept with Bobby, her high school boyfriend, and then she met Steven. How was it possible that she was forty-one and had only slept with three men?

She might not have had much experience, but compared to sex with Steven, it had been painfully awkward. Steven knew her body. He'd seen the little pouch of fat on her stomach, a result of two C-sections. He didn't care that her thighs were thicker than she would have liked, or that she preferred to have the lights off because she couldn't stand being preoccupied by thinking about what facial expressions she was making.

She suspected the sex itself would get better with time (assuming there was another time. She *hoped* there would be another time). What had stunned Libby most was the feeling of Adam's hands on her skin, the realization of how rarely she was touched by another human other than the girls (and Caitlin's touches were growing less frequent by the day). Afterward they'd lain in Adam's bed, Libby's cheek pressed up against his smooth chest. His arm was wrapped protectively around her shoulders, and he played with her hair, and while they hadn't really talked about much, she felt the crush of intimacy in the back of her throat, a closeness both familiar and unfamiliar, something she'd almost forgotten.

Ada sighed. "God, I don't think I'm ever going to have sex again."

"Why not? Are you and Tyler okay?" Libby asked, grateful to have the conversation veer away from her.

"Yeah, I guess. I just don't have any interest. Did that happen to you guys after you had kids?" Ada asked. She looked vulnerable, her face pinched with worry.

"I think so." It all seemed so far away. Bethany was only eight, but her infancy was a lifetime ago.

"Not for me," Ivy said. "I couldn't even get Sebastian to wait until I had my follow-up visit with the OB. As soon as I stopped bleeding, he was ready."

"Ugh, TMI," Libby said, wrinkling her nose.

Ivy shrugged. "We were young though. I was only twenty-four when Jax was born. I'm sure it would be different now. Though the idea of having a baby now is *insane*. I don't know how you're doing it, Ada."

Ada blinked into her coffee cup. Libby waited for Elise to help.

"It's totally normal not to be interested in sex," Elise said, jumping in. "Your whole body is working overtime just to function. Between nursing and changing dirty diapers and sleep deprivation, who has time for sex? For me, it got better with the other kids. Number one just takes it out of you more than the others somehow."

"Well, Sam's probably it for us. Does that mean I'll never want to have sex again?" Ada asked.

"Of course not," Elise and Libby said in unison.

"How often are you guys doing it?" Ivy asked.

"None of our business," Elise added, though again they all waited for Ada's answer.

"I don't know," Ada hedged. She glanced at Sam who was chewing on a rubber book. He was only wearing a wool sweater, and Libby wondered if it was too cold for him out here, though his cheeks were flushed pink. "It's hard. I just don't feel like it."

"How often?" Ivy pressed.

"Like… I don't know…" Ada focused intently on the weathered gray floorboards of the deck. "Twice?"

"Twice a week? That's really good actually," Ivy said.

"No, twice since Sam was born," Ada mumbled.

They sat in a stunned silence, none of them wanting to be the first to comment, each of them doing the mental calculations of how long had passed. Sam was nine months old.

Libby was torn between feeling terrible for Ada and wanting to throw her coffee cup at her. If Libby had a husband in her bed every night, she would have had sex with him whenever possible. Maybe this was the kind of rose-colored hindsight that came only after your husband was dead, but she couldn't imagine being married to Tyler and not wanting sex. Not that she was attracted to Ada's husband, but Tyler was nice, attractive, and helpful, the whole package as far as Libby was concerned. Steven had the kind of boundless enthusiasm for sex as a teenager, and though they'd slowed after the kids were born, until he died they were still doing it at least two or three times a week. Twice in nine months. It really was hard to fathom.

"That's not normal, is it?" Ada asked, her eyes filling with tears.

"What's normal?" Elise asked, sliding closer to Ada. "None of us have had a baby at forty. What do we know?"

Sam let out a wail. "I need to feed him." Ada wiped her face and hoisted Sam onto her hip.

"I just gave him a bottle. He didn't drink much though," Elise said.

"He hates bottles. He just wants to nurse. Besides, I need to get him down for a nap." Ada bounced up and down with Sam, rubbing circles on his back.

"I'll do it," Libby said, standing and holding her arms out to Ada. "It's my turn, remember?"

"It's fine. It will be faster if I do it anyway." Ada hurried into the house, shutting the sliding door between them and leaving the conversation behind. Libby met Elise and Ivy's eyes and waited to see who would speak first.

"Twice?" Ivy whispered. Her eyebrows were raised so high they disappeared behind her bangs.

Libby held up a hand to stop Ivy from saying anything more. "Don't," she said and was grateful that, for once, Ivy listened.

ELISE

Text message: Brad to Elise
Meeting scheduled at Tommy's school for Monday 9AM in principal's office. Call me to discuss.

The baby hadn't wanted to nap after all, and Elise had managed to wrestle Sam from Ada's arms to send her back downstairs for a second cup of coffee. She spread a bath towel out on her bed and laid Sam upon it. He wriggled and whimpered as she slipped off his cotton pants and changed his diaper. He was a fussy baby, there was no question about it, but Elise wondered how much of Sam's temperament was in response to Ada. His irritability was probably because he was tired from waking up so much at night.

It was so easy to judge, Elise knew, when the truth was that your children were who they were from the moment they were born. Tommy was her first and hardest, a boy who was born contrary and unsettled from the day he opened his eyes. He was late smiling, and even after he did, it was more likely for him to have an expression of worry on his face, even as a chubby-cheeked infant. Elise had watched her friends swoon over their firstborns who did everything easily—poop, sleep, socialize, follow directions, use good manners. Elise was certain she had done something to cause Tommy's anxious personality until she had Piper, who was born with a sunny and easy disposition. She smiled as often as Tommy frowned, learned to say please and thank you as if through osmosis, and filled the house with her effortless laugh. It wasn't anything Elise did or didn't do—it was simply who her children were.

She sat cross-legged beside Sam on the bed, steeling herself to call Brad. She knew his voice would have the same detached chilly tone that he'd been using with her for the past two months. At some point they would have to address the gulf between them. Or would they? Some couples lived like this for years, coexisting like roommates who'd met on Craigslist, passing the children back and forth like hot potatoes, all the while creating their own separate lives.

She pulled out her phone and dialed Brad's number.

"Hi, Mama!" Marianna answered.

"Hello, sweetheart," Elise said, grateful that Brad had allowed Marianna to answer, even if it meant he wasn't ready to talk to her. Her heart swelled at the sound of her daughter's voice. "Are you having a nice weekend? Are you being good for Daddy?"

"Uh-huh. Lucy brought me to the park."

"That's nice," she said. Lucy was their frequent babysitter, a sophomore at Harper who sometimes watched the kids. Elise had left her number for Brad, but it still annoyed her. How many weekends had she managed to survive with all three kids without needing to call in a sitter?

"When are you coming home, Mama?" Marianna asked in her soft lisp. When she was younger and first learning to speak, Elise was the only one who could understand her. Even Brad had needed Elise to interpret. Sometimes it felt like she and Marianna spoke their own secret language. Her speech was clearer now, although she continued speech therapy, and Elise knew the other children sometimes had difficulty understanding her.

"Soon, baby, soon. Less than two days." When she returned home, Elise knew that Marianna would wrap her arms around Elise's waist and hang on. Piper would give her a brief hug, and Tommy would wave hello, as if he hadn't noticed she'd been gone. Only Marianna still openly loved her with a wide-eyed abandon.

"I'll see you soon, sweetheart, okay? Can you put Daddy on now? I love you."

"Love you too, Mama," Marianna said. There was a shuffle and then Brad was on the line.

"So what's going on with Tommy?" Elise asked, feeling prickly again now that it was Brad.

"Mrs. Kingsley called," he said.

"Why?"

Mrs. Kingsley couldn't have been more than twenty-five, and Elise was certain she wouldn't last more than three years in the profession. At least not in middle school. Middle school was the dreaded middle child of education, the children no longer cute like in elementary, but not yet maturing into adulthood like high school. When Elise was a teacher, she'd hated even passing her former students in the hall, horrified by what those adorable six-year-olds had become. Yet now that Tommy was in eighth grade, she wished for a teacher made of sterner stuff than Mrs. Kingsley, one who could see past the pale caterpillar of a mustache crawling across his upper lip, the blackheads that decorated his nose like an abstract painting, and the smirk with which he greeted the world.

"Apparently, Tommy's gotten into some computer trouble," Brad said.

"Computer trouble? What do you mean?" Elise asked. Beside her on the bed, Sam grunted in frustration and Elise lowered him onto the carpet.

Brad cleared his throat. "Well, I guess the elementary students use a reading program. LetterBot, I think it's called?"

"LetterBot? Yeah, I know. Marianna's class uses it. What does that have to do with Tommy?" Most students were done with LetterBot by fourth grade.

Tommy was still the most mercurial of the three children, with the potential to become either a sensitive soulful artist or a subversive sociopath. Right now it looked like it could go either way. Elise knew he still battled the anxiety that had plagued him as a boy, but he no longer shared his worries with Elise as he once had. Instead, he put on a front of indifference and shoved down his discomfort.

"It seems that Tommy figured out a way into the system." When Elise didn't answer, he added, "He hacked into LetterBot."

"He hacked into LetterBot," Elise repeated, trying to wrap her mind around it.

"I guess there are magical creatures and each child earns fairies for reading the words correctly. Tommy somehow created a gnome that eliminated the fairies. It's actually quite ingenious, though he obviously shouldn't have done it," Brad said. "At some point, we should talk about sending him to computer camp. Or at least finding an after-school coding class he could take."

"*Brad,*" Elise said, trying to contain her irritation that Brad was off on a tangent, yet also loving her husband for his ability to see the best in each of their children and wishing he could extend the same courtesy to her. "Tell me more about what he did."

"Sorry," he mumbled. "So in addition to wiping out the fairies, he changed all the usernames. Each kid logs in with his own account, and Tommy went in and changed them all."

"To what?" Elise lowered herself onto the floor beside Sam, dreading where the rest of the conversation was going.

Brad sighed. "Well, there's an Asshole, a Fuckface, a Blueballs, a Cock, and a Cunt. Along with a few others."

"Oh my God. Where did he hear those words? We don't talk like that," Elise said.

"He's thirteen, Elise. He's heard the word cunt before."

"Stop saying that word! It's hateful and misogynistic."

"I'm sure that's what the parents of the second and third graders think, too," Brad snapped. "They're calling for Tommy's expulsion."

"Expulsion? Oh, God." Elise covered her face with her hand.

"We have a meeting with the principal on Monday at nine. Tommy's suspended until further notice."

"I'm going to kill him. I'm going to wring his little neck," Elise said softly.

"I think you should come home," Brad said.

"What? I'm not coming home! We just got here."

"There's obviously something going on with Tommy, and I think we need to talk with him. Together." Brad emphasized this last word.

"Oh, together?" Elise felt her anger at Tommy diverting course. "Now you want to do something together? What's going on with Tommy probably has something to do with the fact that his parents no longer speak or sleep in the same room."

"That's on you, Elise. I'm not the one who was stealing money for years and squirreling it away in a private bank account," Brad said. He'd lowered his voice but there was more emotion in it than she had heard in months.

"I wasn't stealing!" Elise insisted, though deep down she knew it was theft, that more than the money, she'd been stealing away pieces of their marriage with each deposit, chipping away at the trust built up over their years together. "How many times can I apologize for this? You need to move on," she whisper-yelled, not wanting the others to hear her.

"It was thirty thousand dollars, Elise. People go to jail for taking that kind of money. It's called embezzlement."

"Oh, so now you want me to go to jail? Are you going to call the police?" Elise asked.

"It's not even about the money, Elise, don't you get that?" he said in an exasperated voice.

"Really? Because it sounds like it's about the money," she said.

"I'm not having this discussion with you over the phone. This isn't even about us, it's about Tommy. I think you should come home," Brad said in his new icy voice.

"No. I will not," Elise said, rising with Sam in her arms. She was braver somehow, holding the child. "*You* talk to Tommy. You're his father. I'll be at the meeting on Monday."

Without another word, she ended the call, dropping the phone on the bed, on the verge of tears but trembling with anger too. She took a deep breath, trying to regain her composure. On the bed, Sam flashed her a rare gummy smile, and Elise bent to kiss his cheek and inhale that unforgettable baby smell, thinking about Tommy and what they would do if he was expelled. Ada thought that parenting an infant was hard, but the truth was, she had no idea how much harder it would get.

LIBBY

Text message: Libby to Adam
Having a great time! Maybe we can do something this week?
Btw—I miss you too.

Text message: Libby to Caitlin
Hang in there—it's only a few days. Please just be nice to Grandma.

"Caitlin told me to fuck off," Libby's mother informed her on the phone.

"I'm sorry," Libby said, by now used to apologizing to her mother for Caitlin's behavior, though this was a new low. Libby had dragged a towel out onto the beach to call and check on the girls. The wind whipped the waves into a froth as they crashed on the shore, and Libby zipped up the collar of her coat against the chill.

"*You* shouldn't be. But I told her if it happened again, I was going to wash her mouth out with soap," Anne-Marie said.

"*Mom.*" Libby could only imagine the battle that would ensue if her mother tried such a thing. Caitlin might punch Anne-Marie in the gut. Libby would never be able to ask her mother to babysit again.

"The girl needs discipline, Libby. You're letting her run wild. I know you're trying your best to be both her mother and father, but letting her get away with everything and treat other people disrespectfully is not going to help her later."

Libby could see her mother so clearly, all that self-righteous judgment on her strong makeup-free face, colorless lips pinched together in disapproval. It was their ongoing argument, though most of it took place in Libby's head. It consisted of Anne-Marie's criticism over Libby's haphazard and lax methods of parenting and discipline, while Libby seethed silently.

As a child, Libby's mouth had been washed out with soap on a single occasion, the one time she dared swear in the presence of her mother, but not for using the F word. Libby wouldn't have dared to utter such a word in her parents' home. She could still taste the bittersweet flavor of Ivory soap, the hard edges of the bar pressing against her teeth and tongue after she'd used the word "suck" to describe her day at school. Today the word was used freely in classrooms, but in Libby's house, it had been a curse.

Part of Libby's parenting style was in direct opposition to the way Anne-Marie ruled her household—all those timeouts and weekends grounded for minor infractions, nightly formal meals around the table where Libby or her sister Karen were scolded for reaching across the table for the salt without saying "excuse me," or for letting their elbows graze the straw placemat.

The trouble was, she knew her mother was right. The girls who wilted in Libby's office, their eyes rimmed in black makeup, faces pulled in permanent pouts—there were times when Libby listened to their complaints and wished she could conjure up her mother. Anne-Marie wouldn't stand for such nonsense—the back talk and cattiness, the self-pity, the desire to inflict pain both inward and outward. Anne-Marie would have prescribed a month without screen time and weekends spent doing chores, reading, and playing outside. Libby wondered if the world had changed so dramatically that these tactics no longer worked, or that parents today didn't dream of doling out such punishment.

Caitlin was on the fast track to being one of the girls in her office. People thought living in a place like Wolf Mountain (safe, picturesque, where mountain met lake) shielded you from the dangers of city life, but it wasn't true. Drugs ran rampant in the town, and teenagers spent weekends partying in the woods and in crumbling mountain shacks. Unemployment was high, and young people malingered after graduation before getting the hell out or finding themselves trapped. It was a fine place to be an adult or a child, but no place for anyone between the ages of fifteen and twenty-five. She and Steven had lived in Dedham, less than a half-hour away from Elise, and Libby hadn't wanted to leave when he died, but it had seemed like the only option. After his death, they'd lived with Libby's parents for six months before finally moving into a house of their own. Libby was grateful to her parents for all they had done and still did for her family, but there was a price tag for such help, and it usually came in the form of listening to her mother's subtle critique of her parenting.

"What am I supposed to do, Mom?" Libby asked, regretting the question as soon as it was out of her mouth. Anne-Marie had a solution for everything.

"Well, first of all, take that phone away. I don't know why she has it in the first place. What does a twelve-year-old need a phone for anyway?"

"They all have them," Libby answered, before she could think better of it.

"So? All your friends had Cabbage Patch Kids when you were a girl too, but did that mean your father or I were going to run out and spend a hundred dollars on a doll? Absolutely ridiculous," Anne-Marie huffed.

Libby tightened her grip on the phone and bit her tongue. What was ridiculous was her mother's solution for the Cabbage Patch Kid Libby had so desperately wanted, the prized dolls with their pungent baby oil-scented skin and moon faces. Instead Anne-Marie bought a homemade version from the church bazaar, a stuffed ladies' nude stocking decorated with limp yellow yarn for hair and unstaring eyes made out of shiny black buttons. Libby had hidden the doll in her closet so none of her friends would see it.

"Right," Libby said, unwilling to follow the Cabbage Patch Kid example any further. "Okay, take away her phone. What else?" As if just that wouldn't start a major rebellion at home.

"You spend time together every night. The three of you. Playing board games, reading together, doing crafts, what have you," her mother said, as if it were the simplest thing in the world.

Libby was glad her mother couldn't see her roll her eyes, as that was another of Anne-Marie's pet peeves. She'd been a stay-at-home mom for most of Libby's childhood, but Libby didn't recall her ever playing games or doing crafts with them. Reading, maybe. *Maybe.* Then again, Libby and Karen had spent most afternoons wandering the woods behind their house, creating elaborate games about fairies and wild animals, sitting on the pine-needled ground and writing in the dirt with sticks and rocks. When Libby and Karen were in high school, Anne-Marie got a job in a doctor's office where she still worked part-time. She was always bringing home back issues of *Psychology Today* and *Parents* magazine. She sent Libby clippings in the mail and dropped tidbits into conversation with the authority of a trained professional.

"We don't have time to play games together every night. The girls have homework. I need to cook dinner." *And I'm too fucking tired*, she wanted to add, but didn't, not wanting another lecture on the ills of cursing.

"You make time. Family is more important than anything else," Anne-Marie chided, and Libby swallowed a sigh because this was her mother's trump card, and Libby knew it was true. Despite her unwillingness to be the kind of mother Anne-Marie was, Libby and her sister had never doubted they were loved, never doubted that their family came before anything.

"I know, you're right, Mom," Libby murmured.

"Anyway, why are you talking to me? You're supposed to be relaxing. Caitlin's potty mouth is nothing I can't handle for a few days. I did raise two teenage girls myself, you might recall," Anne-Marie reminded her.

"Can I talk to her? I'd just like to say hello."

There was a pause, and Libby could see the disapproval as it flickered between her mother's brows. "I'll put her on, but just for a few minutes. Try to relax, okay? Enjoy yourself. Here she is." There was a shuffle, and after a moment Caitlin grunted hello.

"Hi, honey."

"Hang on," Caitlin said, and Libby knew she was waiting till she was out of earshot of Anne-Marie. "Hi."

"How are you? Are you having a nice weekend with Grandma?" Maybe if she pretended everything was fine, so would Caitlin. No such luck.

"It sucks. Grandma seriously thinks we live in the eighteen hundreds. Last night she wanted to teach me how to knit." Her voice dripped with contempt.

"Lots of girls knit these days. You could make all your Christmas presents," Libby chirped, trying to channel Elise's endless stream of goodwill.

"Then she wanted me to cook dinner with her. We were having this disgusting beef stew, and she made me peel and chop all the potatoes. Like, twenty of them!"

"There's nothing wrong with helping out at dinner. Karen and I used to have to cook once a week when we were your age." Libby hated the patronizing tone in her voice, but sometimes Anne-Marie's chipper frankness rubbed off, and Libby found herself speaking in platitudes and clichés.

"Whatever," Caitlin muttered, the last word on everything.

Libby closed her eyes and tipped her face toward the sun, letting it warm her cheeks. She tried to focus on what Caitlin was saying, but sometimes Caitlin's complaining was a monologue she tuned out. Libby half listened to her rant about how there was no cable or Wi-Fi, and she wasn't even able to watch Netflix because it would use up all her data. Libby murmured in sympathy when Caitlin grumbled that tonight was meat loaf.

She dreaded what Caitlin's reaction would be if she knew about Adam. Libby wasn't sure if she would scream and yell or withdraw even further, disappearing more than she already had. She wondered what Steven would have said about Caitlin's constant state of disappointment and surliness, her husband whose optimism and cheer had been boundless. Then again, Libby realized with a pang, maybe Caitlin wouldn't be so miserable if Steven was around. If her husband were still alive, it was possible that Caitlin would be a very different child.

IVY

Text message: Marshall Boyd to Ivy
I had a great time the other night. I have another work event Thursday evening if you're free. We can work something out privately rather than going through the agency.

Ivy closed her eyes and tried to enjoy the feeling of the massage therapist's hands rubbing hot oil into her shoulders. It should have been a simple pleasure, but Ivy couldn't relax. There had been three more 800 calls on the way over, none of which Ivy had listened to. She'd ignored the message from Marshall so far too, but she wondered how much she could ask for the entire evening, especially if she were willing to go back to his apartment—for what, she wasn't sure yet.

The massage therapist smoothed the oil into Ivy's shoulders. For each gentle yet firm squeeze, Ivy knew where it hurt the massage therapist. She knew the burn in her forearms, the way it tingled and spasmed, knew the dull ache in the balls of her feet. She knew the way the mind drifted over the sixty minutes, flitting from grocery lists to life plans as her fingers worked methodically.

Ivy knew everything the therapist felt, and it prevented her from enjoying the luxury of the massage.

Despite all that, being a massage therapist hadn't been a bad job, even if it wasn't what she'd planned. After being expelled from Harper, Ivy had moved back home to Butler. She was so close to finishing her degree, and her mother made her immediately apply to the nearest state university. She lost a few credits in the process but was able to graduate, although a degree from the state university was nowhere near as prestigious as one from Harper. Her mother urged her to apply for teaching jobs in the area, but Ivy didn't want a job that would tether her to Butler or any of the nearby towns. When she finished the degree, she stayed only till she scraped together enough money to move to San Francisco and away from her mother's disappointment. In San Francisco, she found a job in a restaurant and slept on her old friend Gene's couch, sending her resume out to schools in the area. She had a few interviews, but none of them had landed in a job, and after a few months, she stopped applying. The restaurant money was good, and Ivy was no longer sure she wanted to teach. Unrealistic as it might have been, she'd envisioned working in a school with Libby, Elise, and Ada, or if not in the same school, at least in the same area. She'd imagined them having drinks after work on Friday evenings, grumbling over students, comparing notes about their week. The idea of stepping into the classroom by herself, without their support, was terrifying.

Instead, a friend from the restaurant told her about a course she was taking in massage, and Ivy signed up. She got a job working at a high-end spa in the Marina, rubbing the shoulders and backsides of socialites and dotcommers. She kept a few shifts at the restaurant in order to pay her rent (by this time Gene had a new girlfriend, and the couch situation wasn't working out as smoothly). The days passed quickly in the new rhythm of restaurant and spa.

It was at the restaurant where she met Sebastian. He was a few years older and a regular, one of the customers who came in a few nights a week and sat at the bar. His hands were always stained with paint, the fingernails rimmed in indigo, cerulean and fuchsia, like a manicure gone wrong. She stayed to have a drink with him one night after work, and the next night she went home with him. Within the year, Jax came along, and the life she'd had at Harper was as fuzzy and distant as a dream.

"How does that feel?" the massage therapist asked. She was a tiny woman with gray hair shorn into an unflattering buzz cut. She'd introduced herself as Denise and shook Ivy's hand with a firm grip.

"Good," Ivy murmured.

"Is this the right amount of pressure?"

"It's great. Thanks." Ivy spoke her response through the hole in the donut-shaped cushion her face was smushed into.

Ivy was always careful not to talk too much with her clients, unless they initiated the conversation. A well-timed question here and there, and you quickly understood what the client wanted. Most people wanted silence, their slow breathing mingling with the hypnotic background music. Occasionally, though, she'd get a talker. These were the people who could never relax. They treated the massage like a drink at the bar, and Ivy was the bartender, ready to serve and converse.

Denise didn't ask any more questions, and Ivy closed her eyes again, intent on rising above her distraction and "being present." But she'd never been good at being present, making her thoughts go white and empty, and within minutes, her mind started to drift again. She recalled that long-ago February day when she began to unravel the carefully braided strands of her life.

From the day she entered Harper, she'd struggled. In high school, Ivy had never worried about how she stacked up against the other students in her class. She made all As with only minimal studying and she had nothing to prove to her classmates. At Harper, it was different. All of the students were accustomed to doing well, except most of her peers had gotten As at Choate and Exeter, not Butler Valley Regional. From the moment she walked onto the ivied campus of Harper, she knew she didn't belong.

She hadn't realized how hard it would be and how unprepared she actually was, despite the scholarship they'd given her. Her intelligence was the one thing Ivy had always been certain of, but Harper triggered a terrible insecurity in her. She felt like an imposter waiting to be discovered. Her friends worked hard and they moaned about the amount of work, but none of them complained that it was too difficult for them. Ivy seemed to work twice as hard and yet she still brought in only Bs. There was an all-encompassing terror that they'd take away her scholarship.

Then there was the test anxiety. It began freshman year during the Intro to Teaching class all education majors were required to take. She'd feel sick the day of an exam, diarrhea in the public bathroom, her stomach in knots. It continued sophomore and junior year, though a new symptom arrived—floating black dots in her vision and a feeling of lightheadedness, her stomach as queasy as if she'd eaten bad Mexican food the night before. By then she knew she could do the work, but the dread from those first years had seeped into her skin, the fear that she wasn't good enough, that she didn't fit in, that she didn't belong. It didn't matter how prepared she was for the test, and she was *always* prepared. The worry got ahold of her and wouldn't let go, not even after the exam was over. It wouldn't be till the next morning that Ivy would feel like herself again. The more important the test, the more extreme the symptoms. Each exam, each in-class essay, each pop quiz was a fresh opportunity for everyone to discover her secret.

The teacher's exam was the SATs of an education degree. *More* important. It was what they'd been preparing for since day one.

There were two four-hour tests, one in basic language and communication, and one in all areas of science. In order to get a job upon graduation, they each needed to pass the tests. It was the first step in the long process of certification, the first step toward becoming a teacher.

Ivy had been studying for the exam since the beginning of senior year. It was the science test she was worried about. They'd taken several practice tests in class, and even during those, Ivy's anxiety shot through the roof. Not just inconvenient, the side effects of the stress were becoming debilitating. During one of the practice tests Ivy had to use the restroom twice, emptying her bowels of the toxic fear that had been collecting for days. The actual exam was timed, and every bathroom break she took would be held against her, the minutes on the clock ticking away as Ivy sat on the toilet and tried to clear her vision.

She was leaving class one day when the idea came to her. They'd taken yet another practice exam, and Ivy was certain she hadn't passed. She was lightheaded and walked slowly so as not to stumble, like a sorority girl on her way home from a frat party.

"I'm going to bomb this stupid test," the girl in front of Ivy mumbled to her friend. Her long blonde hair was twisted into a perfect French braid. "I wish I could just pay someone to take it for me."

"You can if you want," her friend said in a low voice, tugging down her wool hat. "There's a girl on my floor who takes tests for people. She's some kind of genius."

"Who is she?" Ivy asked, though neither of them was talking to her.

The girl in the hat glanced at Ivy, then back toward her friend.

"I can't take this test," Ivy said, and as soon as the words were out, she knew it was true, and the relief made her feel a little steadier, her equilibrium suddenly returned. It hadn't occurred to her that there might be a solution. There was a girl. Of course there was. In college, there was someone for everything you might need.

"I wasn't talking to you," the one in the hat said as they stepped out into the early February air. Fat flakes fell from the sky, creating white polka dots in the grayness.

"Please. I'll give you my number if you don't want to tell me her name. Just tell her to call me. It has nothing to do with you." Ivy dug through her bag until she found a notebook and pen, hastily scribbling her name and number down on a piece of loose-leaf, which she shoved at the girl in the hat. Snow fell on the paper, blurring the blue ink of Ivy's phone number.

"I'm not making any promises," she said, shoving the paper into the pocket of her enormous black parka. They hurried away into the snow, and Ivy let herself imagine a future where she didn't have to take the test.

The test taker's name was Michelle Hansen. She called Ivy that night, and her nasally voice sounded like salvation over the cordless phone. All Ivy needed to do was give her the details of the test—subject area, time, and location—and two hundred and fifty dollars. Turned out Michelle was only a sophomore, short and freckled in sweatpants and glasses. Ivy brought the details and money to Michelle's dorm room the next day, the folded bills crisp in her jeans pocket, earned from her work-study job in the library. Then she returned to where her roommates were busy studying. Already she felt better.

The teacher's test wasn't a college exam, so it was given on Saturdays at high schools around the Boston area. Back then all you needed was a photocopy of your student ID or another form of identification. Ivy easily acquired a fake Harper ID with her name and Michelle's picture on it. It had only cost her an extra fifty bucks, money well spent.

Ivy was registered for the first Saturday in March. Her roommates all knew the date was coming, though she hadn't told anyone about the dirty deal with Michelle. On the morning of the test, Ivy rose early and showered. She brushed her teeth and blow-dried her hair, feeling calmer than she had in months. On the way out, her roommates wished her luck, and Ivy gave a brave smile, then took the train to Newbury Street. She sat in a café and read magazines for the afternoon. She arrived home a little before four, breathless with relief.

Libby and Elise were waiting for her.

"How did it go?" Elise asked.

Ivy hoisted her bag over her shoulder. "It was fine. Hard, but I think I passed."

"Mark came by looking for you. He wants you to go to his apartment as soon as you get in. We told him you were at the exam and would be home soon," Libby said.

Mark was the director of the dorm. Ivy had only met him once before, the first week of the semester, a pale man with thinning hair who was probably only thirty but seemed ancient.

"What does he want?" Ivy asked. Something turned in her stomach.

"I don't know, but you should probably go down there. He's expecting you." Libby gave a weak smile. They all knew that a visit from the dorm director couldn't be good news.

Ivy took the elevator to the first floor and knocked on the door of his apartment. Mark opened the door and gave her a quick nod.

"Ivy, come in." He led her into the small living room and gestured to an orange corduroy couch. He sat in a worn leather chair opposite her. A box of crackers was on the scarred coffee table next to a Harper College mug and a stack of papers.

"Tea?" He raised his mug to her.

"No, thanks." She shifted on the sofa, and Mark took a sip from his cup and watched her with alert eyes. "Is everything okay? Is my mom all right?"

His gaze softened and he nodded, lowering the mug to the table. "She's fine. I'm sorry if I scared you."

"It's okay."

"Today was your teacher's exam." It wasn't a question.

Ivy bit her fingernail, too close to the quick. A slice of pain cut through her thumb. She nodded.

"Did you go?" He waited.

She'd always figured it was hyperbole when people said their heart stopped beating, but at that moment, Ivy's heart stopped. It quivered in her chest, waiting, waiting, the blood in her veins floating stagnant. "Yes," she whispered, though she knew it was already over.

Mark leaned forward, so close that Ivy saw his nearly white eyelashes. They were so long they pressed up against the lenses of his glasses.

"I'm going to ask you again, Ivy. And I want you to think before you answer. Did you take the test today?"

Her mouth was dry, the stale taste of coffee coating her tongue and gums. He knew. *He knew.* There was no other reason for her to be here. She shook her head but couldn't meet his eyes.

"I didn't think so." He looked down at the coffee table, wearied by her admission.

"I'm sorry," Ivy whispered, the tears suddenly sharp, but it wasn't true. She wasn't sorry she'd cheated on the test. She was only sorry she'd gotten caught.

"Why? Why would you do that?" Mark shook his head in perplexity. "From what I gather you're a solid student. Mostly Bs for the past three years. You're a *senior.* You would have passed. Why cheat?"

Ivy swallowed. Something hot and tart pressed its way into her throat and threatened to erupt. She tried to find the words to explain. "I get test anxiety." Even she heard how flimsy the excuse was. She pressed her lips together, trying to make him understand. "It's really bad. It makes me sick, for days, weeks. It's gotten worse. And my grades are okay, but I never do as well on my final exams as I do on all the other coursework. I was worried I'd be too sick to pass."

Mark sighed and rubbed his eyes behind the small gold frames. The pale stubble of a day's growth shone on his chin. "I wish you'd talked to someone. Your professor. Health services. Me." Ivy would have laughed if she weren't so terrified. Mark had never even spoken to her before this conversation. He'd probably had to look up her picture in the yearbook in order to know who she was. The idea she might have confided in him was preposterous.

"I'll retake it. I'll register again and take it myself this time. I promise," Ivy pleaded.

Mark shook his head. "It's too late for that."

A tear fell in her lap, landing on the nubby polyester of her sweater. Another one joined it. "Please, you have to let me take it. It was a mistake."

"It's not up to me," Mark said.

Ivy let that sink in, turning the words over in her mind. "So what happens now?"

"I don't know. You have a meeting with President Temple on Monday morning at eleven. She's already been informed of the situation. She was the one who called me and asked if I would speak with you first."

Ivy tried to process what he'd told her. She wondered what it was that had given the scam away—if someone had recognized Michelle, or if her fake ID hadn't been as authentic as Ivy had thought.

"But what will happen to me?"

Mark held up an empty hand. "At best, you'll fail the course or the entire semester. But this is a serious breach of Harper's code of honor. You may very well be expelled." He delivered this last news in a hushed voice.

Expelled. The word brought to mind boys with pocketknives and shaved heads, juvenile delinquents skipping high school to smoke on street corners. Ivy's breath caught in her chest.

"I can't be expelled. Please. I can't. Please." She could already picture her mother's face, stained gray with sorrow, her disappointment a living being between them, rattling around the small rooms of their house.

"It's not up to me. I'm sorry."

"There must be something you can do. It was a terrible mistake. It will never happen again. I can't get expelled my senior year. What will I do?" Her voice was high-pitched and unfamiliar. "What will I do?"

Perhaps he took pity on her, or maybe he just wanted to end the conversation as quickly as possible, to return to the mundane stack of papers on the table and refill his tea. Mark leaned forward, his fingers steepled in his lap.

"If you tell me who took the test for you, then maybe, *maybe*, President Temple will take that into consideration."

It hadn't occurred to Ivy that Michelle wouldn't already be in trouble too. How could she not be? She was the one who'd impersonated someone else during the exam. Ivy thought of Michelle and her moon-shaped face decorated with a maze of freckles, how readily she'd accepted Ivy's offer, pocketing the money and writing down the details in her calendar, like it was just another assignment she needed to keep track of. While Ivy understood that what Michelle did was wrong to someone like Mark or President Temple, to Ivy she had offered the utmost kindness for a reasonable price. Whatever the consequences for Ivy, it would likely be doubly hard for Michelle if they learned that this was a regular business for her.

But three and a half years wasted. All that financial aid money, summers spent waitressing in Butler, inhaling the sickly smell of beer ground into damp wood, thousands upon thousands of dollars evaporating, burning up and smoking before her eyes. Her whole future gone, just like that.

"Her name is Michelle," Ivy began, the shame blossoming alongside a slender sliver of hope.

In the end, it hadn't mattered. President Temple expelled her anyway, peering at Ivy from behind her massive desk, cutting her to shreds with just her cold gray eyes and tongue. Libby told her later that Michelle was expelled too, her talent and goodwill wasted because Ivy was bartering for another chance at a future. She couldn't bring herself to apologize to Michelle for ratting her out, and Ivy never even found out how they'd got caught. Within a week, they were both gone.

"You've got a lot of tension in your upper back," Denise remarked, kneading out the knot above Ivy's right shoulder where all of her stress liked to take hold, coiling itself into a hard, pulsing ball.

"Mm hm," Ivy murmured. Her face was sticky against the plastic cushion of the massage table. She wondered if she'd drifted off. For a moment, it was almost as if she were back at Harper, reliving those horrible moments in Mark's cramped living room.

"You should try yoga. It can really help with stress," Denise suggested, pressing harder on the knot.

Ivy didn't answer, focusing instead on the sweet pain in her shoulder as Denise tried her best to untangle the stress. She could work on it all day, and it would never fully go away. It had been there since she left Harper, and each year it only seemed to grow larger. Ivy bit her lip to keep from crying out in pain.

ADA

Facebook status update: Massages??!! Thank you, thank you, Elise Kelly-Ryan!!

Ada lay face down on the massage table, her cheeks pressed into the sticky plastic headrest while Anthony rubbed her back. She was going to kill Elise.

Ada had been so excited for the massage, all of the muscles in her back coiling even tighter, as if in anticipation of someone's hands trying to smooth them out. She'd put on the plush terrycloth robe and sat giddily with Elise, Libby, and Ivy in the waiting room, sipping a cup of cucumber water. Just the eucalyptus-scented room and that new age music they played in spas was enough to help her unwind. Flipping through a magazine, her bare legs crossed under the robe, she waited while a gray-haired pixie of a woman came to collect Ivy and a fresh-faced blonde with a ponytail came to fetch Elise. Ada was in no rush, glad that Sam was out of her sight for the next hour, enjoying looking at pictures of twenty-year-old celebrities, even if they did make her feel fat.

"Ada?"

She looked up to see a handsome dark-haired man in a tight black tee shirt smiling at her. He couldn't have been thirty. *Oh, hell*, Ada thought to herself. It hadn't occurred to her that she'd receive the massage from a man.

"Yes?" she asked, hoping he was just there to tell her they were running late today. She glanced over at Libby who was also still waiting.

He strode across the room and towered over her, his large tan arm extended. "I'm Anthony. I'll be your massage therapist today." He pronounced it "An-tony" and Ada detected a faint accent—Italian?

"Oh. Hi," Ada said.

He flashed another smile and then motioned with his hand. "Please follow me. Right this way."

Ada stood, holding the robe closed at the collar. She looked to Libby, widening her eyes in alarm. Libby gave a sympathetic smile and shrug. Ada followed Anthony into one of the small rooms.

"I'll step outside. You can hang your robe on the door and get under the sheet. I'll be back in a moment," Anthony instructed. Ada nodded dumbly.

The door shut behind him with a gentle click, and Ada dropped the robe and dove under the sheet as quickly as possible, for fear he'd come back while she was partially exposed. *For goodness' sake, Elise*, Ada thought. How could she not have requested a woman? A moment later there was a soft knock on the door.

"Come in," Ada called out. She buried her face into the plastic donut of the table, staring down at the circle of blond flooring, grateful that at least she didn't have to look at him.

Anthony was quiet as he prepared the room. He adjusted the music, bottles clinked together, the faucet ran, and then the lights were dimmed. After a moment, there was a squirt of warm oil at the top of her spine and then Anthony's capable hands on her back.

Ada closed her eyes and tried to relax, but every nerve in her body was on alert.

"How's this?" he asked, his hands polishing the knobs of her shoulders with expert precision.

"Good," Ada mumbled to the floor, as the muscles in her back further contracted. It didn't matter how skilled he was at his job, there was no way Ada was going to be able to relax.

It wasn't just that he was a man. There had been a time in her life when she might have enjoyed a male massage therapist, might have gotten a sexual thrill out of some stranger's hands rubbing her all over, especially if he looked like Anthony. But not now. Not now, when all she could think about was the stippled spread of her thighs against the plastic, when her ass had the same heft and weight as a sack of flour under the starchy sheet, and she hadn't even thought to wear nice underwear. Hers were oversized cotton with little red roses that had faded to pink after too many washings, fraying seams and loose elastic, the underwear of a young girl or an old woman.

In her normal life (as she'd come to think of life before Sam, before her mother's ever-present absence) Ada was tall and a little curvy, at least on her lower half. What the magazines referred to as pear-shaped, as if a woman could be boiled down to fruit and geometric shapes. She would have liked her thighs to be a little more toned, her butt a little smaller and tighter, and she'd never loved her tiny size-B breasts. But in general, she'd been mostly content with her body and hadn't paid it an inordinate amount of attention.

She'd gained sixty pounds during the pregnancy: sixty pounds of peanut butter fudge ice cream after dinner and second helpings of foods she normally ate only occasionally, like steak, burgers, and creamy mac and cheese. She was healthy and active, she told herself. And eating was the only thing that gave her any pleasure during that time, though it was a short-lived enjoyment, always followed by a wave of disgust. Still the weight would fall off after the baby was born.

Except it hadn't. After the initial fifteen pounds of baby, blood, and amniotic fluid, Ada had only lost another ten pounds. She was still thirty-five pounds heavier than usual, not that she'd stepped on a scale in over a month because it only depressed her. She'd imagined long walks with Sam where she'd grow strong and thin again while bonding with her new baby. He was born in July, and by the time Ada was even thinking about exercise, winter had begun to settle in, frost shadowing the streets, leaving them slippery and treacherous. And it wasn't only the weather. Even if she lived in California, most of the time she was too exhausted to imagine walking further than the mailbox or to the coffee shop for a blueberry muffin. Her body was an unfamiliar landscape, lumpy and soft as dough around the middle, purple stretch marks crisscrossing her belly, hips heavy with soft layers of flesh, and then these massive breasts that belonged on a porn star, the consolation prize for the rest of her body.

"You're very tense," Anthony said. "Just try to relax." Ada felt the muscles in her back contract into even tighter knots, if that was possible.

She could only partly blame the excess weight on the pregnancy, because Ada had buried her face in a carton of Häagen-Dazs the night her mother died, the first of many. Ada's mother had been a cook. She spread her love around through the food she made—flaky pies with gooey sweet centers, trays of enchiladas smothered in three types of cheese, homemade fudge at Christmas. Over the years, Ada had learned how to manage her portions and lighten up some of her mother's favorite recipes, but when she died, Ada sought out the comfort of food, the rich succulence of beef, fresh pasta that glistened with oil and parmesan, cakes so sweet her teeth ached in pleasure and pain.

Ada cooked for her father each week, stocking the freezer full of casseroles and meat loaf, dishes that could stretch for several meals. She loved her father, but he was a stoic man, handling grief with the same efficiency that he managed his bills and daily workout schedule at the health club. He accepted Ada's weekly offerings with a dry kiss on the cheek, and then proceeded to talk about the book he'd picked up at the library or an interesting clip he saw on the news. Ada knew he mourned his wife, but it was a private sorrow not to be shared.

"How's the pressure?" Anthony asked, interrupting her private humiliation. His hands were on her lower back, the waistband of her horrible granny panties certainly showing.

"Fine."

As an adult, Ada had talked to her mother every day, calling her in the car on the way home from work to check in. Ada was the youngest and the only girl in a family of four children. Her brothers were all athletes—hockey, football, basketball, soccer; every month brought a new set of athletic gear. Growing up, the house was littered with sports paraphernalia—cleats, helmets, sticks, and gloves. Sundays were for football, her brothers and father gathered around the television in the den while Ada and her mother stayed in the sanctuary of the living room. Ada would do homework while her mother read her own book. Every now and then the den would explode with cheers or boos as a point was made or lost, and Ada and her mother would glance at each other in annoyed affection.

Sunday dinner was a mandatory event, regardless of girlfriends, sports, or friends, and in the late afternoon, she and her mother would head to the kitchen. Over chopped garlic and frying onions, Ada told her mother about school or the boy she had a crush on. Her mother listened as she stirred the tomato sauce. Theirs was a household full of classic gender stereotypes, yet Ada hadn't minded at all.

Her brothers were scattered around New England now, busy with families and careers of their own. Only Ada had remained in the same town they'd grown up in, still seeing her parents weekly if not daily. Even in the months before her death, their mother still hosted the weekly Sunday dinner. Usually it was just Tyler and Ada and her parents, but on the last Sunday of every month, her brothers would come, their spouses and children filling the house. Since her mother's death, Ada didn't have the heart or the energy to replicate the Sunday meals. They'd attempted a few dinners with pizza and store-bought cookies, but it had been a dismal, paltry meal compared to their mother's banquet. Despite the noise of the children and the football game, there was a hollow emptiness in the house without their mother. After a few attempts the monthly family meals had ceased, forty years of Sunday dinners ended, just like that. The loss of her mother was a hole in Ada's heart, the wind whistling through each time she stepped outside.

"Flip over for me, please. I'll hold the sheet while you do," Anthony instructed. "You haven't fallen asleep? It happens sometimes."

"No, I'm fine."

Ada pushed herself from the table while Anthony held the sheet suspended over her body. As she shifted, she felt the telltale tingle in her breasts that indicated impending milk. She willed her body to hold in the milk, knowing it was powerless to obey.

She opened her eyes, shifting gently on her back, trying to avoid any unnecessary movement. The lights were dimmed, though not enough. With her eyes open, it felt as bright as a doctor's office. She shut them again quickly. They twitched with the effort of squeezing them closed.

Anthony's hands rested on her shoulders, making their way down her bicep, kneading her forearm. The first drops of milk dripped from Ada's breasts and were quickly absorbed by the sheet. Ada swallowed, trying to breathe deeply, as if she could meditate through her body's desire to lactate. She pictured Sam's hungry mouth, his pudgy hands reaching for her, lips parted in impatient greed. Another drop fell.

Anthony's hands froze on her shoulder. "Uh…"

The milk spilled forth, soaking through the thin sheet, sliding down the rolls of her stomach and onto the sheet that covered the plastic table. Ada kept her eyes closed, unable to face the look of terror that was surely on his face. She should have left her bra on. She'd even thought about it, then told herself she was being too self-conscious, imagining the hum of maternal solidarity between her and the massage therapist if her milk were to come in. But the decision to leave her bra in the locker outside (a graying industrial-strength nursing bra, not a scrap of lace in sight) was predicated on having a female. If she'd known about Anthony, she would have stuffed the nasty bra full of extra nursing pads. No, if she'd known about Anthony, she would have cancelled the appointment in the first place.

"Is everything okay?" Anthony asked, his chummy confidence cracking just a hair.

"I'm nursing," Ada whispered.

"What?"

"I'm nursing. I'm leaking." Like she was a broken faucet, a pipe in need of repair, someone to flush out all the gunk that was getting clogged, and then take a pair of pliers and tighten her back up again. Even with her eyes closed, she heard him swallow, a lump of revulsion and horror, no doubt.

Anthony removed his hands, and Ada tried to open her eyes but couldn't bear to re-enter the room with him. Her cheeks burned in shame at the way her own body had come to betray her, yet again. The table was wet beneath her. A tear made its way out of the corner of her eye, sliding down her face and landing against her earlobe, making the whole spectacle worse. It was followed by another and then another.

"Are you okay? Can I get you something?" Anthony asked.

Ada shook her head, finally opening her eyes. Anthony looked back at her with concern, his strong arms clasped across his chest.

She sat up, clutching the sheet against her. The milk continued to drip, despite the absence of Sam's mouth. There must have been a quarter-cup soaking through the sheet and pooling on the table.

"I can bring you some towels, if you'd like," Anthony offered.

"It's okay," Ada mumbled. "We can just be done."

Anthony frowned at her in concern, though Ada was certain she detected relief behind the mask of his drawn eyebrows. "Are you sure? We still have another thirty-five minutes."

Damn Elise and her eighty-minute massage. Eighty minutes that should have been pure heaven, and had turned into a humiliating reminder of how her body's sole function was in service to Sam.

"It's fine. I should be getting back to my baby," Ada said, hating Sam for just a moment despite the love that made her miss him even now.

Ada was certain her own mother would never have had such a thought about any of her children. Her mother had been like Elise, competent and in control even when surrounded by the chaos of family life. If her mother were still here, Ada would drop Sam off at her house and then head to the gym to run on the treadmill. She'd return to find Sam napping soundly, her mother in the other room making her a spinach quiche to take home for dinner. If her mother were alive, Ada would be having sex with Tyler again, ordering new underwear on Amazon to accommodate her little bit of extra baby weight, though even that would be melting away each day. If her mother were alive, Ada's love for Sam would be simple and clean, not muddied up with inadequacy, grief, and shame.

But Ada's mother wasn't here.

"Well, if you're sure." Anthony handed Ada a crisp white towel that smelled of bleach. "If you'd like to reschedule for another time, just check in with the receptionist. Take your time in here. There's no rush," he said, before closing the door softly behind him.

Ada lay back down on the table. She peeled off the sheet and looked at her enormous breasts, the veins bulging blue, nipples violet and engorged, large as tea saucers. She held the tiny towel against her body to soak up the endless stream of milk. Then she curled up on her side and closed her eyes.

ELISE

When Elise's massage was finished, she lay on the table for a few extra minutes and listened to the music. There was a whole collection of CDs against the wall, and Elise found it amazing that there were actual musical artists who devoted their careers to creating spa music. It all sounded the same to her—unidentifiable instruments, either real or electronic, like the ocean and sun on a spring day.

It wasn't until she was an adult that Elise had her first massage and she'd been blown away by the experience, how she felt like a new person afterward, her mind clear and uncluttered, all of the tight places in her body filled with a new looseness. When Brad got his last promotion at work, the one that should have meant Elise really didn't have to worry about money at all, ever, it had been one of her gifts to herself, a Friday afternoon appointment at the spa, followed by pizza for the kids and sushi for herself and Brad. And when her saving amped up, it was the first thing she cut, knowing just how much those weekly spa sessions cost.

She felt bad about the way their conversation had gone this morning, but she resented his implication that all areas of the children's lives were solely her domain. When she left her teaching job after Marianna was born, she knew there would be a price to pay, an uneasy balancing of the scales as they reconfigured which responsibilities lay with whom. She just hadn't figured out what that split would do to their marriage.

None of it had been spoken. They were not the type of couple to openly assign jobs, though Elise had some friends who treated their husbands like an additional child, adding their name to the color-coded chore wheel on the fridge. She and Brad didn't divvy up jobs in this organized of a way, but they each had their unspoken roles, and Elise's jobs revolved around all domestic tasks.

Her mother would roll her eyes and point out that she had to do all those same domestic tasks *after* she got home from an overnight shift at the hospital. She'd never gotten comfortable with Elise's decision to stay home with the children. What Elise's mother didn't understand was how the whole day could be swallowed up by nothing and everything—packing lunches and carpooling, helping with homework and prepping dinner and grocery shopping and laundry. Elise tumbled into bed each night, slightly less tired than when she wrangled a group of six-year-olds, but wiped out nonetheless.

Then there was Josie, the woman who came each Thursday to clean the house top to bottom. This was a sin as far as Elise's mother was concerned, allowing a stranger into the house to do the intimate chores that belonged to her family—wiping pee off the rim of the toilet bowl, cleaning toothpaste spit from the sink, scrubbing the film of scum from the walls of the shower. Josie had been working for Elise's family for years, and while they weren't exactly friends, it no longer felt like inviting a stranger into the house. Elise had met Josie's daughter, had bought her a present when she graduated from high school (a tasteful locket necklace).

She gave Josie two weeks of paid vacation every year. Elise knew not everyone could afford such a luxury, but most of the women in Elise's neighborhood had someone who cleaned the house, and even though her mother tried to make her feel guilty, Elise refused to feel bad about it. One of the biggest blessings of having money was being able to hire someone to do the things you detested, like scrubbing the tub or ironing. Elise had spent enough of her life not having money to understand that there was no glory in being poor, no prize for sharing a bedroom with two siblings or having canned soup for the third night in a row. At the end of one's life, there was no gold star for living so close to the edge.

Elise liked being around for the children, to be able to drop them off at all one hundred sporting events and after-school activities. She liked helping Piper with her math homework, and editing Tommy's papers, and making Marianna's lunch every day, tucking in a paper heart and a cookie on Fridays. She *liked* being a stay at home mom.

What she *didn't* like was how Brad thought this gave him a pass for ninety-five percent of the responsibilities around the children. Homework, paperwork, driving, doctor's visits, grocery shopping, cooking, parent-teacher conferences, back-to-school night, PTO, birthday parties, shopping for gifts, and the many other day-to-day tasks fell in her lap, with no six-figure salary to accompany the sixteen-hour days she put in.

Elise took a deep breath and tried to still her thoughts. The massage therapist always told you to take your time coming out, and Elise usually did. There was no need to rush back to all of the things that needed attending. The room smelled like lavender and eucalyptus, and her skin was smooth from the various oils rubbed into her body. She thought about calling Brad back, but didn't feel like spoiling the nice buzz she had going from the massage. She wondered if he would have been as upset by what Tommy did if Elise had been around to deal with it, or if he was just unaccustomed to handling anything relating to school that wasn't a sporting event (though Elise even attended more of these than Brad).

Still, the thing with Tommy was troubling. He'd always been a nervous and anxious child, but as he'd entered adolescence, a new meanness had emerged in him that worried her. He was smart and funny, but his jokes sometimes crossed the line from humorous into hurtful. He had the ability to cut to the core of a person with a few sharp words, finding the soft spot and jabbing at it fast and sharp. Elise suspected he'd learned some of this from the TV shows or videos he watched online—Tommy consumed media on the privacy of his iPad, and even though she had access to all of his passwords, she had a hard time monitoring it all. Things would have been so much simpler if all three of her children had to agree on a show and gather around the living room television, as Elise and her own siblings and every other person of her generation had once done, something that was inconceivable now.

This year was different. Tommy was hanging out with different boys, not the same little gang whose mothers she'd known forever. Even though they were both in eighth grade, Zach and Leon seemed older. They took more care with their appearance than the other kids, and after school they changed out of their uniforms and into name-brand jeans and expensive sneakers. They gelled their hair and didn't suffer from the same maladies as their peers—acne, an awkward body that hadn't yet adapted to puberty, braces, poorly fitting clothes. Zach and Leon looked like miniature versions of the men they'd become; men, Elise suspected, that she wouldn't like very much.

Tommy had latched on to them this year, the awkward third wheel in their trio. It was obvious to Elise that Tommy didn't fit in with them—he was too uncomfortable in his own skin. It was painful to watch him try so hard, laughing at their jokes, adopting their expressions, even while Zach and Leon had a tendency to make jokes at his expense. Tommy laughed along, as if he didn't mind them giving him a hard time, while Elise had to restrain herself from going into full-blown teacher mode and cutting the little brats down to size. She knew Tommy would be mortified if she tried to reprimand them for their behavior, and the last thing she needed was another reason for Tommy not to talk to her.

Zach and Leon had been over to the house several times, and while they were always polite to Elise, she'd overheard them talking about classmates in a casually cruel way that made her sick to her stomach. Tommy was never the one instigating the conversation, but she'd heard his nervous chuckle in response. Just last week the boys were in the basement playing video games, and Elise had been halfway down the stairs to offer snacks when she heard them joking about Lanie Gardner, a girl Elise had known since preschool. Zach called her a fat douchebag, then went on to laugh at her tuna pussy. The easy way he'd said it—*tuna pussy*—had hit Elise hard, as if they'd been talking about her. She stood frozen on the stairs with a plate of bagel pizzas, her face burning in shame for poor Lanie. She knew she should go down there, yell at all three of them, send those little assholes home, but she'd been paralyzed, unwilling to see Tommy's face, too afraid of the smug expression she might find. She'd tiptoed up the stairs and thrown the bagels in the trash, wishing she could talk to Brad about what she'd overheard.

She suspected that Zach and Leon were behind the LetterBot prank, too wily to get caught, too cowardly to fess up to their role. It was also possible that she was being naive, and that Tommy had taken a darker turn than she'd realized. Maybe it *was* his doing.

Elise's mother would blame his cushy upbringing and elite private school, but Elise had known a fair share of public school kids who were selfish scumbags at thirteen. Some of them grew out of it. Others did not. It wasn't only money that determined the course of one's life.

Elise lowered herself from the table and slipped into the ter-rycloth robe hanging on the closet door. You could only linger for so long, even if they did tell you to take your time. She hoped Ada, Ivy, and Libby had enjoyed their massages. Ada's eyes had lit up when Elise told her it was her treat, and God knew Ada needed a treat. Elise had scheduled lunch at her favorite restaurant, a seafood place that served the best lobster rolls around and had the most gorgeous cocktails.

The weekend was off to a rocky start, but it wasn't too late to salvage it. Elise had hoped the three days would be a respite from the rest of their lives, but all of the drama of home was creeping in—the trouble with Tommy, Sam's sudden appearance, those calls that Ivy kept ignoring, not to mention Libby's phone calls to her mother that left her face tightly drawn in worry. It had seemed so simple, three days to step out of their lives and be together, but it turned out that escaping your life was far harder than Elise had realized.

IVY

Text message: SF Elite Companions to Ivy
Just wanted to confirm our appointment this Wednesday
morning. We have several events next weekend if you're
interested.

Ivy spread the linen napkin across her lap and took a sip of ice water while she scanned the menu. It was the type of restaurant she hated—too upscale for its own good, all about ambience and the view (which was admittedly gorgeous, a wall of windows overlooking the sea) with little effort put into the food. It was a place for tourists, where you'd spend twenty dollars on a dry fish sandwich because you could sit on the deck and hear the waves.

Instead of relaxing her, the massage had left Ivy irritable and nostalgic in the worst way, remembering the day when she'd dismantled her own life. Libby was subdued, Ada was quiet and red-eyed, and Elise was fidgety and still chattering away about the goddamn lobster rolls. When the waiter came to take their order, looking bored in his rumpled polo shirt, Libby, Elise, and Ada all ordered it. Ivy ordered a chicken Caesar salad instead, partly because Elise was being so annoying about it, as if she'd hauled the lobster pot herself and then watched it succumb to death in boiling water.

"Did everyone have a nice massage?" Elise asked. Ivy nodded.

"It was great. Thank you again, Elise," Libby said.

"Was yours okay?" Elise asked Ada.

"It was fine." Ada had been surprisingly quiet on the drive from the spa to the restaurant, no more complaining about Sam or how tired she was. She'd slumped against the window in the back seat and stared at the passing trees.

"Just fine?" Elise asked. She looked hurt, as if she'd given Ada the massage herself and gotten a bad review on Yelp.

"You didn't tell me it would be with a man," Ada said. Elise's eyebrows shot up.

"I didn't know you'd mind! I'm so sorry. I didn't even think to request a woman," she said.

"It was just awkward. And then…" Ada's face colored, her cheeks suddenly blotchy. She shook her head.

"Then what?" Ivy asked. It was a free massage, for goodness' sake. How bad could it have been? The waiter reappeared holding a tray of drinks. He placed Ivy's vodka tonic in front of her in a surprisingly generous-sized glass. Maybe the restaurant wasn't so bad after all.

"Nothing. I just started… leaking," Ada mumbled.

"Leaking?" Libby asked, leaning closer to Ada.

"Yeah, leaking. My milk came in. I was dripping all over the stupid table," Ada said. "It was mortifying. I told him not to finish." She rested her face in her hand.

"Oh, please, that's nothing," Ivy said. "I once had a guy who farted for an entire sixty-minute massage. The place smelled like a septic tank by the end of the hour."

"Ew," Libby said to Ivy. She turned to Ada. "Weren't you wearing breast pads?"

"No! I don't know why, but I wasn't," Ada said with exasperation. The elderly couple at the next table glanced over at their group, and Ivy was tempted to tell them to mind their own business.

"I'm sorry, Ada. I would have requested a woman if I'd thought about it," Elise said.

"It's fine," Ada said, waving her hand as if to brush away the entire incident.

Elise held up her glass. "To twenty years of friendship. To reconnecting and relaxing." Ivy wondered if Elise was being sarcastic, but she held her glass up anyway, clicking it against the others.

Elise took another sip of wine and leaned forward in her seat, elbows on the table. She wore a gold bracelet with nautical-themed charms—scallop shells and starfish and one in the shape of Cape Cod. It was the type of jewelry Ivy hated. "I know I keep saying this, but I'm just so happy that we're all here. No matter how much we change, we can still get together and it's like we're twenty years old again."

Ivy didn't feel twenty; she didn't even feel thirty. She felt old, older than her forty-two years, a whole lifetime behind her.

"I wish we could do this more often. Not just every few years, but once a year at least. We need to make this an annual thing," Elise said.

"If only you weren't so far away. I hate that we see you so rarely. I wish you lived nearby," Libby said to Ivy.

"That ship sailed long ago," Ivy said quietly.

They shifted uncomfortably in their plush chairs. Rarely did they discuss her expulsion their last semester at Harper. When they got together, it was as if Ivy had been with them from start to finish. Sometimes Ivy wondered if they'd actually forgotten she'd been kicked out, so intent were they on the years that came before.

"So, Ivy, what's new with you?" Elise asked.

"Me?" Ivy feigned surprise.

"Yes, you. You've hardly told us anything going on with you since we got here." Libby smiled encouragingly and waited.

"Well." Ivy took a sip of her drink, trying to find the words. Everything seemed off limits, even while she wished she could tell it all.

"Tell us about your jewelry business," Libby prompted. Like the rest of them, her hair had a glossy sheen to it from the massage oil. Libby tucked a lock of hair behind her ear.

"It's fine. You know, these things take time, but it's coming along," Ivy said.

"Are you doing it all online or do you have a retail space?" Elise asked.

"She has a little shop!" Libby chimed in, and Ivy's heart sank.

"You do? That's incredible. What's it called?" Elise asked.

Ivy's mind went blank. She glanced around the room, at the white tablecloths and silverware, the ocean view, the cocktails. Finally, she glanced at her phone which was face down on the table, snug in its pink OtterBox case.

"The Otter," she said.

"Oh, that's so cute," Libby said.

"You have to send me the link to your website again," Elise said. "I bet a bunch of the moms at the kids' schools would be interested. We should have had a trunk show while you were here! We could have done it at my house. Too bad." Elise looked genuinely disappointed, but Ivy didn't think Elise's friends would be interested in the type of jewelry she made, with its chunky mosaic cuts and heavy hammered silver, leather cords and glass beads. She imagined Elise's friends were a pearl and diamond crowd, if her bracelet was any indication. Still, it was nice of her to offer.

"Maybe next time," Ivy said.

"So you're really doing it? You've given up the massage and you're doing the jewelry full-time?" Elise asked.

"Kind of," Ivy said.

"That's so great, Ivy. It's really amazing," Libby said.

"It *is* amazing," Ada said, perking up a little. She'd hardly touched her iced tea. "How is that even possible? Isn't San Francisco the most expensive city in the country? I mean, no offense to your jewelry, but unless you're selling diamond necklaces, I don't see how you're making enough to support yourself."

"My apartment's rent-controlled," Ivy snapped. Elise jumped in before Ada could snap back.

"Sebastian must be so proud of you," Elise said.

This was her chance to finally tell them the truth. It was now or never.

"Actually, Sebastian and I split up."

Ada and Libby let out shocked gasps.

"Oh, Ivy. When?" Libby asked.

"Um," Ivy stalled, mixing her drink with the cocktail straw. "Like... seven months ago, I guess?"

"Seven months?" Libby's face was slack with shock. "Seven months?" she repeated.

"Maybe not quite that," Ivy said, though it had indeed been seven months.

"Did you know?" Libby asked, looking around the table. Ada and Elise quickly shook their heads. She turned back to Ivy. "How could you not tell me?"

Ivy had wondered the same thing. She hadn't intentionally kept it a secret, but she and Libby didn't talk often anymore. They texted frequently and sent emails now and then, but their phone calls were far less frequent, and they were usually preceded by weeks of phone tag before they were able to catch each other for twenty minutes uninterrupted. Nonetheless, she'd spoken to Libby at least several times since the split. The first time was only a month after she and Sebastian separated, and it was still too raw. The next time they talked, Libby was going on about Caitlin's surly adolescence. Ivy hadn't wanted to interrupt to say, "Oh, and by the way, my husband got a girl pregnant, and I think I'm getting a divorce." The most recent times had seemed almost too late to bring it up, and Ivy had filled the conversation with silly prattle about her new jewelry business.

"I don't know. It was just never the right moment," Ivy said. Libby averted her eyes and took a sip of wine.

"What happened?" Ada asked in disbelief.

"Oh, you know, the usual. He cheated on me with his twenty-two-year-old student. They're having a baby." Ivy shrugged and tried to be nonchalant, but the gesture rang false.

"Oh, Ivy," Libby said softly. There, *that* right there, was the reason that Ivy hadn't told Libby, though she hadn't realized it until right this minute. She hadn't told her because she couldn't bear for Libby to feel sorry for her. Ivy hated anyone's pity, but none more than Libby's.

"What happened?" Ada asked again, and Ivy suspected she was just relieved it wasn't her. *At least we were still having sex up until we separated,* Ivy wanted to say, but even that wasn't so simple. In those last months, there had been a renewed vigor to their sex life, like Sebastian had started taking Viagra. Foolishly Ivy had let herself imagine that this was the second stage of their marriage, the children getting older and needing them less. It was only later that she realized their sex life had been reinvigorated because he was sleeping with Fauna too.

"It's fine. Really." She tipped her face forward into her drink, inhaling the sharp tang of vodka and lime.

"Tell us," Libby said, and Elise nodded. Even Ada looked regretful. Ivy slumped in her chair, the bravado suddenly gone, replaced with the desire to confide.

Ivy swallowed and then forced the words out, even though the truth sounded like a plot line on a trashy soap opera. "I found the ultrasound pictures." She was certain the ping-ponging gasp was audible several tables over.

"No," Ada whispered.

The sad thing was Ivy hadn't even suspected Sebastian of cheating. She'd found the pictures in the pocket of his jacket when looking for the spare set of car keys one morning. Ivy's fingers had plunged to the bottom of Sebastian's navy pea coat, fingers grappling in the silk lining and closing over a glossy slip of paper. Pulling it out, she stared at the blurry black and white photos, similar to the ones she'd received at doctor's visits practically two decades ago. They were clearly photos from early on in a pregnancy, no curled-up feet or raised arms, no peanut-shaped body or alien orb head, just a foggy gray speck in the center of the black page. The photo was time-stamped, just a few days earlier. *Fauna Frye, eight weeks' gestation*, was typed in the corner.

Ivy had collapsed against the closet, the shiny evidence crumpled in her palm. When she finally confronted Sebastian about it, she still half expected him to give her an excuse or have a plausible explanation as to why he was carrying around pictures of a developing fetus. Instead he told her that he was in love with Fauna, and she was pregnant. He'd been trying to find a way to break the news to Ivy for months.

"Yup. He got her pregnant. *Fauna*." Ivy spat the name out. "She's only six years older than Trina. What kind of man does that? Sleeps with a girl practically the same age as his daughter?"

No one answered, though the elderly couple was openly glaring at them now.

"Ivy, I'm sorry. That's just awful," Elise finally said.

"What an asshole! I never liked him," Ada added.

"Ada, you shouldn't say that. What if they get back together? Then you'll feel terrible," Elise chided.

"No chance of that," Ivy said.

"I'm sorry, but I never liked him," Ada said again. Ivy's friends had only met Sebastian a few times, including their wedding a lifetime ago. "I always thought he was pompous, so pleased with himself for being an *artist*." Ada drew the word out: ah-tist.

Ivy smirked. It was true. Sebastian had always been kind of a jerk about his "job," and though Ivy knew he was respected within the small California modern art world, she'd always found his paintings to be simplistic and messy, Jackson Pollock meets preschool finger-painting. But it was the way his art came before everything else that was so infuriating—dinner plans cancelled because of a student show, escaping from cleaning the house because he had an amazing idea that he just needed to get on canvas. Ivy's dreams, disjointed and unformed as they were, always came second.

She stabbed at the Caesar salad the waiter placed before her, taking a bite. The lettuce was crisp, the chicken charred just right, the dressing creamy and rich. The rest of them were sighing with pleasure as they bit into their sandwiches. Fluffy pink lobster salad overflowed from the rolls. Apparently, Elise had been right about the restaurant after all. Ivy felt a stab of guilt for doubting her.

"How are the kids handling it?" Libby asked, wiping a splotch of mayo from her lip.

Ivy felt a pang as she thought about her kids. "Confused. Pissed off. They're at that age, you know? Sixteen and eighteen. Who knows if they'd be talking to me anyway? The divorce just gives them something tangible to be angry about."

"So you're actually getting a divorce? This isn't just a separation?" Libby asked.

"The papers came last week. I haven't signed them yet, but it's over." Ivy put her fork down on the edge of the plate, her appetite suspended as she thought about the fat packet of papers that had arrived in a manila envelope. So many places for her to sign, so much tiny print, all just to say that their marriage was over. Nineteen and a half years, and it was gone in a puff of smoke and a flurry of paperwork.

"I'm so sorry, Ivy," Ada said, and Ivy was touched by the sincerity in her voice. She and Ada snipped and snapped at each other, but at the bottom of it all, they really did care about each other.

"Thanks. I'm okay though. I'll be fine. Just need to get on with my life. Maybe I should get out there again like you, Lib," Ivy said, eager to move on to other topics. She waggled her eyebrows at Libby who gave her a half-hearted smile.

"Is Sebastian paying child support? How on earth are you managing on just a jewelry business?" Ada asked. She had nearly polished off her entire lobster roll and was quickly making her way through a pile of French fries. Just watching her made Ivy glad she'd ordered a salad.

"It's tight, but we're managing. I've picked up some extra work to help make ends meet," Ivy said. What the hell did Ada know about San Francisco rent? She lived in a condo in western Massachusetts.

"Massage work?" Libby asked.

"No. Something else." She hadn't intended to tell them about the escort job. She wasn't ashamed of it exactly, but she knew they wouldn't approve. A part-time job for these women would have been picking up a few hours of tutoring on the weekend, not getting paid to spend a night with a stranger. Not that Ivy was planning on doing that. She just knew the option was there.

"What is it?" Elise asked.

"My friend works for this company. I can make good money and pick my own hours." Ivy stabbed a spear of lettuce and didn't meet anyone's eyes.

"Doing what?" Ada asked. They all waited.

Ivy imagined she could spin the job, make it seem glamorous or just a laugh. Or give them a thrill, shock them. That's what she'd done in college. If they had been cast in a movie back then, Ivy's description would have been "the wild one." Sometimes she'd played up to the part, doing things that shocked herself, just for the thrill of seeing their reaction.

"It's pretty hysterical actually. I'll basically get paid to attend fancy dinners. With men who are unattached." Already she could tell that her attempt at spinning it would be unsuccessful. There was a silence while they digested Ivy's words, tried to make sense of them.

"Like an escort?" Ada finally said. Her eyes were wide. She'd cleared her plate of all the fries, Ivy noticed.

"No, that's not what she means," Libby said with a laugh. "Right?"

Ivy blinked quickly, finishing the last of her drink and signaling to the waiter for another. A prickly flush crept up her neck and into her cheeks. "It's not a big deal. It's mostly just going to charity events with wealthy men. Last week I went to a charity dinner, and made a crazy amount of money to flirt and make small talk. It's basically getting paid to eat free dinners and drink champagne."

"Ivy, that's like prostitution," Ada whispered. She looked horrified, her dark brows knitted together.

"*No*, it's not like prostitution at all. I wouldn't actually *sleep* with the guys," Ivy said in frustration. She wished they could see what a good opportunity this was for her.

"But you could, right? I've heard about those places. If you're willing to do more, you can. It's basically legal prostitution," Ada continued.

"Where did you hear that?" Libby asked.

"I saw a *20/20* on it," Ada said.

"Oh, well then I guess you must be an expert," Ivy said, fury bubbling to the surface.

Ada rolled her eyes. "They did a whole exposé on it. Most of the girls eventually ended up doing more than going to dinner. I'm just saying." She shrugged.

She wished that Ada was totally off base, but Ivy knew she wasn't. Samantha had made it clear that she didn't have to sleep with the guys, but said that if Ivy wanted to make some extra money, that was often on the table. Ivy had pondered this. How far was she willing to go? She imagined the hands of a stranger on her body, some old fat guy with bad breath and a comb-over. Then she pictured the stack of unopened credit card bills on her dresser at home, the phone calls from the collections agencies. She wasn't certain which was worse.

"Ivy, this is a big deal. Are you really going to take this job?" Libby's eyes were shiny with concern. They weren't going to let it go. As she'd known.

Now they wanted to be there for her. How many times had any of them visited her in San Francisco over the past twenty years? One trip soon after graduation, and then a few visits from Libby, though even she hadn't been in years. Yet here Ivy was, four hundred dollars in the hole so she could spend the weekend babysitting, and now they expected her to act like they were really all best friends?

"Forget it. I don't want to talk about it," Ivy said, waving her hand in the air as if she could swat away their words.

Elise leaned forward and reached out a hand, placing it on Ivy's forearm. The tenderness of the gesture brought tears to her eyes, but she blinked them away.

"It's just us, Ivy. Ada didn't mean anything by it. Did you, Ada?"

Ada was wide-eyed, though she managed to shake her head.

"What part of 'I don't want to talk about it' do you not understand?" Ivy asked. Her voice cracked midway through the sentence in a way that she hated, her own speech betraying her. It was too much, the pain of Sebastian coupled with the stress of keeping afloat, now made worse by their judgment and obvious disgust. Ivy resisted the urge to throw her drink across the room or at the elderly couple whispering. She could get a ride straight to the airport, hop on an earlier flight home.

The waiter appeared with dessert menus, and Ivy could have kissed him. They all focused very hard on the choices, though Ivy barely read anything, the words blurring together on the page.

They always made her feel bad about herself, she realized. As much as she loved them (and she *did* love them, even Ada), there was something about their friendship that made Ivy feel small, the same guilty feeling she'd had when she was kicked out of Harper. The judgment was always there, the peering eyes scrutinizing her every action, their pursed lips and sideways glances. *There goes Ivy again.* Her friends in San Francisco didn't make her feel this way. Even if she'd told them about the escort job, all they would have done was marvel at the amount of money she was making and tell her to be careful. The trouble was, her Harper friends always knew the tender spot of her heart, the things she did that she regretted, the actions she wished she could erase. Maybe they were her conscience, humming in her ear with their disapproval, the little voice that knew when she was doing something wrong. Either way, after any time with them, Ivy was left feeling like she was the dirty one. Yet she also knew their judgment was born out of love, and this was what kept her coming back to them.

"Just forget it. Forget I said anything," Ivy said, picking up her glass to wrench her arm from Elise's grasp. She took a long swallow of her drink, then stood abruptly, folding her fine linen napkin upon the table. "I'm going to the bathroom." She walked quickly, aware of their eyes on her back, certain that as soon as she rounded the corner to the restrooms, the conversation would buzz about her.

Screw them all.

LIBBY

Text message: Libby to Adam
*The weekend's been… interesting. I'll fill you in later. Btw I
miss you too.*

"Seriously, this is not normal. Should we be concerned?" Ada said
when Ivy was out of earshot. Libby bit her lip. Elise looked down
at her plate. Ada leaned closer. "You guys, come on. You don't
think there's something wrong with this?"

"Let's not," Libby said gently, and Elise shot her a grateful glance.

"Okay, fine, we won't talk about the fact that one of our oldest
friends is considering *prostituting* herself," Ada said.

"Ada," Libby snapped, unable to hide her irritation. "What is
your problem?"

"*My* problem? Seriously?" Ada's eyes were suddenly filled with
tears and Libby felt like a jerk, though she wasn't even sure for what.

By the time Ivy sat back down, an uneasy silence had settled
over the table. Ivy's eyes were bloodshot, and Libby wanted to
pull her aside to ask all the questions Ada was wondering, but in
a nicer, less obnoxious way.

The waiter appeared with two desserts and four spoons. Ada
attacked the slice of chocolate cake with surprising force while the
rest of them picked at the plates. Ivy had taken out her phone and
was tapping at the keyboard, avoiding eye contact with everyone.

"So." Elise smiled brightly, but it looked pasted on, plastic and immovable. Her eyes were wide but in a manic sort of way. Libby wanted to tell her to relax, not to worry so much about everything being perfect, but she knew there was no point. The weekend was well past the point of perfect. "We have the rest of the day. What should we do?"

"I'm sure you have some ideas," Ivy said, without looking up from her phone.

Elise blinked several times. Surely she heard the sarcasm in Ivy's voice, but she didn't acknowledge it. "Well, we could poke around town and do some shopping. We could take a walk on the beach. Or we could go home and just hang out."

No one answered. Only a few smears of frosting remained of the chocolate cake and Ada looked freshly miserable. All Libby really wanted to do was read her book in the massive bed and watch some bad TV, preferably alone. Yet somehow, she doubted that the four of them spreading out to different rooms in the house and closing the doors was on Elise's agenda.

"Heading back to the house might be nice. What do we want to do for dinner?" Libby finally said when it became clear no one else was going to answer.

Elise perked up at Libby's interest. "I thought we could stay in and cook. Each of us contribute something? I can pop out to the grocery store to pick up whatever we each need. I can make frutti di mare. Someone can do a salad, a side and a dessert. How does that sound to everyone?"

There were unenthusiastic murmurs of agreement.

"Great." Elise gave a grin so wide and false that Libby wondered if it hurt her face. "Who wants to do a salad?"

"I will," Libby said.

Elise shot Libby a grateful look. "Okay, a side. Anyone? Ivy, how about you?"

"Fine." Ivy said, without looking up from her screen. Libby felt the same familiar irritation rising in her as she did when Caitlin zoned out in front of her phone. She wanted to swat it out of Ivy's hand.

"Ada, you must know some good dessert recipes," Elise said.

"What's that supposed to mean?" Ada asked, narrowing her eyes and dropping the fork to her plate with a clatter.

"Nothing, nothing! Just that I remember all those brownies and pies you used to make. If you don't feel like cooking, I can just grab a pie or something," Elise said quickly.

"It's fine. I'll make something," Ada said.

"Okay! Why don't we go back to the house and make a list of what we'll need, and then I'll run to the grocery store. We've got loads of food there, so we'll probably only need a few things anyway. Does that sound like a plan? We can make an event of dinner," Elise said, giving another forced smile.

"That sounds great, Elise," Libby said, because someone had to. Ada and Ivy continued to sulk.

The waiter came and dropped the bill, and Elise snatched it up. "I've got this."

"No," Libby said, reaching for her wallet. "You already got the massages. We'll split it."

"No no, it's on me. Really," Elise said, clutching the leather billfold.

Libby opened her mouth to protest, but Elise had already plucked out her Amex and was waving toward their server.

"How was your meal?" he asked, pushing Elise's credit card into the device attached to a cell phone.

"Wonderful," Elise said.

"When is the sitter booked till?" Ada asked when he'd left.

"There's no rush. I told her we might not be back till five. It's not even three," Elise said, snapping her wallet shut.

"I should get back. Sam's probably hungry." Ada yawned.

"You left her with plenty of instructions and tons of food. Janie's great, she's been watching my kids forever."

"Yeah, but your kids are older. They're not babies," Ada said.

Libby watched Elise's jaw tighten, though her cheerful face didn't crack. "Well, they weren't always older. They were all once babies, just like Sam. Janie watched both Piper and Marianna."

Ada shook her head. "Sam's really particular. He'll be starting to fuss. He doesn't like to be away from me for very long."

"Isn't that the whole point?" Elise asked. She didn't snap exactly, although her voice had lost its usual calm. "We said we'd watch Sam so you could have a break. Remember? That's one of the reasons why we're all here. So we can get a few days away to relax?"

Ivy let out a noise, something between a cough and a laugh. Everyone turned to her. Libby hadn't realized she was even following the conversation.

"What?" Elise asked, swiveling her head to look at Ivy.

Ivy raised her eyebrows but didn't take her eyes off her screen. "Nothing. It's just, that's not why we're all here."

"Okay." Elise drew out the word. Libby could see her patience withering. "So tell me, Ivy. Why are we here?"

Ivy finally put her phone down on the table with a heavy thud. "For you, Elise. To pretend we're all still best friends."

"*Ivy*," Libby hissed.

Elise was no longer smiling, but her face had gone completely still except for her eyes, which were blinking too rapidly. She didn't answer Ivy, didn't even acknowledge that she'd spoken. She slipped her credit card back in her purse and then stood slowly, winding her scarf around her neck, shrugging into her coat.

"Right then. I'll meet you all in the car," Elise said, then hoisted her enormous leather bag over a shoulder and hurried to the entrance of the restaurant. Ivy glanced at Libby as if waiting to be scolded.

"Go ahead," she said.

"That was rude," Libby answered.

"What? You know it's true." Ivy looked to Ada for confirmation. "It is, right? This whole thing is ridiculous."

Ada shrugged. "I don't know. I was just looking forward to a few days away. It doesn't need to be this whole big thing."

Ivy spun on Libby and Ada. "Fine, I guess I'm just the bitch then, as usual. Isn't that convenient for both of you? If I'm the bitch, then you don't have to be." She snatched her phone from the table and stood abruptly, knocking over a water glass in the process. Libby watched as the water seeped through the thick tablecloth and dripped onto the hardwood floor. Ivy threw her purse over her shoulder and pushed her chair out of the way.

"And you all can just mind your own damn business," she said to the elderly couple as she stormed out. After a moment, Libby and Ada gathered their belongings without speaking and went out to the car, leaving the stunned couple gaping after them.

ELISE

Text message: Brad to Elise
Where are Piper's shin guards? She says her soccer jersey is in the wash. Can she just wear a t shirt?

Elise sat in the parked car and fumed. She was still reeling from Ivy's words. First, that she'd had the nerve to speak them aloud, but second, that it was clear Libby and Ada felt the same way, even if they weren't callous enough to say it.

Elise had friends. Her life was full of friends—other moms she knew from the PTO, the group of women she'd known since she was pregnant with Tommy who she still met up with once a month for drinks, her book club. It wasn't as if she was lonely or desperate. Elise had *plenty* of friends.

But.

If she were honest with herself, Elise knew that none of those relationships were like that of her Harper friends. Monthly cocktails couldn't compare to four inseparable years, where she learned everything about her roommates, down to what type of underwear they favored (Ada and Libby, cotton bikinis; Ivy, lace boy shorts). They had been like sisters to Elise, at a time when she was losing her actual sister.

Elise knew that her attachment to the three of them was connected to the year Jackie was sick, when everything was bound up in a tangled mess of love and loss. It was the same year when her friends from Harper scattered across the globe for their junior semester abroad. Libby went to London, Ada headed to Italy, and Ivy went to Ireland while Elise stayed at Harper, and pretended not to mind that they were gone.

Ivy and Elise were both on scholarship at Harper, but their packages were slightly different, and Elise's plan wouldn't cover all the extra expenses of a semester abroad. Her father was working, but her mother had to cut back on her own shifts at the hospital to care for Jackie.

And then there was Jackie. There was no question of leaving.

It was only a semester. This was what Elise told herself all fall, while her friends opened glossy course catalogs, signing up for art classes in Florence and Irish literature in Cork, "A Royal History" in England. It was only a semester. This was before the days of Skype and FaceTime, when email was in its early infancy and most communication was done over a landline or on paper as thin and sheer as an onionskin.

Elise kept her heartbreak to herself, not wanting any of them to feel bad for her, not wanting any of them to know how much she was anticipating her own loneliness. It wasn't as if she would be bored. Her mother needed her to help with Jackie, who had been in and out of the hospital for the past few months while the doctors pumped her full of medicine that left her exhausted and nauseated, her head smooth and hairless as an Easter egg. But with her closest friends gone, Elise would have no distraction from the fear that clutched her tight throughout the day. The fear that her little sister was going to die soon.

Her sister's symptoms had started her junior year in high school, at the beginning of Elise's junior year at Harper. Jackie was tired all the time. Her skin was gray and washed out, her pallor like a vampire from one of the horror movies she loved. She complained of vague aches and pains in her legs, that no one really paid attention to. In a family of four children where daily survival was stretched to the breaking point, it took more than pale skin and feeling tired for their mother to ring the alarm bell. There was health insurance, thank God, but a trip to the doctor required time off work, and Elise's father had just gotten a job doing electric work for a large apartment complex that no one wanted to jeopardize, knowing its expiration date was already stamped sometime in the near future. And Jackie had never liked school, always the first to complain about a sore throat or upset stomach in the hope of a day in bed.

But then there were the bruises. Dusty purple splotches speckling Jackie's forearms and legs, though she could never recall what had caused the injury. Elise remembered her mother's expression at Sunday dinner when Jackie rolled up the sleeves of her sweatshirt, revealing a connect-the-dots constellation on each arm. At first her mother had assumed that one of them had caused the marks—John, famous for his finger flicks, or Missy, who had a tendency to pinch when she didn't get her way. But Jackie just shrugged, mumbling that she didn't know where they came from, and both Missy and John wore expressions free of guilt.

"Tomorrow we'll go to the doctor," Elise's mother said, placing her fork on the plate and folding her napkin, her chicken barely touched. Elise doubted anyone else at the table noticed, but Elise could sense her mother's fear, a heavy aura that permeated the entire room.

The diagnosis was leukemia, and since the first round of appointments and blood work, life had been turned upside down for Elise's family. Elise hopped on the T to travel across the city every weekend, to offer her parents and siblings some respite and to sit with her sister. When she wasn't in the hospital, Jackie lay on the couch, the TV flickering in the dim living room, an unfinished paperback splayed across her chest. Childhood leukemia was often curable, they were assured, and so Elise tried not to panic when Jackie's thick black hair fell out in clumps, until she asked Elise to shave it for her. To their sister Missy's horror, Elise had shaved her own head too, running the buzzer over her scalp until the hair was just a smooth fuzz against her palm. When it was gone, she and Jackie grinned at each other in the bathroom mirror, their features newly visible without the camouflage of hair. After that, Jackie wore a faded Red Sox cap, a souvenir from one of the only times they'd all gone to a game at Fenway, but Elise only wore hats when she was outside. Otherwise she let her head be exposed, not caring about the looks she received from classmates and teachers who likely wondered if Elise was sick. Feeling the soft stubble on her skull made her feel closer to Jackie.

Of her three siblings, Elise had always been closest to Jackie, even though they couldn't have been less alike. While Elise was the responsible rule-following eldest, Jackie was foul-mouthed and sarcastic, the whole world a black comedy even before her diagnosis. On Saturdays, Elise sat next to Jackie under the crocheted purple afghan and listened while Jackie told cancer jokes. Cancer jokes! Elise didn't even know such a thing existed, but Jackie collected them like playing cards. When Elise arrived Saturday morning, Jackie would whip out a new one before Elise had even sunk into the lumpy sofa, and somehow, despite everything, Jackie would make Elise laugh.

At the end of the afternoon, Elise would kiss her sister's dry cheek, say goodbye to the rest of the family, and let herself out the duplex, walking the three blocks to the train station. The tears started the second the screen door slammed behind her and didn't stop till the train pulled up outside of Harper, the red-brick building glowing in the shadows of dusk like the promise of something better, a world beyond what she'd just left.

When she got back to their dorm, the tears would start all over again as Ada, Libby, and Ivy peppered her with questions about

Jackie, their hands and voices soothing Elise as she dabbed at her eyes with a soggy tissue. Without them, without the refuge of Harper, Elise didn't know how she would survive.

While her friends spent the winter break packing for the semester abroad, buying new suitcases and debating how many pairs of shoes to bring, Elise spent the vacation in the hospital. It was a grim holiday, her family cycling in and out of Jackie's neon-lit hospital room, bearing brightly colored packages and false cheer. Elise's mother insisted on having Christmas dinner in the room, despite Jackie's protestations that "no one could have a Merry Fucking Christmas in the cancer ward, for God's sake." It was a testament to how dire the situation was that their mother didn't slap her across the face for such talk, instead only pursing her lips, and saying she'd get a Tupperware for the roast beef and slice it at home.

When Elise arrived back at Harper in January, the campus felt changed. Without Ivy, Ada, and Libby, without their own private universe, it no longer possessed a hallowed otherworldly feel. It was one of the worst winters on record, the sidewalks slick with ice, the grounds workers scrambling to keep up with the never-ending snowbanks that were heaped around the campus in giant gray masses. Elise began to spend weekends and nights at home, grocery shopping and cleaning for her mother, helping out wherever she could. For the first time, school was a burden, her reading and papers piling up as she struggled to focus.

Elise's campus mailbox continued to fill with postcards. Ivy sent one with a picture of a pub in Cork, its wooden exterior painted a cheerful red, flower baskets hanging from the windows. *I'll have a pint of Guinness for you. Cheers!* Ivy wrote in her neat square print.

Ada sent one from Florence. Her card showed an aerial view of the city, a hundred red-roofed houses dotting the landscape. *Ciao, bella! I'm learning to paint and drinking too much Chianti. Miss you. Xo.* Libby's was from London, on a postcard of Trafalgar

Square filled with bustling tourists and hundreds of pigeons. Elise tucked each postcard into the mirror above her desk until there was no longer room to see her own reflection.

The treatment failed. Each time Elise came to the hospital to visit, Jackie looked frailer. That didn't stop her from cracking jokes with Elise, hurling insults across the room at John, taunting Missy who had taken to wearing halter shirts and baby blue eyeshadow, practically inviting the insults. Jackie was still herself, even if there was a little bit less of her every day.

When Elise tried to remember those last few days with her sister, all she could conjure up was the yellowish color of Jackie's skin and the way her eyes fluttered beneath her closed lids, as if she were unable to rest, even in sleep. Though people shuttled in and out of the room all day long, nurses and doctors, Elise's siblings and close family, the room was remarkably quiet. Not silent because every machine whooshed and beeped and ticked, but there was little talking, save for her mother's whispered prayers. She prayed with her head bent forward, dark hair draped over Jackie's slender arm. Their mother, a nurse, knew by then that her prayers were futile, but that didn't stop her from trying.

Spring finally came. Somehow nearly the whole semester had passed in a hazy blur, and her friends would be back in the country in just a few short weeks. Elise got the phone call from her mother the same week the crocuses outside her dorm room finally poked their stubborn purple heads through the dirt. She should have been prepared but she wasn't. There was no preparing for a phone call like that. Jackie had taken a turn for the worse and Elise needed to come now. She placed the phone in its cradle and prepared to go to the hospital.

The funeral was on a bright morning in mid-May. The sun held tall in the sky, and the air was thick with the rich odor of damp soil. It was the kind of day that felt like relief after a long hard winter, but to Elise it wasn't the beginning of anything. She sat in the back seat of her father's car, squished between John and Missy. For once, they were able to travel in just one vehicle.

They pulled up in front of the church that Elise and her family had attended every Sunday for all of Elise's childhood, and hoisted themselves out of the car in their dark and somber finest. Elise stood on the curb and smoothed the front of her wool dress, the heat already pricking at the back of her neck. When she looked up, her breath caught in her throat. There they were, Ada, Libby, and Ivy, and just a few feet behind them, Steven. Her friends had their arms linked and looked expectantly at Elise. Despite their dark dresses, they shone in the sun, a promise of hope at the other side of this loss. Only Libby looked just the same, square and sensible and herself. Elise rushed from her parents and threw herself into their arms, breathing in the flowery smell of Ada's familiar perfume, and the sweet scent of soap and shampoo. Their hands rubbed Elise's back; their fingers touched the soft fuzz of her head.

"You came," Elise murmured into the tight knot that they formed around her. "You're here."

ADA

No one spoke on the drive. Libby sat up front with Elise, and Ivy
sat in the last row, leaving Ada with the whole middle row to herself.

Ada wasn't quite sure what had transpired over lunch. Ivy's
outburst, her own cattiness, Elise's sudden and dramatic exit. Ada
had hardly even been paying attention to the conversation until the
end of the meal. She'd been focused instead on her embarrassment
over the massage with Anthony. Then the cake had come, and
before she realized it, she'd practically buried her face in it, even
though she wasn't even hungry after the enormous lobster roll.
She hadn't noticed the dynamic between the three of them until
Ivy stormed off to the bathroom; she hadn't meant to be rude. Her
comments about Ivy and the *20/20* special were so second nature
to the way they'd always interacted that Ada hadn't realized Ivy
would be hurt. Ada didn't think she *had* the ability to hurt Ivy.

It scared her to think of Ivy going down this road. Having
sex for money wasn't just gross, it was dangerous. STDs, sexual
violence, not to mention the idea that her children could find out
about it—Ada didn't think Ivy had really thought through what
it was she was getting herself into. Ivy's brazen confidence often

led her to act rashly and without thinking, only later realizing the consequences of her actions. But because it had been Ada who voiced what the rest of them were thinking, Ivy was angry.

It had always been like this between the two of them. They were a foursome, but in many ways, they were two twosomes, with Libby and Elise as the bridges that connected their friendship. Since the first week they met at freshman orientation, Ivy had rubbed Ada the wrong way—Ivy in her short baby doll dress, effortlessly cool in Doc Martens and bracelets that jangled up and down her arms, an air of indifference to everything. Ada had looked down at her own khaki shorts and pale pink tee shirt, her hair secured in a long tidy braid, and felt like she was about six years old.

Part of it was envy. Even back then Ada had recognized it, the tendency to dislike anything that made her question herself, not only her clothes and appearance, but also her own ability. She envied Ivy's confidence, her willingness to dive headfirst into an adventure without needing to weigh every possible outcome. Ivy was brash and bold while Ada was measured and cautious. She both chafed at the differences between them and doubted her own way in the world.

Ada glanced behind her at Ivy, sitting in the back row of Elise's massive minivan. She was hunched down in her puffy winter coat, eyes glued to the screen of her phone, blocking out everyone. She was still exactly the same, squeezed into her too-tight sweater and skinny jeans that she'd probably borrowed from her daughter. When they were together, all Ada's insecurity came rushing back, rising to the surface like curdled cream. She was at her weakest and most vulnerable right now, beaten down by exhaustion and grief, but this wasn't who she *really* was. Ada had almost forgotten who she was in her real life from not so long ago, a person confident and at ease in her own skin. She had outgrown the insecurity, traded it in with her twenty-something self, and the grown-up version was much better. Yet it turned out the needy vulnerable part of her had been there all along, and it returned with a rushing force, overshadowing the other person that Ada thought she'd become. This weekend only amplified it, as Ivy's bullish strength only brought out Ada's weakness.

Yet how much of this was Ivy's fault and how much was Ada's? All Ivy's intelligence and determination gone to waste, and now Ivy was on her way to divorce and getting paid to sleep around. (Ada didn't care how vehemently Ivy denied it. They all knew what Ivy was willing to do, how spongy her moral compass was.) It was so easy to dismiss Ivy as careless, self-destructive, oblivious, but Ada knew Ivy couldn't be boiled down to such simplistic terms. Ivy had also taken notes for Ada the week she got the flu, had spent Christmas breaks at school because she didn't want to go home. When Ada's mother died, Ivy hadn't been able to come for the funeral, but she knew what it was like to lose a parent. She'd sent a giant bouquet of orange lilies and a lovely card, and called Ada every week just to check in. While Ada might not have been responsible for every choice Ivy made, she knew she did have a hand in the way Ivy's life had gone.

The teacher's exams were held at middle and high schools all over Massachusetts. These days they administered the exams in testing centers, secure locations where you stowed all your belongings in a locker and sat down at a computer, but back then it was far more informal. You brought your ID and a number two pencil, and took your test in the same type of classroom where you'd taken the SATs or your high school finals.

Ivy's exam was being held at Natick High School, which happened to be the same school where Ada was doing her student teaching. Ada was working in a freshman English classroom, and the following week the teacher she assisted would be getting knee surgery. She'd be out for the next six weeks and had left all four sections of her classroom in Ada's control. Ada was at school that Saturday getting prepared for Monday, trying not to panic at the idea of twenty-six fourteen-year-olds marching into the classroom, expecting Ada to lead them in a discussion about Holden Caulfield. The students were fine with Mrs. Mucci, but Ada was not so far removed from high school that she didn't recall what happened when the sub took over.

When the test takers arrived to sit the exam, Ada was at Mrs. Mucci's desk, reading *The Catcher in the Rye*, trying to remember why she'd loved the book so much when she read it in high school, when it was clear that Holden was a self-centered, clinically depressed *asshole*. She'd left campus early that morning, before Ivy was up, so hadn't had a chance to wish her luck.

From Mrs. Mucci's desk, Ada watched the students pull into the parking lot. She sipped her lukewarm coffee and then headed into the dimly lit hallway in search of Ivy. Ada's sneakers squeaked against the rubber floors, echoing in the empty stairwell. The teacher's exams took place on the third floor, in a wing Ada rarely visited. There was a young woman at the desk, looking at IDs and checking off names.

"Name, please?" she asked when Ada paused at her desk. The woman regarded her with a bored expression.

"Oh, I'm not taking a test. I work here," Ada said. Even though it was technically true, Ada felt like an imposter. She continued, "I'm looking for a friend who's here. Ivy Thomson?"

"The test begins in ten minutes," the woman said. She pushed her oversized glasses up the bridge of her nose.

"I just wanted to wish her good luck. Can you tell me what room she's in?"

The woman hesitated then dropped her eyes to the list. "Two-o-four. But hurry up," she said, pointing a finger in the direction of the room.

Most of the students were seated but a few were sharpening pencils, and Ada scanned the room. Ivy wasn't there. The tension in the air was palpable. Most of the test takers were women Ada's age, other students nearing graduation. They sat hunched over small wooden desks, tapping their pencils, legs bobbing anxiously, fingers knotted in laps. Ada wasn't scheduled to take her test till the summer.

A thin man sat at a desk facing the room. "Name?" he asked when Ada came in.

"I'm looking for a friend. I want to wish her good luck. Ivy Thomson?"

The man glanced around the room and then gestured toward a row of desks.

"She's over there," he said.

"Where?" Ada asked, scanning the strangers in the room.

"Right there. Front row." He pointed at a chubby freckled girl who Ada recognized from Harper. She was hunched over the desk, oblivious to the conversation.

"Sorry, that's not her. Are you sure she's already checked in?"

The man looked up and seemed to notice Ada for the first time. He shuffled through a stack of papers on his desk. Ada saw photocopies of driver's licenses. He pulled one out and handed it to Ada. "Is this her?" There was the image of the freckled girl beside Ivy's information.

Ada's breath caught in her throat and she knew her face was on fire. "I'm sorry, never mind. Forget it," she said, dropping the paper back on his desk. The man called out after her, but Ada hurried down the hall and out the building, leaving behind the stranger with Ivy's name, terrified of what she had set in motion.

Ada thought back to that day twenty years earlier. It had been an innocent mistake on Ada's part, but one that had cost Ivy dearly. She thought about how Ivy hadn't told anyone about her separation from Sebastian. Then there was her evasiveness about her new jewelry business. For once, she saw Ivy not as the brash and overconfident person that made Ada feel small, but as someone who desperately wanted to be seen as successful whose life was unravelling around her. Getting kicked out of Harper had set off a quick chain of events in Ivy's life that led to where she was today—a middle-aged almost-divorcee struggling to stay afloat financially, considering accepting a job as a sex worker.

Ada had never told Ivy about what she'd done the day of the teacher's exam, too afraid of Ivy's reaction and the magnitude of what she would be admitting to. How did you apologize for a mistake that cost a person everything? How did you say sorry for accidentally ruining someone's life? It was this fear that had kept Ada quiet for so many years, but maybe now it was time to truly make amends. Maybe if Ivy realized getting kicked out of Harper hadn't been entirely her own fault, she might finally be able to move on. Maybe she'd be able to see this time in her life not as a failure but as a fresh start. Maybe she'd finally be able to stop blaming herself for this one mistake.

Ada glanced back at Ivy, who still hadn't looked up from her phone. A few silver strands threaded through her hair and her face was free of makeup, the lines in her forehead and around her mouth more visible than usual. With her head dipped forward and her shoulders hunched, she looked vulnerable; a softer, weaker version of who Ada always assumed Ivy was. She'd tell her, Ada decided. Sometime this weekend, she'd screw up her courage and finally reveal the whole story, and apologize to Ivy after all this time. She thought about getting the words out now, starting with *Do you remember when…?* Or *Look, Ivy, there's something I need to tell you.* Just thinking about it made Ada's palms sweat and heart race, but she'd find a way before the weekend was over. She took a deep breath, willing her fluttering heart to slow. She glanced out the window, focusing on the blue stripe of ocean that flickered past in an unbroken line.

ELISE

For once, Elise didn't feel like talking. When they arrived back at the house after a silent car drive, they all scattered to separate corners to lick their wounds. Libby went to take a shower, and Ivy found a couch to curl up on with her iPad. Ada nursed Sam, and Elise watched him fuss, noticing the slackness in Ada's face. Despite her frustration and anger, Elise insisted on taking Sam so Ada could lie down. Elise bundled him into his fleece and then brought him with her to the grocery store.

She took the long route, using the road that led past the beach. She needed some distance between herself and the others. Elise wasn't prone to anger or rage, but she felt something close to fury vibrating in her body. She clutched the steering wheel so tightly the skin pulled smooth over the knotty bulges of her knuckles.

Elise tried to count the things she was grateful for. It was a practice she had when she started to feel sorry for herself and to feel the petty strains of daily life encroaching. She had two beautiful homes, a happy healthy family, a community of people who cared about her. She had more money than her own parents could even imagine. When she looked at her oldest friends, Elise knew she was the lucky one—Ada with her postpartum misery, Ivy with her defunct marriage and half-baked career, skittering just this side of head-above-water. Libby with her dead husband. And all of them teetering financially, always just this side of afloat. Elise *knew* she was lucky.

But there were still moments when she resented her friends, times when the finely varnished veneer began to crack, and Elise inwardly seethed with everything the others assumed of her, none of which was ever returned. She had planned on paying for lunch, but how hard would it be for Ada or Ivy to at least pretend to offer? Elise might not have had a job like the rest of them, but did they really not notice how much time and effort, and yes, *money* had gone into the weekend? Shopping lists and reservations booked for the massage and lunch, trips for food and alcohol, the caretaker called to open up the house for the weekend, the cleaners hired to make up all the beds, the fresh flowers purchased for every room, the last-minute calls searching for a babysitter for Sam. Elise didn't mind. She enjoyed doing these things for her friends. But it would be nice if they didn't act like they were doing her a favor, humoring her by spending this weekend here at her behest, rather than because anyone actually wanted to.

It was so easy to look in from the outside and assume everything was perfect—the house, the money, the plushy golden comfort of financial security—but there were things in Elise's life that they didn't understand.

She didn't tell them about her ever-present worries for Marianna that lingered around the edges of everything else. No need to share the dark clutch of fear that found her in the middle of the night, or in the early mornings when everyone else in the house lay sleeping. Nor did she tell them about Brad and what she had done, not just the money she'd siphoned from her own husband, but the panicky terror that had led to it. She didn't tell them about her fear that Brad would divorce her, and then where would she be? Easier to smile and play happy host, to let their worries trump hers, and pretend that everything was just fine. But it wasn't, and

Elise was having a harder time acting like it was. A line had been crossed, and now Elise was genuinely pissed off.

Her phone rang, the screen of the car lighting up, indicating it was Brad. Sam let out a squawk from the back seat. Elise answered using the hands-free button on her steering wheel, cursing Brad for waking Sam. Already he was mewling in the back seat.

"You hung up on me. What the hell, Elise?" Brad sounded more wounded than angry.

"I'm sorry. I shouldn't have. It's been kind of a hard weekend," Elise said, surprised how glad she was to hear his voice.

There was a pause and Elise waited to see if he'd ask why. Three months ago, he would have. But three months ago, she wasn't worried he was going to leave her.

"Did you find Piper's shin guards?" Elise asked. They were in her soccer bag, as was her (clean) soccer jersey.

"No, but the coach had an extra pair she borrowed. I didn't realize we were supposed to bring snacks for the *whole team*," Brad said. "Since when do you need a snack break during a one-hour practice?"

Since kindergarten, Elise thought, but kept her mouth shut. She imagined Brad showing up with a single cheese stick for Piper while the rest of the team waited expectantly. Likely one of the other mothers had made a run to the grocery store for pretzels and oranges.

"I want you to talk to Tommy," Brad said. A surge of irritation rippled through her, though she wasn't sure if it was in response to Brad or Sam's high-pitched wails in the back seat. "Why?"

"I want you to figure out what the hell is going on. He claims he had nothing to do with hacking into the reading program," Brad said.

"And you believe him?" Sometimes Brad's inability to see the negatives in those he loved was astonishing. No wonder she'd been able to take the money for so long.

"I don't know. Why would he lie?"

Elise nearly burst out laughing. Why *wouldn't* he lie? Was she the only one who knew Tommy? Was Brad actually fooled by their son?

"Just put him on," she said.

There was a rustling on the line, and then, "What."

God, her kid could be an asshole sometimes. Unconditional love was a blessed thing.

"Hi, honey. Dad wanted me to talk to you," Elise said, putting on her calmest voice.

"Why." His questions weren't questions, just angry one-word statements.

"Because you've been accused of hacking into a computer program, and there's a good chance you might get expelled, or at least suspended. So before I go into a meeting with your teacher and the principal on Monday morning, I want to know what the hell you did," Elise said, her patience worn thin.

"I can't hear you. What's that noise?" Tommy asked. Sam's crying had gotten louder. In the rearview mirror his face was all bunched up and red.

"Ada's baby. I'm driving. Oh, for God's sake, hang on." Elise pulled over to the side of the road and stepped out of the car, closing the door on Sam's cries. The cold air was a welcome relief, the tinge of salt and the ripe smell of drying shellfish. The sun glittered off the ocean, and Elise took a deep breath before bringing the phone to her ear. "I'm here."

"Okay." Tommy's monotone was so flat and emotionless that Elise wanted to shake him until he returned to the fat-faced toddler he'd once been, the same boy who cried every morning of kindergarten drop-off, pressing his wet nose into her skirt.

"Tommy, what did you do?" Elise asked.

"Nothing." A hint of a whine crept into his voice. "Why don't you believe me?"

Because I'm your mother, and I know better. Because I pushed you out of my body with no drugs other than the sheer force of my love. Because I look in your eyes and I worry about who you are becoming.

"I just know," she answered.

Silence.

Elise planted her hand on the roof of the car. The metal was warm under her palm. She was still riding the adrenaline from lunch, and her frustration with her friends buoyed her forward. "If you don't tell me the truth, right this minute, and I find out that you were in some way responsible for this, then I will take away every device you own for the next year. Your phone, your laptop, your video games."

"*Mom.*"

"I'm not kidding, Tommy. I'll write a note to your teachers explaining you'll have to do all your homework by hand or stay after school to finish it. I will not let you see your friends on the weekend. I'm not bluffing, so don't bullshit me." Elise felt her own mother's no-nonsense approach to parenting coursing through her.

There was another long silence, only the gentle sound of the waves crashing on the shore, and Sam's muted cries through the closed window of the car.

"It wasn't my idea. Zach and Leon thought it would be funny," he finally said.

Elise sighed and leaned against the car. "Go on."

As Tommy began to tell the story, Elise turned to look at Sam. Every now and then he let out a whimper, but his cries were subsiding, and he was falling back to sleep. Maybe Ada just needed to let the child cry. Maybe she needed to stop rescuing him every time he felt any discomfort or fear or unease. Maybe she needed to let things be a little hard every now and then, because if she didn't, twelve years from now she might be regretting the big stinky mess she'd made.

IVY

Ivy Thomson's voicemail: This is Louann calling from BDK Financial. I'd like to talk to you about some overdue charges on your accounts. Please call me back at 1-800-929-DEBT.

Text message: Ivy to Marshall
I think we can work something out.

Ivy pulled the cream-colored cashmere throw over her legs and listened to the voicemail from the creditor, deleting the message before writing down the number. She turned the ringer off. The pit of worry that had been with her for months was back again, having receded briefly since arriving at Elise's. Yet the conversation at lunch had reminded Ivy of everything she'd left behind. The phone calls had started a week ago and she hadn't returned a single one.

There was a knock on the bedroom door.

"Come in."

Libby stuck her head in, looking pink and soft from sleep. She plopped on the bed beside Ivy.

"Are you okay?" Libby asked.

"Yeah," Ivy said, even though this was far from the truth. She wasn't okay, not today, not yesterday, not tomorrow.

"You were pretty harsh on Elise. Do you really feel that way? That we're not really friends anymore?" Libby examined her fingernail, averting her eyes from Ivy's, and Ivy felt a pang of guilt.

"I don't know. We're not close like we once were."

"No," Libby agreed. "But we were in college then. We lived together. Just because we don't share underwear anymore, doesn't mean we're not still close."

"Ew. We never shared underwear," Ivy said, wrinkling her nose in mock disgust.

"You know what I mean," Libby said with a smile.

"I do." Ivy tried to explain. "But we don't talk very often, we hardly ever see each other. Our lives are totally different. It's what made it so hard to tell you about Sebastian. I wanted to, but I didn't know how."

"I don't want to make this about me, but I wish you'd told me," Libby said.

Ivy sighed. "I know. I meant to. The longer I waited, the harder it got. The past few months have just really sucked. We don't talk often enough for me to drop a bombshell like that. You have to kind of warm up to that first. You know?"

"I do. I'm sorry about the two of you though," Libby said, her face gentle with concern.

"Thanks." Ivy picked up her phone. The screen lit up with a missed call number. "Were you worried about money when Steven died?" she asked.

Libby pulled the blanket over her lap. "Yeah, it was awful. We didn't have life insurance. How stupid is that? It was one of those things we kept meaning to do and never got around to. When he died, I was only working part-time, and I couldn't afford to pay our mortgage, much less all of the other bills. We hardly had anything in savings, and I blew through it in less than two months. It's why I sold the house and moved back to Vermont."

"I thought you moved back to be closer to your parents." Ivy had always been jealous of Libby's home life, the sturdy comfortable farmhouse in Vermont, her practical and reliable parents. To nineteen-year-old Ivy, it had seemed like an ideal and wholesome life.

"Well, that was part of it, but it was mostly because I couldn't afford not to. It really sucked." Libby shifted on the bed, so Ivy had no choice but to look her in the eye. "Are you really supporting yourself with your jewelry?"

"No. I lied about the shop. Well, not lied, but exaggerated. It's been hard." Ivy fingered the soft spun cashmere of the blanket.

"Tell me." Libby leaned closer, so close that Ivy smelled the soapy scent of her shampoo. She'd used the same brand for as long as Ivy could remember.

"Things have been tight since Sebastian left. I've gotten into some credit card debt." She looked down at her lap, surprised to see a tear fall. She wiped it away before Libby noticed. "I was just really dumb. I can't even blame Sebastian. It was my own fault."

It was always Ivy's fault, that was the reality of it. Every misstep she'd ever made in her life always came down to her poor judgment.

"How much?" Libby asked. Ivy was silent. She twisted her hands together in her lap upon the softness of the throw. When Ivy didn't answer, Libby reached for her hand. "How much?"

"About fifteen thousand," Ivy said, her voice so soft that Libby had to lean close to hear.

"Oh, Ivy," she whispered. "What happened?"

After several months of holding the stress tight in her body, Ivy let herself fall into the telling of it. She still wasn't sure how things had gotten this bad. Three credit cards, all maxed out, nearly twenty thousand dollars in the hole (a little more than the fifteen she'd admitted to Libby). Just the minimum monthly payments were more than Ivy could afford.

It had started with the grocery bill. A hundred dollars here, another hundred there, just to be able to put dinner on the table every night and to keep buying the expensive Greek yogurt and dried mangos that Trina liked, and the cubed cheese and spicy pepperoni that Jax wolfed down. The next month she'd used one of the cards to buy a few things she needed to get the jewelry business off the ground—insurance for the retail space at the mall, a new pair of pliers, and some really beautiful hand-blown glass beads she'd found at a boutique in Noe Valley. The next month she'd barely cleared a few hundred dollars in jewelry sales, so she put the electric bill and cable on the card as well.

"The creditors have started calling," Ivy said.

"Is that what all those calls have been?" Libby asked.

Ivy nodded miserably. "I'm going to have to declare bankruptcy if I can't make the payments."

"Is that why you're thinking about this job?" Libby asked.

"It seemed like the only way to get me out of debt."

"There's got to be another option," Libby said. Her eyes were wide and clear with concern. "What about Sebastian?"

Ivy shook her head. "I could never ask him, not now, but he doesn't have that kind of money anyway."

"Your mom?"

"No." Ivy's mother also wouldn't have the money, and all she would have done was berate Ivy for her foolishness, reminding her that she'd managed to struggle along as a single parent for all those years without ever declaring bankruptcy or becoming a prostitute.

They were quiet for a moment and then Libby straightened up. Ivy could almost see the gears turning in her mind.

"What about Elise?" Libby asked.

Since first stepping into Elise's home, Ivy had been bowled over by Elise's money. It had been in her face all weekend. She'd looked at items in Elise's house and wondered how much they cost, how all those beautiful things stacked up against Ivy's unpaid bills. But she'd never actually thought about asking for help.

"No way. I couldn't," Ivy said.

"Why not? You know Elise, I bet she'd be happy to help." Libby paused, likely recalling the disastrous lunch and Ivy's own nastiness. "Well, maybe not immediately, and you'd obviously have to apologize, but I'm sure Elise would be more than happy to lend you the money."

Libby was probably right, but Ivy's pride would never allow her to ask for help from Elise. She was more likely to declare bankruptcy.

"I don't think so," Ivy said.

"Just think about it," Libby said.

Ivy nodded, knowing she wouldn't.

"But even if you don't," Libby continued, "I don't think you should take this job. It's beneath you."

Ivy bristled, already on the defense. What did Libby know about what was beneath her? Then she softened. Maybe Libby was right. Libby had always seen something in Ivy that she herself couldn't see.

She could always call her old manager at the last spa she'd worked, and there were some private massage clients she could reach out to. She actually liked massage work: the flexible schedule, the physical element of the job, not to mention the gratitude a client felt after an hour beneath her hands. For so long it had been the thing she hadn't intended to do, neither teaching nor jewelry making, a job she'd fallen into after a failure, so she'd left the job easily, not thinking about what it was she was giving up. She wouldn't be able to pay back all of the debt this way, but she might be able to pay her bills more easily.

"I'll think about it. All of it," Ivy said.

Libby nodded, satisfied for the moment. "Should we go see what everyone else is doing?"

"And if Elise is still speaking to me?" Ivy added. *Poor Elise.* Ivy had been so nasty to her at lunch, after all she'd done to welcome them into her home.

"That too."

"I'll apologize," Ivy said.

"Good idea," Libby said, climbing out of bed. "I'm going to see if Elise needs a hand down there."

"I'll be down in a few minutes. And Lib? I didn't mean it," Ivy said. Libby cocked her head in question. "About us not being best friends anymore. I didn't mean it." Libby flashed a smile.

"I know," she said, before she shut the door behind her.

On the bed, Ivy's cell phone rang again, another 800 number illuminated on the small face. She shoved the phone underneath the pillow and lay back down in bed.

ELISE

Elise put Sam down in the bouncy chair she'd dug out of the
basement and began to put the groceries away. The house was
quiet, and she suspected everyone was upstairs, taking some
much-needed space. She dumped the mussels and clams in a
colander and ran them under cold water; the kitchen filled with
the loamy scent of the sea.

"Need some help?" Libby appeared in the kitchen, rolling up
the sleeves of her shirt and washing her hands before Elise could
answer.

Libby got to work on the sauce and salad while Elise debearded
the mussels and deveined the shrimp. They worked in a quiet easy
rhythm. Every now and then Libby asked a question—where the
cutting boards were, how finely to mince the onion—but otherwise
they worked in silence, the hum of the radio the only noise other
than the clip and chop of knives.

Cooking dinner was Elise's favorite part of the day. Not the
actual eating of it, because dinner was a harried messy affair that
involved Elise jumping up to refill water glasses and pile seconds on
plates. Often Marianna and Piper turned up their noses at whatever

she'd prepared, and she spent the meal filling bowls with Cheerios and milk, her mother's voice in her head admonishing her for such ridiculous accommodations. "This isn't a restaurant," her mother would bark whenever anyone dared to complain about dinner.

It was the preparation that Elise enjoyed, the few minutes of quiet when the children knew enough to leave her be, and she was left with just her thoughts and the cadence of work. In the kitchen, Elise felt most at ease, a rare clarity and calmness settling over her as she diced and grated. Perhaps it was the order to it that Elise appreciated, the simple doable tasks before her—a clove of garlic slipped from its skin, a bell pepper chopped, an onion sautéed. Each act required attention, and her own thoughts finally stilled. Watching Libby navigate Elise's unfamiliar kitchen, she imagined that Libby felt the same ease.

As always happened when quiet reigned for more than a few minutes, Elise felt compelled to fill the air with chatter. The silence wasn't awkward or strained, but it was difficult for her to ever shed her role as host. Yet she worried that if she started talking, she might burst into tears and tell Libby everything. She wasn't sure why this would be so bad. She'd seen all of her friends struggle before, but had always had trouble laying herself bare in the same way. In college, it was Elise who created a system for cleaning their apartment, Elise who divided the bills and told them how much they each owed, Elise who planned out weekly meals and made a grocery list, a mother even before she was one. She knew her desire to care for the people around her kept her on track, and kept all those carefully arranged pieces from falling apart.

After Jackie's death, Elise went through a dark period. She barely got out of bed and struggled to prepare for her final exams. Her friends would often return from classes to find her still in pajamas even though it was lunchtime. She cried easily, tears appearing out of nowhere while they were all eating spaghetti in the dining hall. She'd see her friends looking at her sympathetically, and Elise would reach a hand to her face and realize tears were pouring down her face. It scared her, how quickly she'd come undone, her whole world collapsing like a carefully built house of cards. By the time they returned for their senior year, Elise was back to her tightly wound and energetic self, but there was a performance in it, as if she were going through the motions of who they all expected her to be. Over the years she'd become well versed in how to shroud her grief, offering up a smile and favor for someone else in place of true emotion.

So a new guy? Adam? That's exciting. The words were on the tip of her tongue, ready whenever the need to speak grew too great to contain. She wanted to hear more about Libby's new love interest, and Elise would be spared having to talk about herself.

She was happy that Libby finally seemed ready to move on after Steven's death. The shock of it had been stunning, both because it meant that Libby was a widow and single mother, but because it had been *Steven. Everyone* had loved Steven. Handsome and charming but without the cockiness that often accompanied these traits, he'd been the extra limb of their group, steady and reliable, there when you needed him, always making everyone laugh. It was Steven who helped Elise through the awful semester when everyone was away, Steven who contacted them all when Jackie died. It was during this time that her relationship with him changed, developing independent of the others, independent of Libby.

It was junior year when Elise fell in love with Steven, though now she was no longer certain it was love and not a desperate attempt to cling to something good in a time when little else was. It was hard to know how she would have felt if her heart wasn't already so tender and raw, laid bare without her usual filters and defenses. Yet something had crackled between them, an energy that Elise didn't think was only in her head. Maybe he just missed Libby, maybe he wasn't as faithful as they'd always assumed, but Elise knew there was more than friendship in the way he looked at her. She hated herself for it, but it was a reprieve from the storm that raged inside her and outside the walls of Harper.

Nothing happened, not really. There was a kiss one night, after a particularly bad day with Jackie. They had both pulled away before anything more could happen, although Elise couldn't even say she'd stopped out of respect for Libby. She'd stopped because her head was too full of the sight of Jackie's body withering away on the narrow twin bed, skin nearly as pale as the bedsheets. Every time Elise closed her eyes, it was her sister she saw, not Libby, but that had been enough.

It seemed a more treacherous betrayal than if she'd actually gone through with it, knowing how the story ended now. Libby got to keep Steven then, but had to lose him later. Perhaps she would have been better off if she'd lost him to Elise back then. Elise knew that the pain of losing a husband and the father of your children was far worse than the pain of losing a boyfriend and college friend, although her own friendship with Libby might not have survived. If Libby found love again, maybe Elise could let those tender moments with Steven fade into the bank of memory, sweet and innocent, no longer tainted with sadness and deceit.

Elise glanced down at her hands, which had gone numb and red under the cold running water where the shellfish rinsed in a colander. She turned off the tap and dried her hands on a dish towel, rubbing her aching knuckles. She had started to inherit her mother's arthritis.

"How are you?" Libby asked, breaking the spell of silence. Her voice held more meaning than those three little words often intended, but Elise ignored it.

"Great!" she answered, out of habit.

"El." Libby laid down her knife and waited till Elise met her eyes. "How are you really?"

Elise's eyes filled immediately, though she wasn't sure why, other than it was so rare anyone asked her that question and actually wanted to hear the answer. The one time she'd gone to see a therapist, soon after Marianna's diagnosis when the uncertainty of the future was a thunderous crush, the therapist had asked her what had made her come in. Elise burst into tears, her breath jagged and hiccupy, and she'd struggled to find the words. She thought maybe she'd only come to find a place to cry. She never returned, too afraid of what it was she'd untapped, but there had been many times when she recalled the safeness of that room and wished she'd gone back.

"Are you sure? You seem a little…" Libby paused, likely searching for a word that wouldn't upset Elise. "High-strung."

"You know me." Elise pressed her lips together so hard they throbbed, forcing them into a smile that Libby would never believe.

"El, it's me. What's going on?" Libby sat down at the counter and pulled a chair out for Elise. She sat.

"It's been a bit of a hard time lately," Elise admitted, taking a shaky breath and trying to keep her voice light. Libby waited. "Nothing in particular. Well, just a bunch of different things. Tommy's hanging out with a bunch of jerks and getting in trouble." She let out a harsh laugh even as her eyes filled. Easier to start with the small things. She swallowed, working her way up to the troubles that cartwheeled through her mind in the blue-black night. "Brad and I haven't been getting along. Actually, we're barely speaking. He set up a meeting for us this week. I think he's called a divorce lawyer." Her voice broke on this last one, and Elise began to cry, arms clasped around her waist in a futile attempt to hold herself together.

"Oh, El." Libby had her by the shoulders, pulling Elise into a hug. "I'm so sorry."

Elise nodded, burying her face in the softness of Libby's sweater, and neither of them said any more. Elise didn't need the endless hashing it out that Ada or Ivy required, hours spent analyzing every emotion and action, feelings pummeled into submission until they were easily understood and managed. Elise didn't need words, for Libby understood the texture of loss, knew how the anticipation of it was a too-thin sweater on a cold day. All Elise needed was a moment to rest her head against Libby's shoulder, and a place to cry.

IVY

Ivy padded into the kitchen carrying her sneakers. Elise and Libby were shoulder to shoulder at the counter. Elise's eyes were pink and puffy, but as soon as she saw Ivy, Elise jumped up from the stool and resumed chopping a pepper.

"Everything okay?" Ivy asked.

"Sure! We were just taking a little break from dinner prep. All on track though," Elise answered.

"About earlier," Ivy began.

"It's fine," Elise said, avoiding eye contact. Thwack, thwack, thwack, went the knife.

"No, really. I'm glad to be here," Ivy said. It wasn't exactly true, but it wasn't entirely untrue, and it was what Elise needed her to say. "I'm sorry I was so awful," she added, which was the truth. Elise finally looked up. "And before you say I wasn't, I was. I really was, and I'm sorry." Ivy swallowed, forcing herself to get it all out. "I'm still dealing with the thing with Sebastian. It was hard to tell you all, and I lashed out." Ivy waited for Elise to start clucking over her, but she didn't.

"You *were* awful," Elise said, but the edge of a smile played at her mouth.

"I know. And I'm really sorry." She waited for Elise's response. Ivy took their friendship for granted, she realized, always assuming they would be there if she needed them, treating her three oldest friends the same reckless way that you treated those closest to you. Yet they *weren't* family, and there were no blood ties to keep them together if their bonds frayed beyond repair.

"I forgive you," Elise said, and Ivy let out a sigh of relief.

"So are we okay?" she asked.

Elise held her eye for a moment. "We're okay," she said, and Ivy chose to believe her. She bent to slip her feet into her sneakers and tied the laces.

"I'm going for a walk. Anyone want to come?" she asked.

"I could use some exercise." Libby wiped her hands on the flowered apron she wore.

"Me too. I bet Sam could use some fresh air," Elise said. Ivy glanced toward Sam who was parked in his car seat. He was uncharacteristically quiet in the half-awake, half-asleep zone, eyes partly open and glassy.

Ivy unclipped Sam from the chair while Libby found her sneakers and Elise checked on Ada (lying in bed reading). Then they bundled Sam into a full-body snuggly, figured out how to open the stroller, and strapped him in with enough buckles and snaps that Ivy was certain he could survive at high speeds on a freeway. Twenty minutes later, they were finally on the road.

There were no sidewalks in Elise's neighborhood, but the streets were quiet and calm. Through the curtained trees the sky was a pale orange, the air cool but with the faint scent of approaching spring that Ivy recalled from her few years living on the East Coast. In San Francisco, the smell of the air shifted depending on where in the city you were—from the spicy scent of eucalyptus trees to exhaust fumes and piss. But never did she find that particular almost-spring smell.

Elise pushed the stroller, and Ivy peered at the houses in the neighborhood, many of them smaller and more modest than Elise's, gray-shingled capes with a little square of lawn, big enough for a small garden, and a table and chairs. Ivy wondered if things would have ended up differently for her and Sebastian if they'd left the city years ago, bought a little cottage in one of the small towns a few hours north of the city, a place with a little land for a dog to run free and a garage where Sebastian could paint. What if, what if, what if—the broken soundtrack of her life.

"This guy's wiped out," Ivy said once they'd started walking. Sam was awake, but Ivy knew that a few more blocks and he'd be out cold. She recognized the dazed stoned look of a baby on the verge of sleep.

"Ada said not to let him sleep. She said if he naps now, he'll be up all night. And seeing as how I'm with him tonight, let's make sure that doesn't happen," Elise said. She bent down and pulled back the hood of the stroller.

"So what do we think about Ada?" Ivy asked. She'd been wanting to broach the subject with Libby and Elise since they arrived yesterday but hadn't had a chance. "Does she seem off to you?"

"She's just had a baby," Libby said.

"Well, not *just*," Elise pointed out.

"No, but not that long ago either," Libby said.

"She's not herself. You guys have noticed that, right?" Ivy said.

"I guess," Libby said. They rounded the corner and the ocean came into view. The air dropped a few degrees, the chill catching off the waves. Ivy pulled down her hat, wishing she'd thought to bring a warmer coat.

"How worried are you?" Elise asked.

"Well, I don't think she's going to smother him in his sleep, if that's what you're asking," Ivy said.

"God, Ivy, that's not funny. This is serious. That really happens," Elise said, and Libby's eyes flickered toward Ivy with disapproval.

"I know. Postpartum is no joke. I had it with Jax. Things could have gotten bad, but we caught it early enough," Ivy said. Though she rarely talked about it, she had battled postpartum depression with Jax. When he was born, Ivy was terrified. Even two years later, her departure from Harper still felt raw, and many days she awoke shocked that this was her new life. In those first months, she'd looked at Jax's wrinkled red face, his helplessness and vulnerability as he rooted for her breast or let out a high-pitched cry, and all she'd felt was emptiness. She went through the motions—feeding him, changing him, bathing him, waking a million times in the middle of the night to nurse. She did everything she was expected to do, which was miraculous considering that she was only twenty-three but she'd read all the books and gone to the birthing classes, and she was as prepared as any woman could be. What was missing was the feeling of being hopelessly in love that she'd expected. She looked at Jax and thought about everything she'd given up by having him, all possibility for a future as she'd once imagined it. She looked at him and thought that she didn't have anything to offer him. She looked at him and prayed that one day she would love him.

It hadn't gone on that long. Probably only a few months, though those days were under a hazy cloud and not easily remembered. Then one afternoon, Ivy had been giving Jax a bath in the small tub that fit over the kitchen sink. As she'd soaped his belly and rubbed shampoo onto his scalp, she'd imagined letting him go and watching him sink to the bottom of the plastic tub. It had seemed so real that Ivy had gasped out and pulled Jax to her chest, his slippery body scrabbling in Ivy's arms. She'd stumbled into the bedroom, soaking wet, and called Sebastian. He returned home within the hour. Sebastian, her husband for less than a year, was barely an adult himself, but he'd calmly told Ivy he thought she had postpartum depression. He must have been listening during all those birthing classes on the night they'd covered that topic. (It was also the same class Ivy found out what an episiotomy was, so she hadn't been paying close attention, too shell-shocked by what she'd learned.) He took the next few weeks off of work to help with Jax, and brought Ivy to a doctor. Then there was medication and several months of appointments with a therapist, and slowly Ivy began to come back from whatever dark abyss she'd been edging toward.

The love didn't come all at once, not even after medication, but it did come, in little drips and spurts, a sudden and unexpected surge here, a wash of it there. By the time Jax was a year old, she felt the sharp spike of motherhood as she was pretty sure she was supposed to feel it, and had trouble recalling the dim days when she'd looked at Jax like a stranger.

It was so long ago now. Jax had just turned eighteen—he knew how to drive, he had a girlfriend, he shaved every morning, he was going to UC Davis in the fall. He was a man. The days when he was a squirming squalling bundle, defenseless and weak, were so far off. The day when Ivy had imagined him drowning felt even farther off.

Ivy didn't know what she would have done if Sebastian hadn't spoken with the doctor, if he hadn't known what was wrong. Ivy didn't think Ada was a danger to Sam, but what did she know? What did any of them know? None of them were inside Ada's body or her mind; it was impossible to fully understand what she was going through.

"We need to talk to her. And to Tyler. The rest of us aren't going to be with her after this weekend," Ivy said.

"Will she be mad?" Elise asked.

"Who cares?" Ivy asked, and none of them had an answer for that. They walked on, the air colder now that they were close to the water. Night was falling fast.

"Oh no," Elise groaned, peering into the stroller. Sam's eyes were shut. "Ada's going to kill me."

"Wake him." Libby leaned into the stroller and tickled his chin. "Wake up, Sam, wake up."

Sam let out a little whimper but didn't open his eyes.

"Oh, *now* he sleeps. This kid hasn't taken a nap all weekend," Elise said.

"No wonder he's tired. Unstrap him. If we get him out of the seat, he'll wake up," Libby said. Together they unbuckled him, and Libby hoisted him on her hip. Sam let out little mewling noises as he reluctantly woke up. Libby rested her hand against the back of his neck. "Does he feel warm?"

Elise put the back of her hand against Sam's forehead. "Yeah, but it's probably just this bulky suit. Take off his hat, and he'll cool down. We should head back anyway." They began the walk back to Elise's house. Libby carried the baby, Elise pushed the empty stroller, and Ivy carried Sam's soft fleece hat, heading back to Elise's house to carry on their weekend of freedom.

ADA

Ada lay in bed and flipped through the *People* magazine that Ivy had bought for the plane, amazed at how few of the celebrities she recognized. They all looked so impossibly young that it was hard to believe they'd had enough time in their lives to do anything worthy of becoming famous.

She threw the magazine on the nightstand with a sigh. The trouble was she was so used to looking after Sam that she didn't know what to do when given any time away from him. Even now, knowing he was going to be back any minute, Ada felt a little tug of longing, while also wishing they wouldn't be home for hours. Sam managed to leach away her energy to do anything that didn't directly connect to him.

And there had been so much she liked to do! She loved to read but hadn't made it through anything longer than a parenting article since Sam was born. She enjoyed her job, both the teaching elements and also her new role as chair of the department. Except now when she thought of work, it filled her with an uneasy dread.

How on earth would she do it? How did anyone with kids have a job too? Was it possible to be this tired and still function in the working world?

Sleeping on her laptop, the one she only used lately for checking Facebook or searching for sleep training tips, was the first half of a novel she'd started before her mother got sick. The book was a secret, something only her mother and Tyler knew about. Ada hadn't even told Elise, even though she'd quietly dreamed about being a writer since she was a child. She'd become an English teacher not so much because she loved to teach, though that had come later, but because she loved words and what happened when they were strung together, the way a story opened up and it was possible to fall headfirst into it.

The novel she was working on was historical fiction, and it took place during World War Two. It had required huge amounts of research, something else Ada had discovered she enjoyed. For a while there she was really working away on it, spending a few hours every weekend at the library, becoming engrossed as she sketched out her characters and took notes about the time period. It was like a quilt she was stitching together, square by square, each piece nothing alone, but possibly something real when you put it all together.

She hadn't opened the document in months, hadn't done any research or writing since well before Sam was born, too incapacitated in the wake of her mother's death to think about creating anything. Every now and then there were moments when her old pleasures would resurface, glimmering around the edges, almost as if they were trying to catch her attention, flags waving in the wind. Then, just as quickly as they'd appeared, they vanished, and Ada was left with this new person she'd become, someone joyless and worried, afraid of the world.

From downstairs she heard the door open and then voices. Sam was home, she thought with a sigh. She pushed herself up from the bed and padded downstairs to greet him. Libby held him in her arms.

"He didn't fall asleep, did he?" Ada asked, reaching for him. The three of them looked guiltily at each other and Ada's frustration flared. "Oh, come on!"

"I'm sorry, I didn't even notice. He was awake one minute and then fast asleep the next," Elise said.

"That's kind of how it works," Ada grumbled.

"Well, is it the end of the world? He must be tired if he fell asleep," Elise said. Her cheeks were flushed from the cold, and she looked so pretty in her designer jeans and cream-colored fleece that Ada felt a stab of envy, dowdy in leggings and an oversized sweater.

"If only it were that simple," Ada said, unzipping Sam from the winter snuggly. She hoisted him on her hip.

"We want to talk to you," Ivy said, in a voice that was uncharacteristically serious. For a moment Ada felt her heart still and she automatically looked to Libby and Elise, who both looked serious as well. Ever since the day Ivy was kicked out of Harper, Ada felt uneasy in their interactions, worried that Ivy would sniff out the secret she'd kept for all these years. But Ivy didn't look angry, Ada realized, only concerned. She felt herself relax even as she realized that she wanted to tell Ivy what she'd done. But this was not the moment.

"Okay. What's up?"

"Let's go sit down," Libby said. They followed Elise into the living room, and Ada settled on the couch with Sam in her arms.

"We're worried about you," Elise said.

"You don't seem yourself these days," Libby added.

Ada didn't know what to say. She felt tears welling up and she blinked them back quickly. "I'm fine."

"You're not. I think you're postpartum," Ivy said, blunt as always.

"I know I seem like I'm a mess, but I love Sam. I'm so happy he's here." Even as she spoke, the tears started to come, blurring her vision. They dripped down her cheeks and landed on Sam's head.

"I know. But that doesn't mean you're not still depressed," Ivy said.

Ada felt the sobs rising up in her, racking her body in a spasm that was both embarrassing and a relief. "I don't know what's wrong with me," she sputtered between cries.

The three of them crowded on the couch around her. Elise took Sam, and Libby and Ivy rubbed her back.

"Have you talked to Tyler?" Libby asked.

Ada shook her head, wiping her nose with the back of her hand. "I don't want to freak him out. This isn't what he signed up for. I keep thinking that one of these days, I'll get it together. I won't be so sad and anxious and worried about everything. But every day it's the same." She thought about all of the times she'd wanted to turn to Tyler, to allow him to comfort her, and all of the times she'd pulled away instead.

"You just need to get some help. Go to the doctor and talk about it," Elise said.

Ada shook her head, pushing wet strands of hair from her face. "I should be able to handle this myself. You guys all did."

"I know it was a long time ago that my kids were babies, but I had a hard time after Jax was born. I really struggled," Ivy said, and Ada looked up. It surprised her to hear that Ivy, so brash and confident in everything that she did, could have struggled the same way.

"What happened?" Ada asked.

Ivy blinked, and Ada could see how difficult this conversation was for her.

"Nothing happened. But one day I was giving Jax a bath, and I imagined just letting him go. I saw him drown," Ivy said, and from the tremble in her voice, Ada could see how shaken she still was by this vision. From the expressions on Libby's and Elise's faces, she'd never told them either.

Ada had heard of these kinds of violent postpartum fantasies. She'd only had the one, when she imagined throwing Sam against the wall, but she'd pushed it down so deep that she could pretend it hadn't happened. Hearing Ivy talking so bravely about her own experience framed it in a new light.

"Did you hurt him?" Ada asked, her voice barely above a whisper.

"No," Ivy said sharply. "I called Sebastian and I got help. I went on medication and Sebastian helped out more. The medication didn't fix everything overnight, but it saved me. You have to go to the doctor, Ada. This might not just pass on its own."

Ada thought about this. For so long, she'd imagined that she just had to wait, to ride out the storm that raged inside of her. But maybe the storm wouldn't pass. This hadn't occurred to her till now.

"I'll think about it," Ada said.

"No, not think about it. Tell us you'll *do* something about it," Ivy demanded. She crossed her arms and waited. Libby and Elise looked at her.

"Okay. I'll go to the doctor when I get home," Ada said.

"You better not just be saying that, because I'm going to bug you till you go. I'll send you annoying text messages in the middle of the night," Ivy threatened.

"Oh, please, I have a hard enough time sleeping as it is. The last thing I need are your stupid texts waking me up," Ada said, finally smiling. She reached out for Sam and rested her cheek against his. She looked back at Ivy, wondering what it had cost her to share such a dark and private memory.

"Thank you," she said, and Ivy nodded. Ada thought again of her vow to tell Ivy what she'd done and felt worse than ever about this secret, for the way it festered in the face of Ivy's kindness. She'd tell her tonight, she resolved.

Ada kissed Sam's forehead, and Libby put an arm around her shoulders and gave a squeeze. Elise clapped her hands together like a tour guide trying to get the attention of a group of restless tourists.

"Good. Now that we've taken care of that, who wants a drink?" Elise asked, in an obvious attempt to lighten the mood.

They all did.

ELISE

Elise raised her fork, strands of linguini hanging suspended, a
single mussel speared on the prong. "Bon appétit!"

"Bon appétit," the others echoed, ducking their faces toward
the food.

A silence fell on the table and the only sound was the scrape
of forks on Elise's best china.

Finally, Ada broke the quiet. "Oh, I meant to tell you!" She
had perked up since their earlier conversation. Elise wondered if
acknowledging that something was wrong might be the first step
in getting better. "You know who friend-requested me recently?
Mark Wallman. Elise, you remember him?"

When they were sophomores at Harper, Elise was infatuated
with a boy on their floor. It wasn't a relationship, but a series of
late-night drunken hookups, followed by Mark ignoring Elise for
the next few days. Each encounter left Elise moony and depleted,
and she'd lie in bed listening to Tori Amos songs for hours. Ada
tried to convince her that Mark wasn't worth feeling this bad for,

but Elise would just press repeat on her favorite track and stare up at the water-stain marks on the ceiling.

"I haven't thought about him in ages," Elise said. This was a lie. Since the silent rift in her marriage, Elise had found herself googling an inordinate number of former lovers, flings, and passing crushes. She'd already seen Mark Wallman's picture on his Facebook profile, though she hadn't dared to friend-request him, largely because she didn't trust her own judgment while her marriage hung in such a precarious state, and since she'd discovered he lived in Cambridge, less than a half-hour away. His profile was public, and she'd already seen the pictures of his children (no wife visible) and enlarged different photos to see how he'd aged. "What's he up to these days?"

Ivy crunched a crouton. "He's a science teacher at Cambridge Rindge and Latin. Divorced. He looked pretty good in his picture. Not that I ever saw the allure."

Elise sighed. "I don't know what it was about him that made me crazy. It might have been the goatee."

"Soul patch," Ada chimed in. "Isn't that what they call those stupid goatees that are just a splotch of hair in the middle of the chin?"

"Oh, I loved his soul patch," Elise sighed. The others giggled.

"You were crazy about him. I've never seen you get so worked up over a guy. Remember Tori Amos?" Libby asked. Ivy and Ada shrieked with laughter and something in the room shifted, a general loosening as they all remembered how to be together.

The rest of the dinner passed with companionable chatter about Harper and the people they'd once known. Toward the end of the meal, Ada's phone chirped, and she excused herself to take the call. She returned a few minutes later, her face dark.

"Tyler needs to work tomorrow. He's not picking up Sam." She slumped heavily into her chair and took a slug of wine. "I knew it. I knew he wasn't going to take him."

Elise wanted to ask if Tyler really needed to work, if he couldn't just take the day off so Ada could have one child-free day, but she already knew the question would only further aggravate Ada. Tyler was a good guy and he seemed to really get Ada—if he was working tomorrow it was because he had to, and Ada didn't need Elise questioning if they really needed the money.

"Sorry, Ada," Ivy said, and Ada pressed her lips together to hold back the tears. "We'll help. It's okay." Ivy reached across the table and squeezed Ada's shoulder.

The rift between them was because they'd stopped sharing things. Elise wasn't sure when or how it happened. She couldn't pinpoint the exact moment when the person she turned to wasn't Libby, Ada, or Ivy, but it had been years ago, and she knew it was the same for the others. Yet the history was there. It wouldn't take much to revive the closeness, despite the differences in their lives and circumstances.

"I have an idea," Elise announced, trying for spontaneity. "Let's play Truth or Dare!" Groans rippled around the table. "Come on, it will be fun! We haven't played in ages."

"That's because we're not *twelve*," Ivy said, though Elise was pretty sure something wicked sparkled in her eyes, and she knew it wouldn't take much cajoling.

"Come on, this used to be our favorite. You promised." Elise went back to the games cupboard, determined to try again tonight. She withdrew a small cardboard box. "We don't even have to make up the questions."

"Really, Elise?" Libby asked.

"Come on, why not? Are you guys chicken?" Elise asked.

"No," snapped Ada, never one to be called out for cowardice. "It's just stupid. We're too old for that."

"Oh God, Ada, aren't you tired of being too old?" Elise felt a flutter of annoyance—at all of them, including herself, for being so disconnected from something as simple as fun. "Doesn't it bore you sometimes? Can we just try to have a little fun? Please?"

Libby threw her napkin on the table. "Why not? I'm game. Ivy?"

Ivy shrugged. "Sure."

"Okay, I'm in," Ada said.

"Yay!" Elise said, refilling Ada's wineglass. She thought about adding a splash to her own, then thought better of it. Ada would relax more if she wasn't worried about Elise drinking too much. Not to mention that tomorrow's hangover would be wicked if Sam slept as poorly for her as he had for Ivy.

"Okay, who wants to go first?" Elise lifted the lid off the box and pulled out two stacks of cards, one red, one yellow.

"I think you should, since it was your idea in the first place." Ada sat back in her seat and sipped her wine. Finally, she looked more relaxed than she had all weekend, hair falling softly around her shoulders, cheeks flushed. She looked almost like herself.

"Bring it on," Elise said.

"Truth or dare?" Libby asked.

The truths were where friendship was built. Where you whispered secrets—funny and embarrassing and shameful—that allowed others to get close.

"Truth," Elise said.

Libby reached for a yellow card. "What is the most embarrassing thing in your room?"

"Hmm." Elise thought of the bedroom she and Brad shared, the one she'd been sleeping in alone. She mentally scanned the sparse room with its framed photos and jewelry box atop her dresser, a bookcase in the corner, a walk-in closet. On the nightstand was a stack of books, a bottle of hand lotion, and a lip balm. There was no kink in sight. "K-Y Jelly?" she said, thinking of the tube in her nightstand. Rarely used these days.

"Seriously?" Ivy asked. "That's the naughtiest thing you have in your bedroom? No secret stash of erotica or a dildo?"

Elise shrugged. "Sorry."

"My turn," Ivy said, shaking her head in mock disgust. "Dare."

Elise picked a red card. "Do four cartwheels in a row."

Ivy groaned but pushed herself to standing. The dining room opened into the living room, and there was a plush carpet and plenty of open space. "Okay, here goes. It's your fault, Elise, if I break a bone." Ivy raised her hands over her head and proceeded to do four wobbly cartwheels, turning around after two to avoid hitting the wall. She rose triumphantly. "Ta da!" She was red-faced and out of breath, and pushed her hair from her face. "Your turn, Libs. Truth or dare?"

"Oh, truth, I guess." Libby looked nervous, drumming her fingers on the gnarled wooden table.

"What is the most childish thing you still do?" Ivy asked.

Libby squinted her eyes, trying to think. "I still bite my nails. I don't bother getting manicures because I just chew the whole thing apart."

"Gross. My turn," Ada said. "Truth."

Libby reached out and picked a card. "What are you most self-conscious about?"

"That's easy. How fat I am right now." Elise watched Ada paste on a false smile and cross her arms over her midsection.

"You're not fat," Elise said quickly.

"Oh, come on. We all know that's not true," Ada said with a shrug.

"It's just baby weight. It will come off soon," Libby chimed in.

"Sure." Ada ran a finger under her eyelid.

"Come on. No moping around. Let's play the game," Ivy said. "Elise, you're up again."

"Okay. I'll do a dare this time," Elise said. Maybe they needed to ration the truths, let the mood be light before they got deep.

Ivy pulled a card. "Lick the floor."

"What?"

Ivy held up the card. "That's what it says. Lick the floor."

Elise heaved herself out of the chair and lowered herself to her knees, bringing her face to the hardwood floor, grateful that the cleaners had polished it just last week. She squeezed her tongue through her lips, just a tiny bit, until it met the cold wood. It tasted like lemons.

The room felt brighter. The bad feelings and anger from earlier today had dissipated, and all that was left was the four of them. It was what Elise had hoped for in all those weeks of preparation, all those emails and texts sent with dates and lists, extra trips to the grocery shop and liquor store. When she stood up from the floor, she saw the flickering candles dripping in the silver candlesticks, her best friends softly lit by the glow, the warmth of the wine and the seafood and their friendship filling her up and making the room cozy and safe. The four of them together.

IVY

"Have you crapped your pants since you were a child?" Libby asked.

"What? Is that seriously a question? Let me see that!" Ivy
snatched the card from Libby. "Who comes up with these?"

"Stop stalling. Answer the question," Elise prodded.

"Of course not."

"Liar," Libby said with a grin. "Sophomore year? The party
at Beta?"

"Oh, God," Ivy said, the memory of the awful night suddenly
coming back.

"What? I don't remember this," Elise said, leaning in.

"Yes, you do. She got food poisoning. Probably from those
funky meatballs you were eating that had been sitting out in the
sun all day," Libby said.

"Ugh. I still can't eat meatballs. I'd forgotten about that." The
whole day was dredged up from whatever dank repository of
memory she'd filed it in all those years ago. A homecoming party,
afternoon drinking, warm beer in tin cans. Ivy hadn't wanted to

use the bathroom at Beta, too mortified by the idea of taking a shit at a crowded party. Instead she'd tried to hurry back to their dorm room, but when she arrived ten minutes later, clammy and pale, it was too late. She already had diarrhea running down her leg.

"How do I not remember this?" Ada asked.

"It was a bad night. Moving on," Ivy said. Ada had been away the weekend of the crappy pants, and Libby and Elise had both mercifully kept the incident to themselves. Looking back, it was funny, but at the time it had been so humiliating. Even thinking about it brought a little sting of shame, though she was by no means the only one eating those meatballs. She'd always wondered how many other people had gotten sick.

"You're up, Ada," Elise said.

"Is there more wine?" Ada asked.

"That's the spirit! Here." Elise refilled Ada's glass.

"You've got Sam, right?" Ada asked, for what must have been the twentieth time.

"Yes!" Elise said. "You're off tonight. Relax. It's your turn."

Ivy leaned back on the couch and surveyed the room. They'd migrated to the couch, and evidence of the rising state of drunkenness was visible in the mess. The dining room table was still littered with dirty dishes, the remains of frutti di mare gelatinizing in a fishy red glaze on the plates. A half-full bottle of wine had been carried to the coffee table, its level quickly lowering. Elise had started a fire, and it crackled and popped in the fireplace.

"Truth," Ada said.

Ivy pulled a card. "What is something from your past that you feel guilty about?" she read.

"Oh, God. I don't know." Ada took another sip of wine and pulled her legs up into the giant plush chair in which she sat.

"Everyone has something," Ivy said. There were a million and one things in Ivy's past that she felt guilty about. Surely Ada had at least one.

"I'm not sure," Ada said, her eyes skirting Ivy as she tucked a lock of hair behind her ear. Ada glanced at Elise and Libby who seemed to draw into themselves. Something sparkled between the three of them.

Ivy leaned closer, trying to pin Ada in place. "You've got something, don't you?"

Ada didn't answer. She wrapped her arms around her legs and appeared lost in thought, and Ivy had the feeling that she was considering something, flipping an idea over in her mind and rubbing it like a well-worn stone.

"Come on, Ada, you have to. It's part of the game," Ivy prompted, even while she felt alarm bells ringing.

In the glow of the firelight, Ada looked young, the fatigue and wrinkles of time softened. For a moment, Ivy could see Ada at twenty, in her ironed button-down blouse and dark-wash jeans. She had seemed so settled to Ivy, so cared for, her mother sending weekly care packages full of homemade cookies and gum like she was away at summer camp. The cloak of a solid family wrapped itself around Ada and protected her, offering a shield that Ivy had never known. Her jealousy of Ada had been strong, even as they forged a tentative friendship.

"Go on," Ivy said, despite the ripple of unease that quivered in her stomach.

"Okay," Ada said, reaching for her wineglass and draining it in one long swallow. "You're going to be upset, but it was a long time ago."

"Ada," Libby said, and gave a slight shake of her head.

"It's okay," Ada said. "It's time. It's for the best. Really."

"Tell me," Ivy said, even though part of her wanted to flee the room before Ada could speak.

"Okay," Ada repeated, clearly gathering courage. She turned to Ivy and when she did, her eyes sparkled with unspent tears. "I was the one who told that you cheated on the teacher's exam."

Ivy blinked, trying to make sense of what Ada had said, her mind casting back to all those years ago. "What? What do you mean? What are you talking about?" Libby and Elise's eyes met across the coffee table, but neither of them spoke.

"It was an accident," Ada hurried to add. She already looked like she might be regretting this. "I was at the school the day you took the test. Remember? I was doing student teaching there. I went to wish you luck. I asked where you were, and they pointed at some girl. I didn't know. I wasn't even thinking, I just blurted it out to the proctor."

Ivy inhaled quickly, a sharp breath of air. She'd never known how she got caught. She hadn't even spent much time trying to figure it out. Ivy had been guilty, and it wasn't an airtight plan to begin with. She just hadn't imagined that someone she knew had turned her in.

"How could you?" Ivy's voice was tiny.

Ada shook her head. "It was an accident. You didn't tell us you weren't taking the test! I had no idea what would happen after."

Ivy thought of the afternoon she left Harper, the searing sadness and shame she'd kept hidden from her friends as she got in the cab. She thought of the shitty jobs she'd taken over the years, the tiny apartment that awaited her back in San Francisco, her broken marriage, Sebastian's new baby, the piles of unpaid bills, her upcoming date with Marshall and all of the other Marshalls in her future. She thought of her mother in Butler, living a quiet and lonely life that wasn't Ada's fault, but it sort of was, really, because Ivy's mother's happiness had always rested on Ivy. *You're only as happy as your unhappiest child*, wasn't that the saying? And Ivy's happiness was always precarious and ready to topple over. It wasn't all Ada's fault—surely Ivy held some responsibility over the sad state of her current life—but *this* was Ada's fault. Ada, who found every opportunity to make Ivy feel small and worthless, whose eyes were always judging.

"You did it on purpose," Ivy said.

Ada's eyes widened. "I didn't, Ivy! I didn't."

"Why are you even telling me this now? What is the point?" Ivy's voice was shrill.

"Because you don't need to blame yourself anymore! You can forgive yourself and move on," Ada said. Her voice was shaky.

"Forgive *myself*? What do I need to forgive myself for?" Ivy asked.

"Nothing," Ada said quickly, and Ivy watched as she shrank in on herself. "I only mean it seems like you've never gotten over it. And I can't help feeling like taking this job as an escort is partly because of what happened back then. Like you're set on punishing yourself for something."

"You think I'm punishing myself? Taking this job as penance of some sort? God, you really don't get it, do you?" Ivy said, even while she wondered if there might be a tiny morsel of truth to what Ada had said. She knew the lines were not nearly so simply drawn as Ada made out, but it was possible that one bad decision had led to a series of others and at some point, Ivy had stopped trying to determine which ones were wise and which were foolish.

Ivy looked from Ada to Libby and Elise, who both sat still as statues on the couch. "Did you know?" she asked. Neither of them spoke, eyes bright with tears, and it dawned on Ivy. "You did. You both knew."

Libby spoke first. "We didn't see the point in telling you. It would only have made things worse. We were trying to protect you."

"How could you have kept this from me? All these years?" Ivy felt not just betrayed but humiliated, as if she'd been walking around naked for years and only just now had someone bothered to mention it.

"Ivy, I'm so sorry. It was an accident. I never meant for you to get kicked out. The words were out of my mouth before I even realized you could get in trouble. I told Libby and Elise because I didn't know what to do, and we decided it would only be worse if we told you," Ada said. She was fully crying now, and Ivy remembered what an ugly crier Ada was, the way her face turned bright red and her features crumbled like a pastry. She looked so miserable that Ivy would have felt sorry for her if she wasn't so furious. She imagined the three of them talking about her over the years, discussing every life decision she'd made—graduating from a state school instead of Harper, getting pregnant so young, marrying a man she barely knew, giving up a career as a teacher to go to massage school like so many other flighty girls before and after her. Their pity, and the sudden enduring length of it, made Ivy sick to her stomach.

Ivy stood up from the couch, unable to sit for a moment longer. Her body pulsed with the physical craving to hurt someone, the darting and electric desire to inflict pain. She'd slapped Trina once when she was an obstinate toddler, a sharp swat to her bare bottom, a smack that rang out in the small space of the bedroom. She'd felt terrible about it later, but the feeling of release had been strong.

"What's worse is the fact that for twenty years you've all been lying to me." Ivy turned to Elise whose face had gone white. She was frozen in place, fingers gripping the empty wineglass. "You wonder why we're not close anymore? Maybe *this* is why." Before she fully realized what she was doing, the empty wineglass flew from her hand. It sailed across the room as if it had wings. It landed against the wall, shattering into hundreds of tiny shards that glittered in the flickering candlelight.

Elise let out a noise, a gasp of horror, but she didn't speak.

"Ivy!" Libby said sharply, and for once Ivy didn't feel shame about disappointing Libby with her bad behavior. Libby was just as guilty as Ada.

"I can't talk to you right now. Any of you," Ivy said.

"I'm so sorry, Ivy," Ada moaned.

"I'm going to bed," Ivy said and then left the room, climbing the stairs to her bedroom, leaving the others in silence, ignoring Ada's tears, and Elise and Libby's pleas for her to stay.

In the chilly bedroom, Ivy packed her suitcase. A wave of homesickness washed over her, sharp and sweet. She missed her children, Jax and Trina who didn't try to make her someone else. She longed for the safe space of her own cluttered apartment, with its cramped bedrooms and colorful tapestries serving as makeshift doors. This house was too goddamn big, and while Ivy always complained about the lack of privacy in the apartment, the way it was impossible to have anything to yourself, space or belongings or time, she suddenly hated the vast empty openness of Elise's house, the lonely anonymity of each room, as if it were inhabited by designers and photo shoot managers rather than real people. She wanted to go home.

Somehow it was only Saturday, but it felt like they'd been here forever, a time warp where none of them was sure if they were adults or children, because even though they'd been eighteen, nineteen, twenty at Harper, really, they were all just children. They were still children, unsure and scared, bumbling through the world with crossed fingers and frayed hope, trusting that someone or something would guide them to the other side in one piece.

LIBBY

Text message: Caitlin to Libby
Just saw the pic you posted on Instagram of your dinner. Looks
yum. Who's Adam Cole? He commented that he missed you??

"Ivy, it's me. Can I come in?" Libby stood at Ivy's closed door, wondering what she would do if Ivy said no. There was a long silence before Ivy answered.

"Yeah." Her voice was flat.

Libby opened the door. Ivy was in bed, but the light was still on.

"Are you okay?" Libby carried in a tall glass of water and placed it on the nightstand before climbing into bed beside Ivy. She pulled the blanket over them both.

Ivy took a long sip of water. "How could you not tell me? All of you, but especially you."

Libby let out a long sigh. "There was no point in telling you. It would only make it worse."

"How much worse could it get? She got me kicked out of Harper!" Ivy burst out.

Libby tipped her head and gave Ivy a sympathetic yet skeptical look. "Well…"

"What?"

"Ivy," Libby said gently, knowing she stepped in treacherous territory. "You did *cheat* on the test. Even if Ada hadn't told, which *was* an accident, you might very well have still gotten caught. You can't blame Ada for what you did. Or us."

"You should have told me," Ivy insisted.

"Maybe. Probably," Libby agreed. They'd thought about it, agonized over it after Ada had tearfully confessed what had happened. But they'd been too afraid, worried that Ivy, hot-tempered, impulsive, might never forgive Ada. And what would happen then? So they agreed to keep it a secret, something they'd never again speak about, despite the fault lines and fissures it created.

"I never asked you—why did you do it in the first place? You were prepared for that test. You would have passed," Libby said.

Ivy shook her head. "I used to get test anxiety, remember? It was really bad."

"I know, but still. You would have been fine. If you'd only trusted yourself. You never trust yourself." It broke Libby's heart to see all of the ways Ivy doubted herself, always looking for the easy fix, never believing that she could find another way.

"I'm going to leave tomorrow," Ivy said.

"Oh, Ivy, don't. Elise will be so upset."

"She'll get over it," Ivy said dismissively, and Libby wondered if this was true. If any of them would get over this weekend.

"Don't make any decisions tonight. Just get some sleep and see how you feel in the morning. Please?" Libby said.

Ivy sighed. "Fine. But I don't want to talk to anyone else tonight. Especially Ada."

"Okay. Don't you dare sneak out before everyone is up," Libby said. It would be just like Ivy to disappear in the middle of the night, leaving the rest of them to sift through the remains of the weekend. Libby slid out of bed and flipped off the bedside lamp. "Goodnight," she said to Ivy. She hoped she would be there in the morning.

*

Downstairs, Libby found that Ada had already gone to bed. Elise had swept up the broken glass and was now tackling the dishes. Libby went to help her and tried not to mind. She wished she were full of effortless goodwill and cheer like Elise, but there were moments like this that pissed her off. Why should Ivy and Ada get out of all the cleanup, especially after the mess Ada had caused? Not to mention that she and Elise were the ones who had done most of the cooking? Libby sighed and scrubbed the pan, trying to get off the little bits of dried up sauce and garlic that stuck to the bottom after hours congealing. Why did they always have to be the adults?

"Poor Ivy," Elise said, spraying the counter with disinfectant. "I don't blame her for being mad."

"I know."

"Will she ever forgive us?" Elise asked. She pulled off the soiled tablecloth and crumbs sprinkled all over the floor.

Libby thought about it, rubbing a silver scouring pad in the bottom of the pan till it finally shone bright again. "Yes. I don't know. I hope so."

"Ada only told her to alleviate her own guilt. She should have kept her mouth shut. It's like telling your husband you're having an affair just to make yourself feel better," Elise said, shutting the dishwasher door and starting the cycle. "Let sleeping lions lie, I say."

Upstairs the lights were off in the other bedrooms, and Libby brushed her teeth in the private bathroom. She changed into pajamas and checked her phone. She still hadn't responded to Caitlin's questions about Adam. It hadn't occurred to Libby that Caitlin might be monitoring her social media activity as much as Libby kept an eye on Caitlin's. It was after eleven, but there was a new text from Caitlin, sent a few minutes earlier. Just a single line.

Grandma made pie. And it didn't suck. When are you coming home?

Libby smiled, drawing the phone into her lap. *What kind?* she wrote back, ignoring the previous message about Adam.

Little bubbles floated on the screen. There was no way Anne-Marie knew Caitlin was awake and texting.

Caitlin's response came through with a little pop.

apple

yum

how's your weekend?

Libby thought about saying great or fine, but then decided to be honest.

Interesting. A little too much drama for me.

????

It might not have been an actual question or words expressing interest, but Libby couldn't help but be pleased that Caitlin actually wanted to hear about her life, even if only through a one-line text message. At home, it was unusual for Caitlin to ask a question more personal than what Libby was cooking for dinner. Yet the medium of text messages seemed to offer a portal into a rarely glimpsed side of Caitlin. Libby thought about how to respond.

Friends not getting along as well as I'd hoped. Ada just dropped a bombshell on everyone.

She knew she was drawing out Caitlin's interest, teasing her with what the bombshell was. Caitlin had met Ada several times, but she'd only heard stories about Ivy. The stories were usually cleaned up for her daughter's benefit.

what???

Libby's thumbs were poised over the keypad. She felt a pang of disloyalty to both Ada and Ivy that she was using this story as a bargaining chip with Caitlin. Then she thought of the pile of dishes that her friends had left her with, and she began to type.

Ivy never graduated from Harper. She got kicked out for cheating. Ada just announced that it was because she told on her.

Caitlin's response was fast.

what a bitch!

It was an accident. And we all knew and never told Ivy. She had thought about telling so many times and always talked herself out of it.

omg

And then a moment later, *sounds like a crazy weekend.*

Yup. Are you guys doing all right?

There was a long blank pause, and Libby wondered if Caitlin had put down the phone now that Libby had shifted the conversation. Or if she'd been caught by Anne-Marie. After a moment, the little bubbles started bobbing.

yeah. B misses you. me too.

Libby felt a swell in her chest, a rush of love for her tangled and difficult eldest child.

I miss you guys too.

It was impossible to know if her daughter's stormy and short-tempered nature was a result of circumstance or personality. Perhaps even if Steven were here, Caitlin would be on the threshold of a dark and angry adolescence. Yet when she thought back to Caitlin two and a half years ago, just before Steven died, all she could picture was a sunny and carefree ten-year-old who skipped rather than walked. A girl who climbed into Libby's lap unprompted, roping her arms around Libby's neck like a warm human scarf. She was another person entirely.

The texts volleyed back and forth for several more minutes, a few more digs at Libby's mother (Anne-Marie had made Caitlin clean the entire bathroom when she found out that Caitlin had never before done this. Then she'd made beet and carrot juice. Caitlin had nothing nice to say about either of these things) and then a couple more about the characters of a TV show that they watched together on Thursday nights. This was when Caitlin tended to be most loving and low-key toward her, even daring to snuggle against Libby on the couch. Sometimes Libby ignored the show altogether and just focused on Caitlin's face, what it actually looked like when she relaxed enough to smile.

When they finally signed off, nearly twenty minutes later, Libby felt closer to her daughter than she had in months, which was ironic considering they hadn't been this far away in years. Somehow the distance of the text messages allowed for an easy intimacy that wasn't possible when face to face. Caitlin actually signed off with a heart emoji.

Libby switched off the light and pulled the blankets over her. Down the hall, Sam had started to whimper and she hoped he went back to sleep soon, for Elise's sake. Blessedly, all of the bedrooms were equipped with white noise machines. Libby reached over and turned hers on, and the room was filled with a soft whooshing that blocked out Sam's cries. She wondered if Ivy would actually leave early or if she'd stay the extra day, patching things up enough to get through the rest of the weekend.

Despite the sheets that made her own T.J. Maxx ones feel like sandpaper, despite the ocean view she would wake up to tomorrow morning, despite being surrounded by her oldest friends, all Libby felt like doing was getting home to her daughters. She fell asleep, for once thinking about how lucky she was to have them, rather than thinking about what they all were missing.

ELISE

Elise climbed into bed as quietly as possible. She didn't want to risk
any sudden noises that might wake Sam up. In the porta-crib, he
snuffled and whimpered in his sleep. She closed her eyes, praying
that Sam was just a noisy sleeper. She was tempted to march into
Ada's bedroom and hand the baby over to her, so pissed off was
she that Ada had sabotaged the weekend, just when things were
finally starting to turn around. Long ago they'd decided not to tell
Ivy, and while Elise had also doubted the decision over the years,
she'd kept up their pact. Still, it was hard to be mad at Ada. She'd
looked as devastated as Ivy, if not more so.

Elise closed her eyes and tried to sleep. She wanted to call
Brad to ask him why the hell Josh Parker was calling her phone
number. If Brad wanted to divorce her, she wished he'd have the
balls to tell her himself rather than setting up a meeting for her to
be blindsided. She wondered what would happen if Brad divorced
her. Would she stay in the house with the kids or would he try

to make her leave? Would he want full custody? Elise didn't see how Brad could accuse her of being a bad mother. Everything she'd ever done was for her family. Still, he was the one who'd used the term embezzlement, and Brad was a lawyer. He knew the ins and outs of the legal system and how to manipulate it to his advantage. Elise lay in bed, her heart pounding so hard she wondered if she was having a panic attack. She listened to the sounds of the others in the house, the toilet flushing, the water running, someone brushing their teeth. In the crib on the other side of the room, Sam whimpered and cried every now and then but never fully awoke. Finally she drifted off into a fitful sleep.

She awoke several hours later to Sam's full-blown cries. She sat up, head pounding, hoping that his cries hadn't woken Ada. She'd forgotten how brutal these middle-of-the-night wake-up calls were. She should never have been so dismissive of Ada's exhaustion. Elise stumbled into the bathroom and turned on the overhead light, blinking in the sudden brightness. Ada had given her a bottle and a can of formula in case Sam woke up. Elise squinted at the directions on the side of the package, trying to remember the proportions of powder to water. Finally, she flipped off the light and headed back into the bedroom, shaking the bottle to mix up the clumps of powder.

Elise peered into Sam's crib. In the darkness, she couldn't make out his face, only see his round shape beneath the blanket. Maybe she wouldn't even need to feed him. Reaching her hand into the crib, she hoped to calm him down with just a rub on the back or a few soft shushes. Sometimes that was all babies needed, just a reminder that you were nearby. Elise's fingers grazed the soft fleece blanket and then made their way up his body, finding Sam's head.

He was burning up.

Her hand froze, a dozen ER visits and sleepless nights tumbling forward from the depths of memory, nights spent doling out droplets of Tylenol, the nighttime nebulizer when Tommy got pneumonia, the barking-seal cough when Piper got croup, the time Marianna got the stomach bug and threw up fourteen (fourteen!) times in the course of one night. Her children were older now, sturdier and able to tell her when they didn't feel well, but it was muscle memory, the familiar heat on the back of the head that was the first indication something wasn't right.

She clicked on the bedside lamp and drank down a whole glass of water, suddenly fully sober and awake. Sam blinked back at her, face damp and red, mouth puckered into a cry. She scooped him from the bed in one quick movement, freeing him from the hot blankets and bringing him into the bathroom. In the medicine cabinet, she found a digital thermometer and jar of petroleum jelly. Even as she made a mental note to replace the thermometer, she knew she'd forget until someone else needed it and then she'd be scrubbing it down with antibacterial soap, trying not to recall its last use. She brought Sam back into the bedroom and laid him down on the bed, unsnapping his pajamas and diaper, dipping the thermometer into the petroleum before carefully inserting it into Sam's bottom.

When the thermometer beeped, she peered closer, squinting to make out the numbers, hoping her instincts were off and the fever was lower than it felt. She blinked, clearing the sleep from her eyes, unwilling to believe she was reading the temperature correctly.

104.6 degrees.

A terrible fear gripped Elise, even as she sprang into action. She tried to recall if Sam had seemed sick earlier today, kicking herself that she'd been so preoccupied with Tommy's drama, and the trouble with Brad, and creating the perfect weekend. She'd barely thought about Ada's baby as much more than a burden and accessory. He'd fussed in the car with her that afternoon, but it hadn't occurred to her that he was actually sick. If he'd been coughing or crying a lot, surely one of them would have noticed. Wouldn't they?

Elise quickly put on a new diaper, refastening the pajamas, and then she lifted Sam up, resting his warm head against her shoulder.

His sobs were jagged and half-hearted, too miserable to even cry properly. Still in pajamas, Elise shoved her feet into a pair of sneakers and stepped into the hallway, hurrying down the hall to the bedroom where Ada was staying. In her haste, she hadn't turned on the hall light, and she gripped Sam tightly, worried she might trip in the darkness.

She knocked on Ada's door. When there was no answer, Elise knocked louder. "Ada? Ada, wake up," she called. Bedroom lights clicked on, slender strips of yellow appearing beneath the doors. Ada appeared, bleary-eyed and mussed in an oversized pair of what had to have been maternity pajamas. Her hair was tangled, and she rubbed her eye with the heel of her palm.

"What's wrong?" Ada asked, just as Libby and Ivy appeared in their own doorways. Elise felt a rush of relief that she didn't have to handle the situation alone.

"Sam's sick. I just took his temperature. It was high," Elise said. She tried to speak calmly so as not to panic Ada, even though the situation warranted a certain level of panic.

"How high?" Ada asked, stepping forward and reaching for the baby.

Elise's heart pounded in her chest as she handed him off, racking her brain as she tried to remember the exact numbers on the thermometer. "One-o-four point something. Six, I think? Or seven. No, it was six. One-o-four point six."

"Oh my God. That's really high, isn't it?" whispered Ada.

"It's high," Elise agreed.

"Do you have any infant Tylenol?" Ivy asked, stepping forward.

"I don't know. Tyler packed his stuff. I didn't check." Ada's face had gone completely white.

"It's a high fever, but babies often get high fevers. We should retake his temperature in a few minutes to see if it's gone down," Libby said, resting her hand along the curve of Sam's neck.

"We should still probably get him to the ER just in case," Ivy said.

"Ada, go check if you have any Tylenol. Strip his clothes down to his diaper and see if he cools down at all. I'll get the thermometer and we can retake his temperature," Elise directed. Ivy and Libby ushered Ada back into her bedroom with Sam, and Elise hurried to get the thermometer. When she returned to Ada's room, Sam was wailing hoarsely, his face blotchy and red with the effort. They'd removed his pajamas and he wore just the diaper, his round body limp in Ada's arms. She clutched him to her chest, eyes frantic.

"I don't have Tylenol. Tyler must have forgotten it," she said in a voice thick with tears. For once, none fell, and Elise was relieved to see that Ada was keeping it together.

"Here. Let's check his temp again." Elise handed Ada the thermometer and jelly, and Ada laid Sam down on the bed to remove his diaper. Her hand trembled and Sam squalled, but she managed to slide in the thermometer. When it beeped, they all peered forward to read the number.

104.8.

Ada inhaled sharply but didn't speak. She met Elise's eyes.

"Let's get in the car," Elise ordered.

IVY

Google search for 'high fever, nine-month-old': If your baby is 6 to 24 months old and has a temperature higher than 102°F that lasts longer than one day but shows no other signs or symptoms, contact the doctor. If your baby also has other signs or symptoms—such as a cold, cough or diarrhea—you might contact the doctor sooner based on their severity.

Text message: Sebastian to Ivy
Ivy, the divorce papers. PLEASE.

Ivy sat in the back seat next to Ada and the baby. Sam's breath came in shallow pants, like an injured animal trying to stave off the pain. She cooed softly in Sam's ear, a torrent of reassurances. Ivy put her hand on Ada's knee and gave her a reassuring squeeze. Ada turned to her in the dim light of the car. A sick fear was visible in her eyes.

"He's going to be okay, right? This is normal?" Ada asked.

Ivy nodded. "He'll be fine."

Most likely, it was true. But what Ivy was thinking about, what she didn't tell Ada because she wasn't a sociopath, was the time that Trina got sick at this age. The symptoms had come on suddenly—a high fever, crying, her pale blue eyes glassy and unfocused, her whole body floppy like her bones were made of bread dough. Luckily, she and Sebastian knew something was wrong and got her to the ER. Bacterial meningitis, they were told. She could have died if they'd waited even a few more hours. They put her on heavy antibiotics, and Ivy and Sebastian were able to walk out of the hospital several days later with Trina, but Ivy never forgot how close they'd come to losing her.

Sam's moans were weak, a chesty wail that filled the car and made it seem smaller. Elise said the hospital was only ten minutes away, but it felt like they'd been driving for hours. It was after midnight and there was no traffic, yet they managed to get stuck at every red light.

"Does he feel any cooler to you?" Ada asked.

Ivy brought her hand up to the back of Sam's neck. It was smooth and hot, a little furnace burning beneath her palm. "Maybe," she lied.

"I'm so stupid," Ada said under her breath. "So selfish and stupid. What was I thinking, pawning him off on you guys? If I'd been taking care of him, I would have noticed something was wrong."

"He wasn't sick earlier, Ada. He really wasn't. These things come on suddenly in babies." Ivy thought about how quickly Trina's illness had appeared, how she'd been babbling at breakfast and eating a mashed banana, but by the time she got up from her morning nap she was lethargic and glazed over. "You're not selfish for wanting a weekend to yourself. Having a baby is hard. Harder than anyone ever tells you." Her anger at Ada from just hours ago suddenly seemed far away, lost amidst the chaos of the emergency.

Ada nodded and clutched Sam tighter. "I've been a mess lately. Obviously. Tyler keeps asking me if I'm okay, and I keep telling him I'm fine, but I'm not. I'm really not. And now I've put Sam at risk because of it." Ada bent forward, burying her face in Sam's neck. Ivy could almost feel the heat against her own cheek.

"Sam's going to be fine, okay? And we're going to get you some help too. It's not too late for anything. We just need to get through the next few hours, okay?" Ivy said, squeezing Ada's forearm. Ada nodded, her face still hidden behind Sam as they pulled up to the circular drive of a large brick building. A white sign read EMERGENCY in glowing red letters.

"You guys go in. Elise and I will park and meet you inside," Libby said.

"Let's go." Ivy jumped out of the car and held the door open for Ada. Ada struggled out, holding Sam awkwardly in her arms, and then they hurried toward the hospital.

Ivy glanced around the ER while Ada registered at the intake desk. Compared to the San Francisco ER, a Cape Cod hospital in March was a peaceful haven. A few people sat hunched in chairs, but no one was bleeding from the head or throwing up in a bucket. The room was quiet, other than Sam's crying, and there was hardly any sense of urgency at all.

"Ada's registering," Ivy said a moment later, when Elise and Libby appeared.

Ada came and took a seat next to Ivy, jostling Sam back and forth in her arms. "They said the doctor would be out soon."

They settled into an uneasy quiet, punctuated by Sam's breathy sobs. Within a few minutes, a young doctor appeared, hands deep in the pockets of his white coat. He was younger than them, only thirty or so, with thick dark hair and a day's stubble on his face. "Ms. Clark?"

"Yes?" Ada stood up quickly, swaying slightly on her feet with Sam in her arms. Ivy stood up too, reaching out a hand to steady her.

"I'm Doctor Campbell. I'll see your baby now. You can follow me." He gestured to a set of double doors.

"Someone should come with you to hold Sam so you can listen to the doctor," Elise said.

"I'll go," Ivy volunteered before anyone else spoke. She followed Ada, the doors swinging behind her, not certain why she had volunteered other than because she needed to know that Sam was okay. The doctor led them into a large room and over to an examining table. A nurse in bright pink scrubs pulled a fresh sheet of paper over the table and took Sam's temperature. The room was bright and fluorescent, ripe with the scent of rubbing alcohol and hand soap. As the doctor asked Ada questions, Ivy did a mental inventory of all the ER visits she and Sebastian had over the years.

There was Trina's meningitis, but there was also Jax's skateboarding accident when he was twelve. His forearm snapped in half that time, the bone poking through the skin. Then there was Trina's sprained ankle from ballet just last year, Jax's accident with a pickle jar that resulted in six stitches in his hand, and Jax's *other* skateboarding accident where he got eight stitches up the length of his shin. Each visit had been harrowing despite the happy ending. The word *family* flashed through Ivy's mind, quivery and pale.

Just the previous year, Ivy had her own ER visit. When she woke up in the middle of the night with stabbing abdominal pain, Sebastian drove her to the ER and squeezed her hand while she waited for a doctor. Unlike tonight, they'd had to wait for what felt like hours (and may very well have been), and Sebastian had tried to keep Ivy's mind off the pain by showing her silly videos on YouTube. He slept in a chair while Ivy had an emergency appendectomy, and when she woke, thick and woozy with painkillers and anesthesia, Sebastian looked rumpled and worried, yet his face flashed with relief when she croaked for a glass of water. Through the haze of medicine, she'd been so grateful to see him there, keeping watch over her in the gray light of dawn. It had never occurred to her that someday he might not be in that chair, standing guard.

Thirteen months later and he was waiting for his unborn child with another woman. In retrospect, surely the affair must have been going on that night. Ivy hadn't suspected a thing. When she'd seen Sebastian looking at her with an expression of melancholy affection, she'd assumed he was thinking about how lucky they were that it was only her appendix and not something worse. In reality, he was probably thinking about how to tell her about Fauna and the new life he had embarked on without her.

A marriage was a world. It had its own weather patterns and terrains, shifting tides and places of shelter. Ivy had spent so much time these past few months being angry with Sebastian that she hadn't thought about what she'd lost. Yes, Sebastian could be a self-centered, self-absorbed jerk. But he was more than a caricature of a cheating husband. In her fury, she'd allowed herself to forget the details that she'd fallen in love with—the way he was constantly singing around the house, how he always got up first and put the coffee on for Ivy, bringing a mug back to bed for her. Sebastian did the laundry every week without being asked, folding Ivy's clothes into neat stacks that he left on the bed. She'd pushed aside memories of Sebastian in bed, the feel of his body against hers, the musky smell of his skin. She'd tried not to think about him as a father, the patient way he helped Trina with her homework, the easy way he had with Jax, the two of them going for long bike rides through Golden Gate Park, returning home sweaty and cheerful. The tang of salt on his skin when he'd grab Ivy around the waist and kiss her. She had let herself forget, too, afraid of the sweep of pain that remembering would bring. There was a whole world in a marriage, one that throbbed and pulsed with life, until it drained away and stopped beating.

Ivy swallowed it all down and tried to pay attention to Ada and the doctor. That's why she was here, she reminded herself, to help Ada, not to wallow in self-pity.

"Has he been eating normally today?" the doctor asked.

"Um, I guess," Ada said, then paused, reconsidering. "Now that I think about it, he wasn't very interested in food today. He only wanted to nurse." She turned to Ivy, a stricken look on her face. "I thought it was because there were more people around and he was distracted. I didn't realize he was sick."

"It's okay," Ivy said.

"And how has he been sleeping?"

Ada looked to Ivy. "He was with you last night. You said he slept well?"

Ivy looked back at her guiltily. "He actually woke up a bunch of times, but I didn't want you to feel bad about it."

Ada looked back at the doctor. "He had a hard time napping today too. We're visiting friends. I just thought he was out of sorts because of the travel."

"Have you given him any medicine? Tylenol or Ibuprofen?" the doctor asked.

Ada shook her head miserably. "I don't have any with me."

"I'm going to give him some Tylenol to bring down his fever and to make him more comfortable. If any of us had a fever this high, we'd be feeling pretty awful too." The doctor motioned to the nurse who guided a dropper of red liquid into Sam's mouth. Sam paused in his crying to swallow the medicine, then resumed his half-hearted wail.

"We'll do a throat culture, but I'm pretty sure he has strep," the doctor said.

"Strep? That's serious, isn't it?" Ada asked.

"Not if we get him on antibiotics. We'll keep him for the next few hours to monitor him, until the antibiotics kick in." The doctor smiled at Ada, his eyes softening in reassurance. "He's going to be fine. You did everything right."

They hadn't, though. Could he tell they'd been drinking, their tongues and teeth still stained with wine, despite haphazard teeth brushing? Did he know that Sam had been little more than an inconvenience all weekend, that they'd babbled at the baby in an automatic way, fingers flying as they changed his diaper, bouncing him on their hip or knee in the practiced way of seasoned mothers, despite their eyes barely taking in more than the fat smushy oval of his body, its warm roundness lost in the past of all their own grown children? This was Ada's miracle baby, yet they'd been too caught up in their own resentments and ancient squabbles to properly marvel at him, to offer Ada or Sam their full attention.

The Tylenol seemed to be kicking in, and Sam had finally stopped crying. Ada sat slumped in a chair nursing, while the doctor went to check on the next patient. Ivy lowered herself to a seat beside Ada, the weight of her fatigue returning now that she knew Sam was going to be all right.

"Are you okay?" she asked Ada.

Ada nodded. "Thanks. For everything tonight."

"Of course."

"About earlier," Ada started, but Ivy cut her off with a wave of her hand.

"Forget it."

Ivy didn't want Ada's apology. She didn't need the explanation. What she needed was to move on from that day. She didn't need to forgive Ada or Elise and Libby. She needed to forgive herself.

Ada blinked her bloodshot eyes at Ivy and then looked down at Sam, lifting him to burp. The baby slept soundly now, finally. His skin was still pink with fever, but his face had lost the beet-red color he'd had when they arrived. With parted lips, he breathed deeply, and Ivy found herself looking at him, really looking, for the first time. He was beautiful.

"Do you want me to hold him?" Ivy asked.

Ada shook her head but smiled. Then she rested her chin upon Sam's head and closed her eyes.

LIBBY

Text message: Caitlin to Libby
You never told me who Adam is! He commented on another
photo—stalker??

Libby helped Ada carry her bags to the front door of Elise's house, where Tyler waited. He'd arrived early Sunday morning, saying he couldn't work after all, and though he was now free to care for Sam, there was no way Ada would leave the baby. Sam was much better this morning after two doses of antibiotics, but Ada wanted to get him back to their own house. She would return home with Tyler, the two of them together caring for Sam.

After a night spent at the hospital, Ada must have been even more worn out than the day before, and she fell gratefully into Tyler's embrace when he arrived at Elise's. Libby sat at the kitchen counter, sipping her coffee and watching the easy practiced way he held Sam in his arms, rubbing the baby's back, pausing in his conversation to murmur in Sam's ear. Tyler was a good man and a good father. Ada would be all right.

"Can I talk to you a minute before you go?" Libby said to Tyler. Ada was in the driveway strapping Sam into his car seat, and Elise and Ivy hovered outside the car. The sun was bright in the sky but the air was crisp, and Libby rubbed her hands along her arms, trying to warm herself up without a jacket.

"Sure." Tyler followed Libby back into the house, tipping his head so he didn't hit it on the doorway. Libby hadn't remembered how tall he was, probably at least six four, thin and lanky. Tyler had the kind of face that was always on the verge of breaking into a smile, kind of like Steven. Deep laugh lines were carved into the skin around Tyler's mouth and at the corners of his eyes. There was something lighthearted in his demeanor, as if he could take the weight of the world on his back and never give any hint of the heft of his load. Libby had never thought of Ada as fun-loving or carefree, but maybe she was both of these things in her real life. Maybe after all this time, the four of them brought out the traits in each other that had mattered when they were twenty, even if that was no longer who they were today.

"What's up?" Tyler asked.

"She should see her doctor. For postpartum depression." Libby eyed Ada through the open door. She felt bad about going to Tyler after they'd already talked to Ada, but she didn't trust that Ada would get herself to the doctor on her own. Tyler's face softened in concern, and he instinctively turned to look at Ada. She was smiling, more relaxed than Libby had seen her all weekend.

Tyler nodded, and Libby wondered if maybe he'd been wondering the same thing all along but had needed someone to give him direct orders. "She's been having a hard time. With the baby and with her mother gone. I've tried to talk to her about it, but she just tells me she's fine," Tyler said.

Libby nodded. "She's not. She really needs some help. With the baby, but also from a doctor."

"I wish you all lived nearby. She doesn't have that many close friends at home. At least not like the three of you," Tyler said.

Libby smiled, swallowing down her desire to tell him that maybe that wasn't such a bad thing after all. "I'm always here. And so are Elise and Ivy."

"We'll go to the doctor this week. I'll take care of her," Tyler said, and Libby knew he would. He peered outside. Ada was in the car, but she was sitting in the back seat, next to Sam. "We should get going."

"I'll come say goodbye," Libby said.

She followed Tyler out to the car. Sam sucked away hungrily on his pacifier, eyes already getting heavy. Tyler got in the front seat and Libby knocked on Ada's window.

Libby opened the door and hugged Ada tightly. There was so much she wanted to tell her. That Sam was going to be okay, that Ada would get through this tough time, that it was okay to ask for help, okay to hire a babysitter or tell Tyler when she was teetering on the brink.

"You can sit in the front seat," was all she said. "Sam will be fine."

"I know. I'd rather be back here where I can see him," Ada said, and there was no reason to argue or say more. You could preach all you wanted from the seat of experience, and none of it would matter at all. They each had to stumble through on their own, flailing around, figuring out their own imperfect way.

ADA

Ada sat in the back seat beside Sam who snored lightly. The weekend had fallen apart, and Ada hadn't had the much-needed break she'd anticipated, yet she felt more relaxed than she had in months. She was sorry to say goodbye to her friends, but she was grateful to return home. And while Ada knew that her nerves were a delicate thing, that tomorrow she'd likely feel depleted and wound tight, today she felt an unfamiliar ease settle over her, a confidence she hadn't experienced since Sam was born.

There was a slight rattle in Sam's breath, but he slept soundly. From her view in the back seat, Ada could see her husband's profile, his strong jaw, the slight bob of his Adam's apple. He adjusted the radio until he found something quiet and unobtrusive that wouldn't wake Sam, though Ada was certain the baby would sleep the whole way home.

Sometimes when Ada looked at Sam, she caught a glimpse of her mother. Tyler didn't see it, certain that Sam's pale blue eyes came from him and his full mouth belonged to Ada, which she'd inherited from her father. But every once in a while, she saw a glimmer of her mother, usually when Sam was sleeping, which seemed odd, since the only time she'd really watched her mother sleep was at the end of her life when sleep was the only respite from the pain, and even then, not a very good one. But looking at Sam now, she was reminded of another time she'd seen her mother sleep, when Ada was a very young girl and her father took her brothers to a game—baseball or football or hockey, it didn't matter; the sports all blurred together in Ada's mind. On these infrequent occasions, Ada and her mother were left together, just the two of them alone, the house uncharacteristically quiet.

Usually her mother would engage her in some activity, a baking project or board game, something that was difficult to do with the cacophony of her brothers around. Always at some point during the afternoon, Ada would see the weariness on her mother's face that she normally didn't notice, the way the afternoon light caught the lines in her forehead, the dark circles beneath her eyes. When the sky was hinting toward the pale gray of late afternoon, when the quiet was nearing its end, her mother would take her hand.

"Nap time, baby girl," she'd say, and lead Ada into the bedroom that her parents shared. Ada's father's side of the bed had a sharp human smell that she didn't like, so Ada would press her head against the pillow her mother usually used, inhaling the faint powdery smell of face cream and some other scent that lived deep inside her mother. Unlike her father's smell, which reminded her of locker rooms and dirty laundry, her mother's odor was calming and comforting. Ada breathed deeply.

Within minutes, her mother drifted off, the wear of the day and the previous days and years of caring for four small children guiding her into an easy rest. Ada wouldn't sleep, instead hovering somewhere on the brink, a pleasant half-sleep where she watched her mother's face in repose and felt the warm blow of breath on her skin.

Ada thought about this as she watched Sam sleep, the way her mother was here in this car with them, even though she was not. She was in Sam's face and by Ada's side, guiding her forward, even if she couldn't hold her hand. Ada leaned against the car window, propping her coat beneath her head, eyes half closed as she watched Sam sleep. She knew it was only in her head, but she heard her mother's voice, steady as a hand on her back.

"Nap time, baby girl."

Ada closed her eyes and slept.

ELISE

Text message: Piper to Elise
It was our turn to bring snacks for soccer practice and Dad
forgot. When are you coming home?

Elise poured herself another cup of coffee, and joined Ivy and
Libby at the kitchen counter.

"This wasn't exactly how I'd expected the weekend to go," she
admitted, taking a sip.

"No one can predict babies," Libby said sympathetically, as if
Sam were the only unpredictable element of the weekend so far.

"I'm sorry about last night," Ivy said, having the decency to
blush. "About throwing the glass, I mean."

"Don't worry about it. You were upset, and you had every right
to be," Elise said, though she'd been annoyed by the broken glass.
They were part of a matching set and now she'd have to find a
replacement.

"You're going to be mad," Ivy said. "But I'm leaving later today.
I changed my ticket last night."

"It's fine," Elise said, surprised that it was. "I have to go to a
meeting at Tommy's school tomorrow morning anyway. Apparently, he might get expelled."

Libby and Ivy's eyes widened. "Why?" Libby asked.

"Because he and some friends hacked into the reading program
the elementary students use. Changed all the usernames to curse

words. Now the class is full of Fuckfaces and Assholes." She didn't mention Mr. Prick or Twathead. She'd made Tommy give her the full list.

Ivy let out a suppressed laugh. Libby elbowed her. "Sorry," Ivy said.

"No, it's fine. If it were someone else's kid, it would be pretty hysterical." Elise rested her mug on the granite counter with a heavy scrape. She stared into her mug, unable to meet either of their eyes. "Brad and I are having problems."

"Did he cheat on you?" Ivy asked, and Elise wondered if Ivy was hoping the answer was yes so at least she wouldn't be the only one.

Elise shook her head. "It's my fault. I'd like to blame him, but I can't. I really can't."

"What happened?" Libby asked.

So she told them—all of it. Her savings as a child and the fear that had gripped her then, and the strange way it had returned as Marianna got older. She told them of the money she'd started to skim from their account, of Brad's face when he found out. It felt good to finally say it out loud, all those long months keeping it to herself, the two of them not speaking about anything except what the children required, avoiding each other in the house, moving from room to room. She told them about the message from Josh Parker, the vague meeting Brad had set up for tomorrow, her fear that he was divorcing her. The secret of their crumbling marriage expanded in Elise's chest like a balloon inflating. It wasn't just that things at home were terrible, she realized, but that no one knew about it. With each sentence Elise uttered, she felt the balloon deflating a tiny bit so that the pressure on her heart wasn't so great.

"But why did you steal? Why not just tell Brad how you felt?" Libby asked. There wasn't disapproval on her face, only disbelief. How to explain that silence could be protective, that sometimes there was so much you weren't saying that the idea of beginning was terrifying, unsure what else might tumble forward.

"I didn't want to worry him," Elise said. "I didn't want him to think that I couldn't handle it. I didn't want him to think that I don't love Marianna just the way she is."

"I'm sure he wouldn't think that," Ivy said.

"Have you ever thought about joining a support group for parents with special needs children? It might be good to have other people who know what you're going through," Libby said.

Brad had suggested the same thing early on, and Elise had been resistant. She didn't need to sit around and wallow about the genetic hand Marianna had been dealt. Better to get on with things and focus on moving forward—the physical therapy and speech therapy and occupational therapy and play therapy (so much therapy!) that would help her make gains in the world. But maybe Libby was right. Maybe the time had come for her to pause and allow things to be hard sometimes, without automatically trying to fix them. Perhaps something good could come from talking about her worries with other parents who shared the same fear of the unknown, even if it wouldn't come easily to her at first. And while it wouldn't change anything for Marianna, maybe it could change something for Elise.

"It must be hard not having anyone to talk to about all this. It sounds like when you were younger, saving was your way of controlling the financial fear that you felt. And it became your way of managing this fear as well, even though your worry over Marianna has nothing to do with money," Libby said.

"Is that your professional opinion?" Ivy asked with a wry grin.

"It is, actually," Libby said. "Don't you think I'm onto something?"

"So now what?" Elise asked.

"I think you need to talk to Brad. Explain to him what you've told us. He's a good guy, Elise. He'll understand. He probably has a lot of the same worries. Rather than hiding them from each other, maybe you can talk about it," Libby said.

"And you need to find out if he really does want a divorce. If he does, you at least deserve to know," Ivy said.

"Talking about it sometimes makes it worse. It makes it real," Elise said, blinking back the tears that sprang into her eyes. She stared into her empty coffee cup.

"Maybe. But sometimes talking about it makes it better too. Even if it's worse at first," Libby said, and she reached over and gave Elise's hand a squeeze. "And that is also my professional opinion."

"What are you going to do about Tommy?" Ivy asked, the conversation that had started this one.

"Oh, Tommy," Elise groaned. "First of all, I'm going to do what I should have done months ago and forbid him from hanging out with Zach and Leon. And that's for starters. He's grounded, indefinitely. He's not going to know what hit him." Elise still didn't know what that would mean, having never grounded any of her children before, but she was determined to figure it out.

"You should call Brad," Libby suggested.

"Now?" Elise asked.

"Why not? Tell him everything you told us. Take the first step."

"Okay. Okay, you're right. I'll call him," Elise said, suddenly nervous about the conversation. But for the first time in months, she could see the next steps of her life clearly, each foothold placed carefully before the next, and while she was certain that the pieces wouldn't line up quite as neatly as they did in her mind, there was relief in at least being able to take a tentative step forward. She thought of Sam, a sweaty little bundle in her arms last night as the fever racked his body. It was like a storm, dark and tumultuous, until it finally broke and the glimmer of a new day was suddenly visible.

In the privacy of her bedroom, she dialed Brad's number. He answered after the second ring.

"Piper's still pissed about the snacks at soccer," Brad said.

Elise let out a laugh. "She'll get over it. Eventually."

"What's up?" Brad asked.

Elise adjusted the pillow she'd propped up behind her and tried to find a way to begin. There was so much she needed to tell him. So much she wanted to say.

"I'm sorry," she began. "About the money, but also about not telling you how I felt. I should have told you how worried I've been about Marianna."

"But Marianna's doing great. She's never going to be like other kids but she's making gains every day," Brad said, which was true. Elise pulled her legs in close, and leaned her chin against the tent of her knees.

"I know. I do understand that. But I worry about her all the time. Her health, her development, what happens when we're gone. I wanted to tell you, but I didn't know how. I really didn't know how," Elise said, and she felt the tears coming. She was glad that Brad couldn't see her. She could count on one hand the number of times she'd cried in front of him. On the rare occasions that Elise did cry, she did it in the shower. But maybe that was part of the problem. She hadn't allowed Brad—or anyone—to know how she really felt.

"I just need you to talk to me," Brad said, and his voice was gentler than it had been in months. "You get so fixated on making everything perfect and organized that you never stop to reflect. You never let me in. If you're scared, if you're upset, if you're angry—I want to know. I'm your husband. We're supposed to be partners."

"I know," Elise said, closing her eyes and pressing her face into her knees. She didn't point out that a partner would know where the sports equipment was kept and would take the kids to the dentist occasionally. She understood what he was saying.

"I need to ask you something," she said, and felt the pulse of her next question beating alongside her own heart.

"What?"

"Are you going to divorce me?" She held her breath, willing herself to be prepared for any answer. She stared at the shimmer of ocean out the window.

"What? No!" Elise heard the surprise in Brad's voice, and felt the muscles in her back and shoulders begin to relax. "Why would you think that?"

"Well, we haven't exactly been communicating well lately. Most of the time you don't talk to me at all," Elise pointed out.

"I know," Brad agreed. "I was upset. I've been trying to deal with it. But I don't want to divorce you. Why would you even think that?"

"Well, you're sending me cryptic messages about a meeting you've scheduled, and I've got Josh Parker, highly successful divorce lawyer, leaving me messages," Elise said. She slid her legs down the length of the bed and leaned back against the stack of propped-up pillows.

"Oh, that," Brad said, sounding chastened. "Josh's wife is pregnant. They just found out the baby has Down syndrome."

"Oh," Elise said, feeling a stab of sympathy.

"I told him he should talk to you. They're obviously upset, but I thought you could help them to understand how incredible Marianna is. How she's so much more than any diagnosis. She's *herself*. I figured you could help them to see that more than anyone. You're an incredible mother," Brad said, and Elise's throat thickened with tears.

"Thank you," she whispered.

"You're welcome. And the appointment is for us to see a marriage counselor. I know it's not really your thing. It's not really my thing either, but I thought we should give it a try," Brad said.

Elise nodded, feeling dizzy with relief. "Okay. We can try. I don't think I'll be very good at it though."

"You can try though, right?" Brad asked. There was a note of impatience in his voice, as if he could sense that Elise had already dismissed the idea.

"Of course," Elise said quickly, and she would. She would try to be the best therapy patient around. Or maybe not the best. Maybe trying to be the best was part of the problem. She would try to be herself.

"Good. That's all I ask," he said. They were quiet for a moment, before Elise thought about what had brought them here in the first place.

"What about the money?" she asked.

Brad's voice was steady when he answered. "I don't care about the money, El. It was never about the money. You can do whatever you want with it—keep it, donate it, I don't care. Whatever will make you feel better about all of this."

Elise nodded, wondering just what that would be.

"Listen, I'll let you go. I've got to figure out breakfast for the kids. We'll probably just go to Butter," Brad said.

"Don't go there," Elise said with an automatic grimace. "It's called Butter but all of their food is either deep fried or smothered in syrup. It should be called Heart Attack."

"Elise." She heard the warning in his voice. The exasperation that rippled so close to the surface in so many of their recent interactions. This too would take time. But at least her marital worries had not proven true. They had time to piece their relationship back together.

"Never mind! Go to Butter," she said. She pressed her lips together so as not to give him the rundown of the different toppings everyone liked. If he didn't order a plain cheese, he could deal with the aftermath. Then, as an afterthought, and because she really couldn't help herself and it would make things easier for him, she added, "Just don't let Marianna order the French toast.

She'll forget, but she didn't like it last time. And there's a coupon on the fridge."

Brad let out a little sigh—of frustration or exasperation or affection, she wasn't sure. "Thanks, hon," he said.

LIBBY

Text message: Adam to Libby
*No pressure, but last-minute schedule change and the kids are
staying with their mom tonight. Feel like coming home a day
early and spending the night?*

Libby was reading Adam's message when a text arrived from Caitlin.
She still hadn't responded to her question about Adam.

Miss you. Are you having fun?

"I think Caitlin likes me better in text messages. She's much
nicer to me when she can't actually see my face," Libby said, without
looking up from her phone. They were in Elise's car, heading to
the airport to drop off Ivy.

"I read a whole article about that last month. Something about
how kids these days can't deal with real communication because
they've grown up behind screens," Elise said.

"That's messed up. And I'm not sure if it's true," Libby said.

She looked down at the phone. Caitlin had written again, three
question marks, waiting impatiently.

*Yes?? A little complicated. I'll tell you the whole story tomorrow.
Ok, xo*

Elise went on. "The article talked about parents using texting
as a way to bring up difficult subjects. Things that their kids might
want to discuss but feel uncomfortable with. One mom wrote

how she had a whole conversation about birth control through text messages."

"That's crazy!" Libby said.

"Maybe," Elise said with a shrug.

It was crazy, but so was the little pink heart that Caitlin had sent. Before she could think too much about it, Libby wrote back. Inspired by the conversation with Elise, Libby plowed ahead.

You asked about Adam.

Yeah. Who is he?

Libby paused, wondering if she should lie, deciding Caitlin deserved the truth.

Well, he's not a stalker.

Ok. So?

He's someone I've been seeing recently.

There was a moment's pause while Libby held her breath, waiting for the bouncing bubbles. Finally, they appeared.

Like a boyfriend?

Kind of.

Libby's fingers hovered over the keypad before she tapped out, *How do you feel about that?* The conversation would have been awkward in person. Libby was grateful for the refuge of Elise's car with its heated leather seats. Caitlin's response came a moment later.

Kind of weird. I mean, I don't want another dad.

I know! No one can ever replace your dad.

NO. THEY CAN'T.

They were only three little words, but Libby felt the anger in them and was glad of the distance. A moment later, Caitlin started typing again.

I'm not psyched about it, but I want you to be happy.

Libby felt a surge of gratitude for her oldest daughter, for her big and broken heart.

Do you love him? Caitlin asked.

The question took Libby's breath away. She hadn't even had the courage to ask herself this question, and she was terrified of the answer.

I don't know, she finally wrote, and it was the truth.

Ok.

I love you though. I know that, Libby wrote.

Yeah. Me too, came Caitlin's reply. Libby could almost see the eye roll it came with.

We'll talk more when I'm home, Libby wrote.

"What are you smiling about?" Elise asked, glancing over at her.

Libby clicked a smiley face and the double purple heart, and hit send. "Nothing. Just talking to Caitlin."

She clicked back over to Adam's text. She wondered what Steven would have thought of Adam. Steven could make a joke out of anything, and Libby knew he would have been baffled by Adam's quiet seriousness, his careful introspection, so different from Steven's carefree and outgoing manner. Adam was not Steven. They were so very, very different. But love didn't have one single recipe. It didn't look the same at eighteen as it did at forty-two. Allowing herself to love Adam didn't mean erasing her love for Steven, and it didn't mean dismissing all of the things she'd loved about her husband that were different from Adam. She'd always known this in her head, but it felt like her heart might finally be catching on too.

She dropped the phone to her lap and turned to Elise. "Would you be really upset if I left today?"

"What? Really? Why?" Elise asked. She didn't look upset, but Libby wasn't sure. Sometimes it was hard to tell with Elise.

"Well," Libby drew the word out, embarrassed to say the rest. "I was thinking I might take advantage of the kids being with my parents for the night. I thought maybe I'd spend the night with Adam."

"Woo hoo, go Libby!" Ivy cheered from the back seat.

Libby rolled her eyes and turned to Elise. "Would you mind?"

Elise took her hand off the steering wheel and waved. "No, it's fine. You should go. Who am I to stand in the way of early-relationship sex?"

"Elise!" Libby said, blushing.

"I'm kidding. It's fine, I'm happy for you. You deserve it."

"Okay, only if you're sure," Libby said. She bent over her phone and typed out a message.

Change of plans. Be there in a few hours.

His response was immediate. *Can't wait to see you.*

"All good?" Elise asked, glancing over.

"Yup," Libby said, pressing her lips between her teeth to prevent the smile from overtaking her face. "All good."

IVY

Text message: Ivy to Jax and Trina
I'm on my way home. I can't wait to see you both. Love you
so much!

Text message: Trina to Ivy
Thank God! Get me away from Dad's crazy girlfriend. She
made me come to her prenatal yoga class. SOS!

Ivy sat in the back of Elise's minivan as they made the drive to the airport. Elise seemed lighter now that the weekend was coming to a close, all that upbeat tension finally slackening a bit.

"This isn't quite the weekend you had in mind, is it, El?" Ivy asked.

Elise shook her head, but she was smiling. "No, not exactly. But you know, in some ways, it was actually better than I'd expected. Except obviously Sam getting sick. And the baby being there in the first place. He's very cute, but next time there needs to be a strict no babies policy."

"Agreed," Libby said, eyes on her phone. "I wish you lived closer," she continued, looking over her shoulder at Ivy. "I hate that we only see you every few years."

"I know. You could come to California next time," Ivy said, and she realized she'd never actually invited them.

"Yes! We'd love that!" Elise said, so quickly that Ivy wondered if maybe she'd been waiting for the invitation all these years.

Tonight, she'd arrive in San Francisco. Ivy was always amazed that, despite the fog and rain that often plagued San Francisco, it was always sunny when she landed. The plane would pass over the Pacific and touch down on another perfect sixty-five-degree day, blue skies and sun. In her past life, Sebastian met her at baggage claim, looking rumpled and happy to see her in paint-covered jeans and an old sweater. Today it would be dark by the time she landed, and Jax would pick her up.

"I haven't signed the divorce papers yet," Ivy said, leaning forward so her head was in the space between the two seats. "I'm not sure why."

"Maybe you're still hoping to get back together," Elise said.

Ivy shook her head. It wasn't that. Even if Sebastian wanted to come home, which she doubted, it was no longer that simple. More than the fact that he'd cheated on her (easily, at length, and with practically a *teenager*), there was the new baby. There was no way Ivy could be stepmom to her husband's love child.

"It's not that. Signing just makes it so permanent. So official. Right now, I'm separated, but as soon as I sign the papers, I'm divorced," Ivy said.

"That's true. But once you're divorced, you can start thinking about what you want next. Until you do that, you're just stuck. What *do* you want to do next?" Libby said.

"Maybe you should move out here." Elise met her eyes in the rearview mirror. "I mean, if you and Sebastian are splitting up, maybe it's a good time to make a change."

Ivy smiled. "Too far."

She couldn't move to New England. Not now. Her mother was in California, and so were Jax and Trina and all of her friends, the friends she talked to every day, not the ones she saw once a year. She couldn't move to Massachusetts.

She'd already contacted her manager from the spa she'd last worked at, and he was going to add her to the rotation of massage therapists. That would bring in some money, at least enough to pay the rent this month. She'd ditch the jewelry cart at the mall. It wasn't making any money, and spending all day at the mall made her feel like a failure. Instead she'd beef up the website, try to promote herself better on social media. Trina and Jax could probably help her with that.

But maybe it was time to think about leaving the city, to one of the little towns that peppered the north coast. Years ago, her old childhood friend Gene had moved with his family to a funky surfer town an hour outside the city. He'd been divorced for several years now, but still lived in the same town, the children shuffling back and forth between him and his ex-wife on weekends. He and Ivy exchanged emails every few weeks, and Ivy knew there was a yoga retreat center in the town, one of those artsy places with spa treatments and yoga classes, somewhere Ivy might be able to get a job. Ivy's friend Samantha had expressed interest in finding a place where the rent was cheaper, a place less busy, where life was quieter. Jax was graduating high school this year, and Trina only had two years left. Soon enough, the world she and Sebastian built would be gone completely. Life was like that, measured in chunks of sameness, until things changed. Maybe her next chunk would offer something unexpected.

She wondered what her life would be like if she had graduated from Harper. Would she be a science teacher? Would she live in the Boston area, near Elise, or in Wolf Mountain, with Libby? Would she have a husband and children, younger children, because certainly she wouldn't have gotten married and had kids so quickly if life had followed the course it was supposed to. She imagined that Ivy, the imaginary version of herself who woke early every morning to dress in khakis and a sweater, who dropped the kids at school on the way to her job at the high school. She imagined the black marble desks in her classroom, the shelves lined with beakers, a closet locked with chemicals, dusty rows of crystals and bones and feathers. She could picture the classroom so clearly, yet the life beyond the walls of the room was empty, a blurry mystery.

She had stepped into a dream for her four years at Harper, tried on an outfit to see if it would fit. It was the right size but it was never comfortable, always a little tight around the shoulders, the material too itchy at the neck. Perhaps she'd shed the unfortunate garment on purpose after all, exchanged an expensive yet ill-fitting outfit for something sloppy but comfortable. A fitted tee shirt that was so soft you never wanted to take it off. Though she might covet what others had, what she had almost had, it was possible that Ivy had been wearing the right clothes all along.

"Sign the papers before you get on the plane. With us," Libby said. They were nearing the airport, the bright green signs alerting them to the different airline carriers. "Go on, hurry up."

Ivy reached into her old leather bag and pulled out the manila envelope she'd been carrying for weeks. When she slid the papers out, she saw that Sebastian's lawyer had marked each page with a plastic sticky arrow, indicating where she needed to sign.

"Here." Libby handed her a pen.

Ivy didn't read the writing. They hardly had any assets between them, just the car that Sebastian had given to Ivy. Other than that, their worldly possessions consisted of the apartment full of crappy furniture and sentimental items.

She signed the first page.

She wouldn't cry, but she did blink a little faster, holding the papers awkwardly on her lap, trying to write neatly despite the moving car.

She turned the page and signed again. And again and again and again. Libby faced forward, but she turned around every few moments to check on Ivy's progress. Ivy was glad she wasn't alone.

She signed the last page just as Elise pulled up at the terminal, putting the car in park.

"I'm done," she said, an odd feeling of emptiness settling over her.

"You're done," Elise repeated. Ivy slid the papers into the envelope and handed Libby her pen. Her friends stared back at her expectantly.

"How do you feel?" Libby asked.

She shrugged. "Not sure yet. But thanks." She knew the moment was significant, but Ivy had never been good at significant moments. It would be a while before it really sank in. She shoved the envelope back into her bag. "I should go. You're going to get a ticket if you wait too long."

They both got out of the car to say goodbye to her. They held Ivy tightly between them, and she wondered when she would see them again. The last time had been at Ada's wedding. Would the next be at Libby's? She hoped it would be a joyous occasion that brought them together, as she doubted Elise would try to plan another weekend like this. Though you never did know. Maybe if they hadn't tried so hard, they would have gotten it right.

"Love you," Libby whispered in Ivy's ear, and now the tears did come—for the effortless way Libby expressed her affection, for the way she tossed the words off so casually but they still meant so much.

"Love you too," Ivy whispered back, giving her friends one last squeeze. Then she lifted her bags and headed through the glass doors into the terminal. She kept walking and didn't look back, not wanting to see Elise's car pull away.

Once on the airplane, she settled in her small coach seat, arranged her book and in-flight magazines, her water bottle and bag of nuts that she'd purchase at the airport store. The seats were the same nubby polyester of every flight she'd ever taken, the flight attendants cheerful and polite as they ushered people into seats and went about the business of instructing them on what to do in the event of an emergency landing. As if the flimsy life jackets would offer any protection in the case of a disaster.

"Ladies and gentlemen, please turn off all electronic devices before takeoff."

She reached into her bag for her phone, but her hand folded around an envelope tucked into the side pocket, her name written on the outside in purple pen. When Ivy opened the envelope, she withdrew a check. It was for fifteen thousand dollars made out to Ivy, and Elise's name was printed at the top. A pink Post-it note was stuck to the back. In Elise's careful swirling script was a message.

Ivy, Libby told me about your money troubles. Please, please accept this. Don't worry about paying me back. I'm happy to give it to you. Love you. ~E

Ivy felt her breath catch in her throat as tears spilled forth. The relief was so intense she thought she might be sick, and then she felt the laughter bubbling up from the back of her throat. The man beside her likely thought she was crazy, but Ivy couldn't help herself. *Thank God for Elise*, Ivy thought. What would they ever do without her? She found her phone and tapped out a frantic message. The first was to the escort agency.

I'm not going to be able to make it in for our meeting this week. You can take my name off your list of possible escorts. Thank you for your time.

She pressed send and then sent another off to Marshall.

Thanks for the offer, but I'm not available after all. You can contact the agency for this weekend and other future dates.

The flight attendant was coming up the aisle, asking people to turn off their cell phones, but Ivy tapped out another message to Sebastian.

It's done. Papers are signed. Tell the kids to come home.

She felt a stitch in her chest, a little flutter of regret and relief, and the tiniest tug of hope. It was a start.

"I'm sorry, ma'am, but you need to put your phone away," the flight attendant said, pointing an impatient finger at Ivy's phone.

"Sorry, sorry," Ivy muttered but didn't turn off her phone. She tapped a final message to Elise, ignoring the pointed stare of the flight attendant. Finally, she switched her phone back to airplane mode, hands trembling in her lap.

The engine roared to life and began to tear down the runway. Ivy held the check in her hand and laughed quietly to herself as tears streamed down her face. And then they were aloft.

Facebook status update: What a fabulous weekend with my oldest friends, despite a few unexpected turns. #grateful

Group text: Elise to Ivy, Libby, and Ada
Well, it wasn't quite the weekend I had planned, but I'm still glad we did it. California, same time next year? Kidding not kidding? Love you all. xx

Text message: Ivy to Elise
Thank you, El. Thank you thank you thank you. Xo

Elise waved at Libby's car as she pulled out of the driveway. Once the car was out of sight, she walked back into the house, smiling at Ivy's message, then typed a quick text to the three of them before turning her phone to silent and laying it on the counter. There would be an endless ricochet of texts in response to hers, but she didn't need to read them now. Instead she headed outside to one of the deck chairs that overlooked the ocean. The day was the warmest they'd had all spring, and Elise sank into the chair, closing her eyes and tipping her head back to feel the softness of the sun on her face. The waves crashed along the shore and Elise felt a wash of peaceful relief float over her. There was no denying that she'd felt lighter since she wrote the check to Ivy. The money had felt tainted all along, a physical manifestation of something toxic, and she was glad to finally be rid of it, especially since Ivy actually needed it. She had asked Brad first, after a long conversation that had not come easily to her, and that she knew was only the first of many they would have. The money that she'd given Ivy was only a portion of what was in the account. The rest she'd deposit into their joint savings account, and then she'd go ahead and close the other account once and for all.

She could fall asleep here in this perfect sunny spot, the warm wood cradling her in place. She thought about all the empty rooms in the house, with no one for her to worry about. Instead of driving back today, she'd stay an extra night alone, rising early tomorrow to make it to the meeting at Tommy's school. The rest of the day unfolded before her—a long walk on the beach, a simple dinner, a movie before bed, the glorious sound of nothing but the wind and the waves.

She wondered if they'd really do it again next year, if they'd salvaged the weekend enough to try. It hadn't been what she'd envisioned but it wasn't possible to control everything. Try as she might, Elise knew she needed to learn to loosen her grip, to let go of the perfect in exchange for the messy, because in the heart of the mess was sometimes where goodness lay.

Upstairs the sheets needed to be stripped and the laundry started, but Elise remained where she was, fighting whatever impulse urged her inside, instead turning herself over to the sun and the sea and the crashing waves. It was a rhythm more powerful than her own chugging heart, if she could only learn to listen.

A LETTER FROM EMILY

Dear Reader,

I want to say a huge thank you for choosing to read *Her Guilty Secret*. If you did enjoy it, and want to keep up to date with all my latest releases, just sign up at the following link. Your email address will never be shared and you can unsubscribe at any time.

www.bookouture.com/emily-cavanagh

One of the best things about being an author is hearing from readers. I hope you enjoyed spending time with Elise, Ada, Libby, and Ivy, and if you did, I would be very grateful if you could write a review. I'd love to hear what you think, and it makes such a difference helping new readers to discover one of my books for the first time. You can also get in touch on my Facebook page, through Twitter, Goodreads or my website.

Thanks,
Emily Cavanagh

emilymcavanagh77

@emilymcavanagh

emilycavanaghauthor

emilycavanaghauthor.com

17634058.Emily_Cavanagh

ACKNOWLEDGMENTS

The idea for this book came at a time when I was just emerging from the daze of early motherhood. Parenthood is its own bubble of joy and exhaustion, love and irritation. It can be all-consuming and, at times, lonely. When I first started writing this book, my babies were no longer babies, and while they were still the center of my world, I knew it wouldn't be long before I was no longer the center of theirs. It was around this time when I started thinking about the importance of female friendships. I no longer had the kind of intense friendships that blossom when you live on top of each other in a small apartment or dorm. However, my female friendships were in some ways even more important to me, despite the challenges of maintaining those connections at this busy stage of life. I wanted to write a book about friendship between women and how those relationships can change yet endure over time.

While Elise, Ivy, Ada, and Libby are fictional, the friendship between them was inspired and informed by many. Thank you to my oldest friends, who helped me to imagine the world of Harper, and thank you to my newer friends, who sustain me through the highs and lows of this stage of our lives. And an even bigger thank you to the few who have traveled with me from one stage to the next. You know who you are.

I am grateful to my early readers, who offered to read this novel when it was rough and ragged, and whose editorial suggestions helped to make it stronger and more real: Amelia Angella, Lynda Bernard, Sarah Smith, Mathea Morais, Stefani Cavanagh, Laurie Hark, Mary Cavanagh, and my parents, Pam and Tom Cavanagh.

Thank you to the fabulous team at Bookouture, including Natasha Hodgson, Noelle Holten, Kim Nash, Peta Nightingale, and Alexandra Holmes. A huge shout-out to Cara Chimirri, my fabulous editor. Your spot-on editorial guidance helped to give the book a heft and shape it lacked before. I'm always thrilled to read your feedback because it makes so much sense that I wonder why I didn't think of it before. A big thank you to my agent, Marlene Stringer, for her unwavering commitment and high standards that help to make me a better and more focused writer.

Thank you to Nevah and Olivia. Being your mother is the best job I could ask for. And to Reuben—for truly being an equal partner, for supporting me in ways both big and small, and for always reminding me how lucky we are.